By CINDY DEES

STUD GAMES
Poker Face
Dead Man's Hand

Published by DREAMSPINNER PRESS
www.dreamspinnerpress.com

DEAD MAN'S HAND

CINDY DEES

Published by
DREAMSPINNER PRESS

5032 Capital Circle SW, Suite 2, PMB# 279, Tallahassee, FL 32305-7886 USA
www.dreamspinnerpress.com

Dead Man's Hand
© 2020 Cindy Dees

Cover Art
© 2020 L.C. Chase
http://www.lcchase.com

Trade Paperback ISBN: 978-1-64405-240-2
Digital ISBN: 978-1-64405-239-6
Library of Congress Control Number: 2020934716
Trade Paperback published July 2020
First Edition
v. 1.0
Previously published by Dreamspinner Press as Seven-Card Stud by Ava Drake, November 2016.
Printed in the United States of America

CHAPTER ONE

COLLIN CALLAHAN stepped onto the beachside veranda and turned his face up to the warm sunshine. The south of Europe was a blessed relief after England in winter, which had been even more gray and dreary than usual at this time of year. A tiny bit of the anvil that had been sitting on his chest these past, long weeks lifted as he soaked up the vitamin D. Out with the old. In with the new.

Although what form new would take, he hadn't the slightest idea.

One thing he was sure of, though—he was ready for more than a change in weather.

The Mediterranean Sea crashed against the seawall that formed the outer edge of the veranda. A torrential rain had passed through last night and although the skies were bright blue, the weather was still blustery today. Curving away from him in each direction from Gibraltar's El Rocca Resort was a man-made beach of pale gold sand. The massive, dark hulk of the Rock of Gibraltar rose behind the resort, which was tucked up against the base of the mighty limestone rock formation. The waves rolled ashore gently along the shallow incline of the beach. But here, beside a vertical sea wall, the transition from veranda to water was abrupt, with waves smashing into the concrete and shale barrier.

He spied a swimmer a ways out in the choppy water, moving from right to left, neon -yellow wet suit and blond hair bright against the black sea. His body was long, his swim strokes angular and even. *Strong swimmer.*

Christ, the water had to be freezing, though. Just the salt spray on his face was bone-chilling. He was glad he'd donned a warm jumper under his suit coat before he came out here. What nut ball would go out for a swim in such bitterly cold surf?

From his left, beyond the far end of the sprawling beach, he heard the rumble of a Jet Ski emerging from the El Rocca marina. As soon as the vehicle cleared the docks, the driver gunned the motor, and the watercraft shot out into the ocean, the front end jumping up and slapping down on the choppy water. The driver wore a black wet suit complete with a hood and goggles.

And his craft was headed directly for the swimmer.

Collin rushed over to the edge of the veranda and waved his arms, trying to get the Jet Skier's attention, but to no avail. The guy seemed oblivious to the swimmer now directly in his path. How in the hell didn't he see that bright slash of yellow in the water? Not only did the Jet Ski driver not seem to see the swimmer, but as Collin looked on in dismay, the bastard turned slightly, lining himself up even more exactly on a collision course with the swimmer.

Collin shouted futilely in hopes of the swimmer or driver hearing the warning, but the driver kept on going, picking up speed if anything, and the swimmer just kept his head down in a crawl stroke, only turning his head to the sides to breathe, and plowed onward, unaware he was about to die.

The gap between Jet Ski and swimmer evaporated in what seemed like the blink of an eye. *Crap, crap, crap.* That Jet Ski was *flying.*

His gut cramped with suspension of time, anticipation of disaster, and a sickening rush of helplessness. A flash of a mangled car passed through his brain. Blood all over the deflated air bag. Yellow crime scene tape. Did Steve see it coming? Have this same moment of frozen horror just before the end?

Collin desperately didn't want to watch this new calamity, but he couldn't have looked away from the unfolding disaster if he'd tried.

At the very last second, the swimmer lifted his head. Perhaps he heard the motorized vehicle approaching. He treaded water and waved his arms frantically, but it was too late for the poor guy to do a damned thing to save himself. The Jet Ski ran directly over him.

No no no no no no....

The call from the police. The frantic drive to the accident scene. The news that Steve had died instantly. Never had a chance....

Agony slashed across his belly, physically doubling him over with the searing pain.

But what of this person out in the sea all alone, dying?

Collin was too far away to see a blood slick in the water or chewed up bits of human being and yellow neoprene, but they had to be there. Nausea flooded his gut and vomit filled his mouth. He spit it out without taking his eyes off the spot where the collision had happened.

And then he registered a bizarre thing. The Jet Ski driver hadn't stopped. Hadn't even slowed down. *The bastard had kept right on going.*

Surely the driver had seen the swimmer in those last few yards, when the guy would have been looming directly in front of him, waving his arms. And yet there hadn't been a swerve, a reduction of engine power, or even an attempt at a turn. Son of a bitch.

The rage of being told it had been a completely avoidable tragedy—that the other driver had been distracted… texting on her phone… drifted into Steve's lane—roared through him. It was so goddamned senseless! Why in the hell hadn't that Jet Ski driver at least tried to swerve?

Staring at the spot where the swimmer had last been, Collin muttered urgently, "C'mon, mate. Surface. Pop up and let me see you're okay. Be alive, dammit."

But no matter how he cajoled the swimmer, there was no sign of the blond hair or yellow wet suit. The seconds ticked away as panic climbed his chest wall and clawed at the back of his throat. He couldn't wait any longer. He kicked off his shoes and stripped off his sweater. Down to just slacks and shirt, he climbed the railing and launched himself into the water.

The cold shocked him into immobility, but the trajectory of his dive had been shallow and he arced back up toward the surface, breaking through, gasping. He sighted off the corner of the veranda and headed for the spot he'd last seen the swimmer.

He'd never swum in full clothing that weighed down all his limbs, or in water that turned him into a human ice cube, numbing his fingers and setting his teeth chattering uncontrollably. But he pressed on in spite of every cell in his body screaming at him to turn around. Go back. Get the hell out of this dangerous, even deadly, water.

Thing was, the swimmer would die if he didn't find the guy and fast.

He was the only one who'd seen the collision, the only person who knew the spot the swimmer had gone down, the only one with a chance to save the victim. There was no time to go get help. It was him or nobody to save the swimmer's life.

It took a never-gonna-be-warm-again eternity to get to the spot where he estimated the crash had happened, and he treaded water, turning in a circle in search of evidence of the collision. Or of a body. Hell, he'd settle for body parts or a blood slick. Anything.

Instead, he saw nothing. Nothing at all. Just the dark, angry surface of the Mediterranean rising and falling around him, trying to drag him down, freeze him into immobility and suck him down, down to his own death.

Crap. He took a deep breath and dived. The visibility sucked, and the frigid salt water burned his eyes like fire, but he doggedly stayed under, searching until his lungs felt as if they would explode. He popped up to the surface, took several gasping breaths, and went down again. He swam in a circle around the area where he'd seen the swimmer go under. The guy had to be here, somewhere. Deeper and deeper he spiraled, praying the guy hadn't already gone down to the bottom of the Mediterranean. But surely the combination of neoprene and the oxygen in the guy's body would keep him from sinking like a rock.

Around fifteen feet down, if the painful pressure in his ears was any indication, it got too dark for him to see a thing.

If the swimmer had already lost all buoyancy and gone down to the bottom, the man was a goner anyway. He had to confine his search to the first fifteen feet or so of water but widen the search area.

Collin ran out of air again, his lungs screaming for oxygen, and he swam for the surface and burst clear at the last possible instant before his chest exploded. He took a bunch of fast breaths and went down a third time.

He wasn't able to stay down as long this time, but he swam in a wide circle around the impact point. No sign of the swimmer. *Dammit!*

Surfacing again, he paid close attention to the current, trying to sense which direction the guy's body might have drifted. Time was running out for the swimmer. He *had* to find the guy, and soon, or resuscitation wouldn't do any good.

He dived yet again, angling toward the current flow, his body growing sluggish with the cold and oxygen starvation. But a man's life depended on him. He pushed through the pain with grim determination.

Despair heavy in his mind, he was rising toward the surface yet again when something large rocketed at him from above. He jolted, fearing the return of the Jet Ski. The object slammed into him, knocking what little breath he still had out of his chest. Something gripped his left arm in a viselike grip.

Holy cow. Had sharks been drawn to the accident site already? Maybe by the scent of blood in the water? Memory flashed through his mind of television documentaries where sharks went into violent feeding frenzies and attacked anything that moved. Panic for his own survival roared through him. He punched at the attacking fish with his free fist, writhing and twisting to free himself of its grip.

The beast breached, yanking him up and breaking the surface of the water. He dragged in a desperately needed lungful of air. He managed another breath before the beast tried to roll him over onto his back. Muscles temporarily refueled with oxygen, he fought harder to release himself. He must get free before too much damage was done. Before he bled out.

"Jeez, quit fighting already!" a voice complained behind him. "I'm trying to help."

It took his cold-numbed mind a moment to register that a human being had spoken the words, not a great white shark.

He grabbed for the chokehold around his throat and realized it was an *arm*. Not a tooth-filled jaw. And that was a big, warm, hard body spooning against his in a way that would have been provocative as hell in any other circumstances.

"Let me go!" he rasped past saltwater and that damned arm all but choking him to death.

"You need help to stay afloat. I've got you."

"A swimmer got hit by a Jet Ski, you moron. I'm out here to save him!"

"You're drowning, dude."

"I was *diving*. Intentionally. Let me go and help me find the guy before he dies!"

"I'm the guy that asshole almost ran over."

Collin's already sluggish mind went blank. "He hit the swimmer. I saw it. The guy went down."

The arm around his neck finally loosened enough for Collin to tear away and tread water under his own power. He spun to face a blond guy with a deep tan, who floated easily behind him. And he was wearing a neon-yellow wet suit, the hood pushed back.

The blond said, "The Jet Ski *almost* hit me. I dived and got out of the way at the last second."

"But you didn't come up. I watched for well over a minute."

"I'm a surfer, man. I can hold my breath for three minutes, easy. I stayed under and swam away from where he hit me in case he circled back to check on me and accidentally hit me the second time around."

"But—" Collin broke off, at a loss for words. His brain was barely functional in the cold grip of the sea. "So you're okay?"

"I'm great. You, however, look like shit. Your lips are blue, and your arms are noodling bad."

If, by that, the swimmer meant Collin's arms were weakening and starting to feel like noodles, the chap was entirely correct, dammit.

The swimmer added helpfully, "This water's too cold for anyone to be out here without a wet suit."

"No. Fucking. Kidding," he managed past the chattering of his teeth. "I was trying… to save… your life."

"If we don't get you to shore pretty quick, I'm going to have to save yours. C'mon. I'll swim you in."

"I can… swim by… m… myself." Although the way his arms and legs were abruptly refusing to cooperate, he might be overstating the truth.

The blond guided him toward the beach, swimming easily alongside him as he flailed like a wet dog. To distract himself from the frigid misery, Collin asked, "How d… did… you f… find… me underwater?"

"Easy. I'm wearing goggles. Visibility's not bad here. I saw you surface and then go down again. Looked for all the world like you were drowning. So I came and got you."

"I was d… diving."

"Yeah, I got that memo. Tell me something. Did you see where the Jet Ski came from?"

Between exhausted pulls with his arms in a modified breaststroke that kept his head out of the water but minimized the need to lift his arms, he gasped, "Marina. Came f…flying out."

"Interesting. Did you see where in the marina it came from?"

"No."

"Too bad."

Something in the swimmer's voice sounded like more than idle curiosity. Collin struggled to make sense of why that was important, but his mind wouldn't compute complex logic analysis right now.

"It was insane of you to jump into the Med after me, you know."

"Gee. Thanks."

"No, really. The water's dangerously cold at this time of year."

"So I n... noticed," Collin managed to retort.

"Have you got a death wish or something?"

More like a hero complex, but that was none of this fellow's business. "Why were you s... swimming... out here if it's so... c... cold?"

"Because I'm wearing a wet suit, and the temperature of the water won't *kill* me."

Irritation warmed Collin enough to say all in one burst, "If I knew it would be so cold, I'd have let you drown." His teeth started chattering again, and he finished lamely, "There. D... does that... m... make you feel b... better?"

"You're lying," the swimmer declared. "You'd have jumped in anyway."

"How do you know?" Collin exclaimed.

"You're a terrible liar. Even half frozen to death, you have tells all over your face. I sure hope you're not here to play in the poker tournament, because the other players will eat you alive, the way you give up a bluff."

He stared in dismay at the swimmer. Of course, he'd read in the poker manuals he'd been frantically studying for the past two weeks how important it was to control his facial features and expressions, not to give away when he was bluffing or had good cards. The books said experienced poker players were masters of reading facial nuance, but he'd had no idea how masterful until this moment.

If he hadn't already been chilled to the bone before, he was now. On multiple levels.

"You need some help there, Skippy?" the swimmer asked. "I don't mind pulling you in. You look totally wiped."

The swimmer would be correct. But damned if he would let the man whom he'd dived in to save rescue him instead. He had a little pride, after all.

It took considerably longer for him to make his way to shore than it had for him to get out to the collision site. But the swimmer stayed with him patiently as he labored ashore. Whether or not he'd have made it back on his own without the motivation of anger and stung pride, he would never know. As it was, he was deeply resentful of the gratitude he was forced to acknowledge toward the swimmer.

The last guy he'd hooked up with in an effort to move past his grief and loneliness, a one-night stand who made him feel even more like shit than before, had called him ungrateful after their horrendously awful encounter. In truth, it hadn't been the guy's fault that he was an emotional wreck and not the least bit ready for a relationship of any kind, casual or otherwise. Hell, maybe the guy was right. Maybe he didn't know how to share emotions, let alone show vulnerability.

He was completely wrung out by a year of grieving the death of his longtime partner. He wasn't sure he had any emotions left. Even he knew that a strange, brittle quality clung to him all the time now. As if any real emotion might shatter him into a million little pieces that could never be put back together again into a whole human being.

Thank God for the job. It had been the only thing that kept him sane, kept him getting out of bed in the morning. Without it, he might have just lain down and died.

And here he was, floundering in the frigid surf, swallowing far too much salt water to be healthy, struggling toward shore, and unsure he would make it. This moment was a hell of an analogy for his entire life.

By the time his feet touched the sandy bottom of the engineered beach, Collin would have been hard-pressed to spell his own name. He staggered through the waist-deep surf, which was more a swaying of the water than actual waves rolling in. But still, it was enough to knock him off his exhausted feet time and again. Each time he toppled over, it was harder to force himself upright, to clear his face of the chilly water while swallowing copious mouthfuls of the foul salty stuff.

"Hang in there, dude. I've got you."

If only.

He would love for someone to swoop in and take care of him for a change. To feel loved again. Hell, just to feel safe.

Without asking, the swimmer he'd set out to save wrapped a powerful arm around his waist and helped him the last few yards to shore. It galled him to allow it, but it wasn't as if he had the strength to fight the guy off.

Left to his own devices, Collin would have collapsed onto the faintly warm sand to rest and catch his breath. But swimmer dude was having none of that.

"You're hypothermic as hell, man. We've got to get you inside and warmed up. No resting for you. Upsy-daisy, English."

"Upsy-daisy?" he echoed wryly.

"Hey. Whatever gets the point across, dude. One foot in front of the other."

"My jacket. Jumper. Shoes. That way…," he mumbled, gesturing at the veranda to their left.

"My room. Hot shower. This way," the swimmer disagreed. "C'mon."

With that shockingly strong arm pulling him along like the limp rag he was at the moment, Collin didn't have much choice in the matter. His entire body was so fatigued and cramped with cold, he could barely move of his own volition. The guy dragged him through the lobby of the resort and pushed him into an elevator. If the other guests noticed him or gave a damn for his half-drowned-rat state, he couldn't tell and didn't care. The idea of a hot shower sounded better than just about anything in the world right now.

At the moment, he had no idea where his room key was or what his own room number was. He was only vaguely aware of going to an unfamiliar floor in an unfamiliar wing of the resort and of being herded down a long hallway into a strange room.

"Can you get your clothes off and get into the shower by yourself, or do you need help?" the swimmer asked.

"I've got it," Collin mumbled. He shambled into the guy's bathroom and managed to get the faucet turned on, but the buttons on his shirt almost did him in. He might have torn off the last couple of them, he wasn't sure. His hands were shaking too badly to control and his fingers too numb to feel what he was doing. But eventually he got the damned shirt off and peeled down his sodden wool trousers and briefs.

He stepped into the shower.

Too hot. *Too hot!* He cringed away from the jet of water.

He cooled the shower down until his half-frozen skin could stand the temperature, and then gradually warmed up the water as his body could take the heat. Convinced he was never going to feel warm again, he turned the water up hotter and hotter until steam filled the bathroom. Water flowed over his head and beat at his neck and shoulders, releasing the terrible tension he hadn't realized he'd been holding. The panic of seeing that swimmer go down and then of thinking he was under attack and going to die finally seeped away under the pounding water.

He hadn't been there when Steve died. The police said death had been instant when his car was hit head-on, both vehicles traveling at roughly one-hundred-kilometers per hour. But when he'd seen that Jet Ski run over neon-yellow guy... it had brought everything back. His desperation to have been there with Steve, to have done something, anything, to save him, or even to have died with him, to feel something other than utter helplessness in the face of random, unkind fate.

At length he began to warm up until he felt semi-human. Normal brain function reengaged. He felt waterlogged but reasonably close to the temperature he was supposed to be. He climbed out of the shower, toweled off, and looked down in dismay at his wet, ruined clothing in a pile on the floor. No way could he put that stuff back on. He got cold just looking at it, not to mention it was saturated with salt water.

Irritated at needing help from the swimmer yet again, Collin wrapped a towel around his hips and stepped out into the hotel room.

His rescuer had stripped the wet suit down to his waist, baring his entire darkly tanned torso and revealing a tantalizing line of light brown hair running down toward that impressive bulge of neoprene-clad junk Collin also couldn't help but notice.

The swimmer was tall, six-foot-two or so, and ran to the lanky side. But he looked hard and fit from head to, umm, crotch. His shoulders were broad and angular, but when he moved, Collin realized they were sheathed in more muscle than initially met the eye. Maybe it was the guy's height that made him look deceptively lean. Abruptly Collin recalled feeling that hard body pressed against his from the back of his neck to his ass in the water when the swimmer had mistakenly thought *he* was drowning. Even through the neoprene, he'd been warm. Vibrant. Sexy as fuck.

Startled at the spark of interest, greater than for any other man since the accident, he went very still inside, unsure of whether to stomp it out or to huddle close over it, protect it, and try to nurse it and grow it more.

The guy's blond hair was dryish now, shaggy, and in need of a trim. That lean jaw could use a decent shave too. His beard stubble was blond with a faint hint of strawberry in it. Swimmer Guy hadn't gotten up close and personal with a razor for several days, at least. He looked like a beach bum—admittedly a hot one—beneath the scruffy exterior, but a bum nonetheless. Collin's preferences ran to elegant men. Neat, sophisticated, put-together men. Not the rough, natural, outdoorsy vibe this man was practically oozing.

Those eyes, though. Mother of God, they were the brightest blue Collin had ever seen. The fellow was totally not Collin's taste, but those electric cobalt peepers were almost enough to make him consider taking a walk on the wild side.

After clearing his throat uncomfortably, Collin asked, "Any chance I could borrow some dry clothes for long enough to go up to my room and change?"

The swimmer's gaze, which had been roaming up and down Collin's towel-clad physique in open appreciation, lifted reluctantly to meet his stare.

"Yeah, sure. Help yourself to anything in my drawers." The swimmer smirked at his own joke, which Collin might otherwise have found mildly amusing but rubbed against his mind like sandpaper now. Christ. Was he actually attracted to this messy beach bum?

The American, assuming his drawling accent didn't lie about his country of origin, was not only physically not his type but also not his type in attitude. A casual, loud, far-too-forward vibe clung to the swimmer. Personally, he preferred his lovers intellectual. Civilized. Restrained.

Apparently, he was expected to paw through the swimmer's clothing by himself. Reluctantly, he opened a drawer and found a wide selection of brightly colored logo T-shirts and lightweight surfing shorts.

Bitchin', dude. Not.

Hiding his distaste, he picked out a relatively sedate T-shirt in faded pink advertising some professional surfing event at the Banzai Pipeline, wherever that was, and a pair of khaki shorts.

He retreated to the bathroom to drop his towel and don the beachwear. Wrapping his own sodden clothing in the towel, he stepped back out into the main room, carrying the bundle.

"Lookin' good, dude."

He glanced up at his rescuer and replied dryly, "Thanks."

The swimmer, now divested entirely of the wet suit, wore faded, torn jeans and a ratty T-shirt. The clothing hung just loosely enough to be sexy. One good tug and those pants would slide off those narrow, hard hips, and that killer ass would be exposed. Ten to one the guy was a freeballer....

"What's your name, English?"

"Collin Callahan. You?"

"Gun."

"As in Big Gun?" he guessed. "Top Gun? Going, going, gun?"

Gun rolled his eyes. "Naw, man. As in long gun. It's a surfboard used for riding big waves. It's built long and narrow, kinda like me. Comes from elephant guns, which are long and strong and drop the big ones."

"I gather you surf?"

Gun laughed and replied, mimicking Collin's British accent when he answered, "I gather I do."

Offended but not interested in showing it, Collin said formally, "Thank you for the clothes. I'll send these out to the laundry and return them to you by tomorrow."

"Why?"

"Why what?" he echoed, a bit flustered.

"Why wash 'em? You just got out of the shower, and they'll touch your skin for about two minutes total. And I've got more shirts and shorts. Unless you've got cooties, just bring 'em back when you're done with them."

"Uh, thank you…." He paused, hinting that he needed an actual name to complete the sentence.

"Gun."

"Right. Gun." What a jerk. Wouldn't give up his real name, not even after Collin had jumped into the Mediterranean on a cold-ass day, fully dressed, to save said jerk's life!

More irritated than he'd been in a long time, he marched up to his own room indignantly. Ungrateful, arrogant, obnoxious… athletic, hot, mesmerizing… no! *Jerk.* That was the final word. Gun was definitely a jerk.

Thank goodness the fellow had shown his complete lack of couth before he'd gone too far down the road of making a terrible mistake with the American surfer.

By some small miracle, Collin's room key was still in the pocket of his wet pants. He pulled out the magnetic card and swiped his way into his room. After dropping his soaked shirt and pants on the floor of the bathroom, he immediately and with great distaste stripped off Gun's clothing and gratefully pulled on his own neatly pressed wool trousers and a freshly starched dress shirt. His normal armor back in place, he headed down to the veranda to fetch his sports coat, cashmere jumper, and Italian loafers. Thankfully, they were still where he'd left them in a pile on the porch.

Now to return Gun's shirt and shorts, and he would be finished with this whole unpleasant little episode. And the hot swimmer could take his smug attitude and shove it.

CHAPTER TWO

OLIVER "GUN" Elliott opened his door at the knock and stared. Day-um. The tense British lifeguard-wannabe looked even better in clothes than he did wearing nothing but a towel. And he'd been freaking hawt, rocking terry cloth that clung precariously to his hips and showed of a six-pack of abs that any surfer would be proud of. Looked as if he worked out a lot. Not a Muscle Beach bodybuilder type… more the running and calisthenics type. Maybe a martial artist. He looked supple enough for something like judo or kung fu. The dude had a seriously cut body. Body fat: none. High-protein diet: totally.

"That's why you got hypothermic so fast, you know," he said.

"I beg your pardon?" Collin replied, managing to look both confused and uptight at the same time.

"No body fat."

"Um. Perhaps a context for your comments would be helpful?"

"I was thinking about how you looked wearing that towel before. You're ripped, dude. No body fat. That's why you got cold so fast when you jumped in to save me. Thanks, by the way. Square of you to come in after me like that."

"Square?"

English sounded pissed off, so Oliver explained. "Yeah. You know. Square. As in cool. It was cool of you to come in after me."

"Ah. In that case, you're welcome. And thank you for making sure I got back to shore safely."

Jeez. The guy sounded like a walking Debrett's British Etiquette manual. "No prob."

"And thank you for lending me the clothing."

English held out a glossy paper gift bag, the kind high-end boutiques used, and Oliver took it, peering inside. His Banzai T-shirt and khaki surfing shorts had never been folded so neatly in their entire lives. "Anytime."

One corner of—Collin, that was his name—of Collin's mouth turned up in wry humor. "I sincerely doubt I will be borrowing your clothes again anytime, but thank you for the offer."

"Too bad."

Oh fuck. The words were out of his mouth before he stopped to consider them. This wasn't California, where anything went and casual propositions were a way of life.

For just an instant, he thought he saw a spark of heated interest in Collin's cool gray eyes. Nah. He hadn't seen that. It was just wishful thinking. This guy was way too classy to slum around with a guy like him. A pang of disappointment startled him. Usually, he wanted no part of uptight pricks who reminded him of the world he'd left behind for the beach life. Once upon a time, a man like this wouldn't have been at all out of his league. But now....

He ran a hand through his long hair that he'd been trimming with a pair of dull scissors for the past couple of years.

Oddly enough, he didn't want to run screaming from this uptight Brit. There was something about the guy. Something tragic, broken even, about the man that called to him. Maybe he tuned in to the guy's pain because he'd lived in a similar headspace until he'd finally ditched the life his family had shoved down his throat for so long.

"What do you do to work out, Collin? You obviously don't surf."

"I study martial arts. I find that they calm the mind and center my focus."

Boom. Nailed it. "Sweet! Which one?"

"Traditional judo, some tai chi, and a variant of jujitsu taught by the British Special Forces."

"You're not a soldier, are you?" Not that he would've been surprised to find out Collin was one. He just would've been surprised to find a soldier in this particular location with such an illegal event about to begin.

"No. I'm not military."

"Whew. Had me worried there for a minute. I mean, you could definitely pass for a military type."

"Why do you say that?"

He tilted his head, considering. "Well, there's the short hair and the guy-who-works-out-a-lot thing. But mainly it's your intense, poker-up-the-ass bearing."

The guy's spine stiffened even more, going ramrod straight. Fuck. Oliver had stuck his foot in his mouth *again*. Most of the surfers he hung out with were too stoned or too brain-fried from being stoned to give a rat's ass when he said stupid crap that could be interpreted as insults.

So touchy, this guy was. Or maybe Oliver had become that big a social klutz when he'd checked out of real life and moved to a shack to surf his days away.

"Can I buy you a drink or a meal or something to say thank you for trying to save my life?" Oliver asked belatedly. Dropping the invite like that into an awkward silence probably would prove to be colossally bad timing, and he wouldn't blame the guy for saying no. He had a hard-core zig going every time he should be zagging with this man.

"That would be nice."

Whoa. Wait. What? English had accepted?

"You sure?" he blurted, incredulous.

"Is there some reason for me to be apprehensive over or turn down the offer to dine with you?" Collin asked cautiously.

"Hell no—uh, no. Lemme grab a real shirt. This joint's restaurant has a dress code and gets picky about it."

"You would know," the Brit said mildly.

He shot an amused glance at his guest. Nobody could deliver a sarcastic put-down quite like a Brit. Good thing he didn't have an ego—at least not about his wardrobe.

He did, however, take pride in his fit physique. He figured English had earned a bit of payback by way of a striptease. He pulled his T-shirt over his head and reached into the closet for a polo shirt with an actual collar, which was about as formal as his attire ever got. He'd heard that the El Rocca was old-school European, though, so he'd broken down and invested in a few garments that actually passed as *not* T-shirts.

A sharp breath sucked in behind him.

Hah. Take that for popping off about my shitty clothes.

His face emerged from the polo shirt's neck, and he grinned over at Collin. "Like what you see?"

Collin's facial muscles twitched infinitesimally. Just enough to indicate a frown without actually being one. So damned British polite, this man was. Which gave him an irresistible urge to poke until he got a rise out of Collin.

"Either you're straight and my gaydar has gone completely haywire, or else you're gay and severely uptight. Which is it?"

"Those are not the only two alternatives to explain a startled reaction to a strange man undressing in front of oneself," Collin declared, a shade defensively.

"Doesn't it get uncomfortable having that stick up your butt all the time?"

"I beg your pardon?"

"No reason to ask for my pardon. I'm pretty hard to offend." He knew damned well that wasn't what Collin had meant, but the guy really needed to loosen up. Or more accurately, he had a perverse urge to force the guy to loosen up. Weird. Usually he didn't get into debauching the closeted and uptight homocurious members of the male population. But damned if this one didn't make him think all kinds of lecherous, cherry-popping thoughts.

"While you're changing, you might want to consider a less… well-ventilated… pair of pants. I doubt they'll let you into the restaurant in those jeans," Collin said.

"Well-ventilated?" He looked down at the holes in his knees and the worn spot on his thigh, where only the white cotton cross threads remained, and grinned. "I paid good money for these holes. They're designer fashion, you know."

"On what planet?" Collin snapped.

Oliver burst out laughing. "It's called California. It's in a galaxy far, far away about a hundred years in the future from your existence."

"Just change, will you?"

"Me? Change? Never." Just enough of a pause to let indignation build in those sexy gray eyes, and then Oliver added, "If you mean I should change the pants, sure thing." Oliver unbuttoned his pants and dropped the offending jeans then and there before reaching into his drawers for another, less worn pair. Too bad he hadn't gone commando today.

It was a blatant come-on, and more hot than he'd expected, to undress in front of Collin Callahan, but the man rubbed him every wrong way with all that stuck-up British manners stuff. He totally wanted to knock the guy out of his comfort zone. To shock him.

Another sharp inhalation announced that Collin was not unmoved by what he saw. Dude was definitely gay or possibly bi. Question was, did Mr. Fussy Pants know that? Or, more important, was he willing to admit to it?

Oliver finished zipping and buttoning his newest and least-ventilated pair of jeans, skipping his usual flip-flops for a more sedate pair of deck shoes. He didn't even own a pair of socks at the moment. And frankly, he planned to keep it that way.

"Am I acceptable now?" he asked wryly. The last time he'd dressed to please someone else had been when his father insisted he put on a suit and tie for his college entrance interview. He'd been fourteen, frighteningly intelligent, and browbeaten into a pile of pubescent goo. That kid had been so damned confused—starting to realize he was gay, desperate to get out from under his family's iron fist, with no idea what to do with his freakishly brilliant mind, and looking for someone to love him before he found a compelling reason to kill himself. Sometimes he wondered if he'd changed all that much from that unhappy kid of long ago.

Collin was speaking. "...as for me, your attire was entirely acceptable before. But now the manager may actually let you eat in his establishment."

He was acceptable, huh? Good to know. Oliver would bet if he got the guy naked in bed, Collin would find him more than merely acceptable. The way he figured it, English would be either a total wild child or completely repressed in bed. But he couldn't for the life of him decide which. And it was starting to make him a little crazy.

He followed the Brit down the hall to the elevator. He had to admit, Collin's glutes made those ultraconservative dress pants look pretty damned good. Martial arts, huh? The guy must be good at it to have an ass like that. That stuff made a person flexible too. Opened up some interesting sexual possibilities....

Stop. The guy was clearly neurotic as hell about sex. Oliver had thrown out blatantly obvious love-to-do-you signals at him, and he hadn't even blinked, let alone responded in the affirmative. Too bad. He would've enjoyed knocking a little of the starch out of Collin Callahan.

COLLIN LED the way into the restaurant, more nervous than he'd been in a long time. Gun was the kind of guy who would let it all hang out in bed, hold nothing back, and enthusiastically embrace being gay, not shy away from it in shame. What would it be like to live like that? Even with Steve, they'd been circumspect, only going to private parties at the homes of friends who knew and approved of their relationship. They'd rarely gone out in public, never gone to his or Steve's office parties, never visited each other's families on the holidays.

He'd grown up furtive and ashamed of being gay, and so had Steve. While they'd been intensely grateful to have found each other, neither of them had been comfortable with sharing their love with the rest of the world. Steve had been even more private about their relationship than he had.

And he'd only come to work for Wild Cards, Inc.—a company run by a pair of gay men whom he was convinced were secretly in love with each other—after Steve's death.

He tried to imagine taking Gun home to his family and literally tripped over his own feet at the mere thought. He jerked his attention back to walking down the hall without falling over.

His family was deeply traditional, which translated to conservative and homophobic. He'd never dared to tell his parents about his proclivity for other boys, although they had probably guessed if their stiff disapproval was any indication. He'd quietly gone off to university, explored his preferences there, and stayed away from his family.

He would lay odds that Gun didn't have a shy bone in his body about being gay. He'd probably exuberantly fucked every liked-minded kid he'd come across in school. And under his parents' noses to boot. Although Gun's parents had probably embraced the whole idea of having a gay son. No doubt it would have immeasurably increased their liberal credentials in California.

He had no business whatsoever pondering a dalliance with Gun. None.

As titillating as it was to consider taking Gun up on his flagrant flirtation, he was better off sticking to his own kind—the semicloseted and deeply guilt-driven. Better the occasional secretive hookup where no one would ever breathe a word of it than a messy, doomed relationship with an uncouth heathen like Gun.

Opposites might attract, but that would only last up to the point where they attacked and killed each other. The scandal it would cause if he got caught messing around with Gun on the job made him faintly nauseated to even consider.

He led the way to a small table in an inconspicuous corner of the restaurant.

"Huh. Went for the romantic table in the corner, did you, English? Didn't see that one coming."

He started. Oh Lord. Was that what people would think? "We can move to a more conspicuous table. Better lit—"

"Relax already. This is fine. Might as well lurk in the corner and study the competition while we're at it."

The very private, very illegal poker tournament he'd been assigned to infiltrate started tomorrow at the exclusive El Rocca Casino in tiny Gibraltar, perched at the junction of the Atlantic Ocean and Mediterranean Sea.

The cover story circulating about this gathering of the world's best poker players was that an Arab prince had rented out the entire resort and casino for a private party with his friends. Although who knew? That might actually be the case. Nobody had any idea who was behind this ultra exclusive, invitation-only event.

He supposed it was possible that the prince existed and that his friends were several hundred of the world's best poker players, each of whom had paid a million dollars for the privilege of participating in this little shindig.

He hadn't personally coughed up that kind of money, of course. The British government had staked the cash in return for information about who was here, who was behind the tournament, and why it had been arranged.

Of course, he wasn't even close to being a professional poker player. He was, however, a quick study and the best mental mathematician in the Wild Cards organization. Contrary to its name, the company provided security and discreet problem solutions to high-end clients, not gamblers. But apparently the British government hadn't known that when they'd come calling with a very off-books request of the firm.

The Home Office was very interested in getting a man inside the tournament and finding out exactly what prize the players were competing for. They seemed convinced that the alleged prince had not created this tournament for his hypothetical personal entertainment.

He was inclined to agree with the government. A great deal of time, trouble, and expense had gone into gathering this collection of the world's best card sharps. And, given that there was no advertising, no television coverage, and no audience, whoever had put this thing together certainly wasn't looking to profit from it. Which left the great unanswered question of why it was taking place at all.

If, in fact, a prince did exist, Collin supposed it was possible the guy merely wanted to pit his own card skills against those of the best. In that case, why not invite the top six or eight poker players on earth to his home for a simple private game? Why an entire tournament? Surely, the prince could have much more easily just entered the World Series of Poker that took place every year in Las Vegas if he was interested in measuring himself against the big dogs of the poker world.

Regardless, when he'd been offered an opportunity to get out of his intel analyst's cubicle and take this once-in-a-lifetime opportunity to be a real spy, he'd leapt at it. Honestly, it was a win-win for everyone. Wild Cards did a favor for the Home Office, maybe got itself some future business from that quarter, he did a favor for his employer, and they gave him a shot at doing more, at being more than a boring, dead-end desk jockey. Steve had wanted him to be more daring. Get out in the field. See more of the world.

Well, Steve. You're going to get your wish for me, for better or worse.

Collin glanced up and realized Gun was, indeed, studying the other people in the restaurant intently. He did the same, staring at the other patrons. With a start, he realized he recognized many of the faces in here from the dossiers the British government had provided to Wild Cards, Inc. of likely attendees at this illegal gathering.

The Home Office anticipated that most of the men and women here would be professional hustlers. Not the kind who starred in Texas Hold'em tournaments on TV, although a few of those were here, too. These would be the hard-core gamblers who took casinos and rich amateurs for all they were worth and never looked back. Tough men and women, unashamedly brilliant sharps, who lived down to the traditionally seedy reputation of professional gamblers.

He leaned forward and asked Gun in a low voice, "Do you suppose most of them are here for the tournament?"

Gun leaned in as well. He was close enough that Collin could see his individual eyelashes. Gun murmured, "*All* of us are here for it. The tournament director has rented the whole place for the next two weeks. The only nonplayers here besides the hotel staff are the card dealers, security guards, and, umm, professional entertainers the director brought in."

So those rumors were true. The Home Office was also interested in the list of the names of the sex workers who showed up here. They were expected to be high-end escorts who catered to the wealthiest criminal elements in Europe. If MI6 could approach a few and talk them into becoming informants, they could be a treasure trove of information to the British government.

He asked lightly, "Who exactly is the tournament director?"

"No idea. I don't think anyone knows. Only invitation I got to this bash was an anonymous email."

"Me, too," Collin lied. "Do you suppose all of these people really have a million dollars to spend on a poker tournament?"

"Any poker player worth his salt is probably sitting on a bank at least that size."

Right. The bank was a player's personal stash of gambling money. It was kept entirely separate from the player's salary and living expenses. The idea was for the bank never to hit a zero balance. Otherwise, the player either sucked and needed to improve or needed to leave the profession and go look for a real job. Having a separate bank also prevented potential gambling addictions from getting out of control.

"So tell me, Gun. What's your guess as to what we're playing for?" The invitation had been mysterious about the winner's prize, hinting that it went well beyond simply the lion's share of the pool of entry fees.

Gun leaned back in his seat, withdrawing abruptly from the intimacy of the conversation. Interesting. Either the surfer didn't know what the prize was or didn't want to talk about it. Gun's cobalt eyes practically glowed in the flickering light of the candle sitting in the middle of the table. Even in this dim light, his eyes were shockingly blue. Collin could gaze into them all night.

A waitress came, and they ordered drinks. Then Gun surprised him by ordering two surf plates. The waitress smiled, obviously flirting with Gun, and retreated.

"What did you just order for us?" Collin asked.

"Surfers work up a big appetite and need to carb—and protein— load. The local version involves steak and potatoes. You burned a crap-ton more calories than you realize staying warm in that cold water, plus flailing around trying not to drown. Trust me. You need to refill the tank."

The surf plate turned out to be a mountain of mashed potatoes topped by a boneless rib eye steak, topped by three fried eggs, the whole thing drenched in hollandaise sauce.

"There must be two thousand calories on this plate!" Collin exclaimed.

"Oh yeah. Easy."

He shook his head, pushed aside the eggs and as much of the sauce as he could, and carved neatly into the steak. He polished off the meat and shocked himself by finishing most of the potatoes. And then the eggs.

A while later, stomach full to bursting, he stared down at his mostly empty plate in minor disbelief. Good call on the huge meal. His body *had* been craving the energy. He pushed his plate back and restrained an urge to loosen his belt a few notches.

"So. What brings you to the El Rocca?" he asked Gun. "Are you a dealer or a player?"

"Player. You?"

"Same."

Gun grinned. "So I guess we'll be, like, mortal enemies."

"Assuming we end up playing at the same table at some point. And odds of that are—"

Gun interrupted, "Approximately fifty to one in the first round, say a diminishing player base of twelve per round, ten or so rounds of play summed—"

Collin interrupted back, "I get the idea." That flash from Gun of the math genius poker player he would expect at a tournament like this one was more intimidating than he cared to admit. *Note to self: don't underestimate the competition, even if they come off like brain-dead surfer bums.*

"Bitchin' good times," Gun drawled.

Aaand… the surfer bum was back.

"Didya get a load of the monster yacht that pulled into the marina overnight?" Gun mumbled around a mouthful of eggs, potatoes, and sauce.

Collin bit back an urge to suggest he chew with his mouth closed and only speak with his mouth open. He wasn't the chap's mother, after all. Not his job to teach the barbarian basic table manners. "Sorry, no, I didn't notice any yacht. I was busy watching you nearly get killed and then trying to save your life. Or at least find your body."

"Thing's a beast. Has to be six hundred feet long."

"That's not a yacht. That's practically a cruise ship."

"No shit, Sherlock. And nobody seems to own it."

Collin frowned. "How do you know that?"

Gun shrugged. "While you were boiling yourself like a lobster in my shower, I did some online research. Boat's called the *Erebus*. No ship by that name is registered anywhere I can find. And I'm a great researcher."

Huh. Collin was a professional intelligence analyst. He would stack his researching skills up against this guy's anytime. When he got back to his room, he'd have to look up the yacht himself. And if he couldn't find it, the entire Wild Cards, Inc. staff bloody well could. "*Erebus*?" Collin responded aloud. "As in the Greek god of darkness?"

"Yuppers."

Huh. That was a rather sketchy mythological reference to choose for a boat name. "Maybe it's registered under some other name but displays the name *Erebus* to protect its owner."

"Yeah, but who needs that much identity protection? Especially because it's bad luck to rename a seagoing vessel."

"Maybe a player in the tournament?" Collin guessed aloud. Privately he hoped it was the director of the tournament making a grand entrance. Maybe his or her arrival would signal the beginning of some answers about who was behind this whole affair, what that person wanted, and why it was being run so secretly.

Gun shrugged. Even hidden by soft cotton, the guy's shoulders were gulp-worthy. He might not be planning to bed the man, but he could at least enjoy the view. Steve would have approved. He'd been fond of saying that he would quit looking at handsome men when he was dead and buried.

A wave of grief rolled over Collin. He held his breath as he always did and waited it out. Thankfully, this one passed relatively quickly.

Changing subject to distract himself he asked, "Have you heard anything about the rules for the tournament?"

Another shrug from Gun. "They don't really matter, do they? The cards will be dealt, the bets will get made. Shit'll happen."

"Are you mainly a Hold'em player?" He'd read that it was a variant of the older poker standard, seven-card stud modified to make play faster and the betting more interesting.

"I prefer straight poker. Made my living at it until—" Gun broke off.

Until what? Collin sensed a mystery. "Why the shift to Texas Hold'em?"

"It got popular a few years back and all the big casinos started running nothing but Hold'em tournaments. From a bettor's standpoint, the better statistician you are, the more you win. Fewer cards dealt means less luck of the draw in play. So professionals prefer Hold'em to regular poker games—" He broke off again. "Christ, I'm rambling. Of course you know that."

Collin circled back to the question that had brought him here. "Aren't you the slightest bit curious about all of the mystery around this tournament?"

Gun's expression went guarded. Closed. *Whoops.* He'd pushed too hard. Collin backed off, saying, "I'm just impatient to get going. I don't like to wait while everyone sits around sizing up the competition."

"I hear ya, bro. That's why I swim. I surf when I can. I'm told there are decent waves over by Tarifa, but I haven't had a chance to check them out yet. Surf report yesterday over there was for glass and bad fetch."

"What, pray tell, are those?"

"Glass as in glassy calm water, and bad fetch means the wind's blowing onshore. An onshore breeze knocks down the waves and turns them into unsurfable mush."

"Ah."

"You've never seen *Endless Summer*, have you?"

"The movie?" Collin frowned.

"Classic surfing flick. Legit stuff. Shows why surfing rocks. You should give it a look."

He couldn't tell if Gun meant the movie or surfing, but either way, he'd skip the look, thanks.

A group of men came into the bar, talking loudly in a tongue Collin recognized with a start as Albanian. He'd worked a case last year that required him to pick up a bit of the language.

Gun murmured, "The mob contingent."

"Excuse me?"

"Way I hear it, they're Albanian mafia. Staked several players to the tournament."

Collin leaned in close enough to Gun to smell the salt in the guy's hair and muttered, "There's such a thing as an Albanian mafia?"

"Fucking A. Their players band together against everyone else in card tournaments and trash the betting like nobody's business. The enemy of my enemy is my friend and all that crap. After all the outsiders are taken down, then they'll turn on each other. They'll go at it like rabid dogs and tear each other apart until one of them is left standing at the end of the tournament."

"Lovely," Collin replied dryly.

"Watch out for them. If a group of them are playing together, they'll cheat the table big-time."

"How?" he asked in surprise.

"They'll signal cards back and forth, and they'll gang bet against a single player to squeeze him or her dry."

"Aren't tournament referees supposed to prohibit that kind of behavior?"

Gun gave him a strange look, like that had been a deeply amateur question to ask. "Of course, they're *supposed* to. Doesn't mean that the tournament referees always see it or that they choose to take action once they spot it. The house gets the same cut of the pot no matter who it goes to."

"What's the house cut in this tournament?" Collin asked.

"One hundred percent, the way I hear it. Rumor is we're not playing for the stake money."

"What, then?"

"No clue."

"Doesn't that worry you at least a little?"

Gun grinned. "Hey, I just came to play some cards." But his eyelids flickered as he said the words. This surfer dude was hiding something. He knew more about this weird tournament that he wasn't sharing. Not that Collin had any business casting the first stone over secrecy. He wasn't about to go around announcing that he was the British government plant at this event.

As he pushed the last mashed potatoes around his plate, Collin considered the revelation that there was no monetary prize at the end of this event. Who in their right mind tossed away a million bucks just to play some cards? Gun was surely in it to win, or he wouldn't be here. Behind that casual facade had to lie an intense but well-concealed competitor. Why else would he be here pitting himself against the most skilled, ruthless card sharks on earth?

"Do you know any of the other players?" Collin asked.

"Some of these pros were around when I used to play."

"Used to?"

"I've been out of circulation for a while. Thought I might stick my toe back in."

Collin was not a highly effective intelligence analyst for nothing. A person did not stick his toe back in by ponying up a million bucks to play in an illegal, cutthroat poker tournament. Gun's story was not adding up. Collin glanced around the restaurant. Who else's story here was a lie?

Was *anybody* here who they appeared to be?

CHAPTER THREE

OLIVER LOOKED around the ballroom, crowded with semicircular poker tables overseen by silent men openly carrying sidearms. It was loud and already smelled of sweat and testosterone, and they hadn't even started dealing cards out of the shoes—the wooden racks that held decks of preshuffled cards.

Women floated around the room, leaning down far enough in their skimpy dresses to flash their assets, both front and back. Those were undoubtedly some of the eye candy brought in especially for the pleasure of the players. Several very attractive young men also cruised the joint wearing equally skimpy outfits. But strangely enough, none of them did it for him. Instead, he saw an uptight Brit in his mind's eye.

Of course, the more unattainable a guy was, the more Oliver enjoyed falling into bed with him. He'd always been a rebel that way.

Speaking of unattainable, he didn't see Collin. But the Brit had to be here somewhere. Poor guy was going to get chewed up and spit out by this bunch. The man wore his emotions on his face like a regular human being, and he didn't seem to have the Off switch for them that the best poker players all mastered. He obviously wasn't skilled enough to hang with the big boys once this tournament really got rolling.

Hell, he didn't know if *he* was skilled enough anymore. He couldn't bring himself to consider the idea of getting old, so he settled for wondering if he was past his prime. Which begged the unbearable question of was he finally growing up? He'd vowed in his early teens never to become like his father—responsible, boring, and bossy. In fact, he'd made most of the major decisions in his life by asking himself what his father would have done and doing the opposite.

It had been years since he'd run the complicated, lightning-fast mental calculations of odds and percentages required to excel at Texas Hold'em. It took practice to weave the math of poker with the psychology of the game, practice he hadn't had in a long time. Could he get the old mojo back? This was his last chance to find out.

He honestly didn't want to think about what came next for him if he failed.

Excitement rippled across his skin as tournament employees came around, placing wire baskets of chips in front of each player. Everyone would start with a stack of chips in denominations that added up to one million dollars. The first thing he'd learned long ago was not to think of the chips as money but only as numbers printed on disks of clay. At the end of the day, poker in any form was just a bunch of mathematical calculations with an element of chance thrown in. And even that chance had its own mathematics if a person was skilled enough at the required calculations.

Which he was.

He sized up the other players at his table. He knew two of the five from his days as a pro in Las Vegas. They were both competent, if not the most imaginative of players. A third player looked and acted like a rich businessman who probably kicked all his poker buddies' asses back home, wherever home was, but who was too excited to actually belong here. Players four and five were unknowns. One was a burly German, and one a stone-faced Asian who wasn't giving away a thing with his expression. Trick with guys like that was to watch their fingers and not their faces. And right now, Asia was fiddling with his chips compulsively.

A male voice boomed over the public address system. "Good evening, ladies and gentlemen. Welcome to the World's Ultimate Poker Tournament. The game is Texas Hold'em, no-limit pots, ten thousand to open, minimum raise twenty thousand. We will play ten-hour sessions starting at 4:00 p.m. each day with a one-hour break halfway through. We will take a one-day break every three days until the field is reduced to one hundred players. When you are eliminated from the tournament, you will be expected to pack your bags and leave El Rocca immediately. Transportation to the airport will be provided."

All pretty standard.

The announcer continued, "Once the field has been cut to one hundred players, there will be modifications to the rules, but those will be announced at that time."

Interesting. He'd never heard of a tournament that changed things up midcourse. Maybe it was arrogant of him to assume he would be around to find out what those rule changes would be, but at one time he'd been one of the best poker players on earth. Before the burnout set in, and the drugs and sex and bad life decisions.

German dude was pulling at his shirt collar. A tell perhaps? Oliver turned his attention to the players he knew. Neither of them appeared to have any immediate tells. Which meant he got to beat them the old-fashioned way—with better cards and playing the odds smarter than they did.

Idly, he rolled a chip back and forth on its edge as the dealer got set up. At least he'd gotten past his self-destructive period. He'd gotten sick to death of his father continually interfering with his life, pushing him to enter the family business, demanding that he monetize his talents. The man was always nagging him and yanking his chain. Eventually he'd rebelled against all of it. For a few years there, after he'd been banned from most of the casinos in North America, he hadn't been sure he would make it to his thirtieth birthday.

Nowadays, he scraped by doing odd jobs, fixing peoples' computers, and tutoring math to a few rich brats he met on the beach. All in all, it was a good life. No commitments, not beholden to anyone for anything, drifting along free of everything and everyone who'd made him crazy.

Although recently, he'd been considering getting a real job, finding a way to use his talent with math and computers and his first-class Stanford University education to make a decent living. He was ready to rejoin the real world, but on his own terms this time.

And then that invitation had come in an email to him, asking him to play at the most exclusive poker tournament ever put together and offering to pay the stake money for him. Whereas the world championships of poker that were widely publicized only attracted the relatively honest players from around the world, this one promised to pull in the best of the best regardless of moral or ethical compasses. Not that the invitation stated the case so baldly. It merely emphasized that the tournament was open to all players, regardless of their standing with casinos or other gambling establishments.

Which was lucky for him. It wasn't that he cheated. He simply was too good a card counter and too good a mental mathematician for casinos to let him play. So this tournament had been right up his alley. The question was who knew that about him and had sent him the invitation?

Moreover, who had known where to find him and how to contact him? He'd been completely off the grid for years. At least until one of his surfing buddies announced that he'd gotten an email containing a request to pass it on to Oliver Elliott. It was all very mysterious, which also was totally irresistible to him. He'd never met a puzzle he couldn't solve, and this one would be no different.

He had his suspicions as to the identity of the invitation's sender; he only hoped he was wrong.

The announcer called the start of play, and cards were dealt, chips pushed out, and bets made. He folded out early in the first couple of hands on mediocre cards, which gave his stomach time to settle and his nerves time to steady before he actually started betting.

He won the next hand he played on a pair of queens. In the following hand he went to work on, he got an unlucky turn on the river card—the fifth and final board card exposed—but he won the hand after that easily, raking in a big pot.

The overexcited businessman turned out to be a shrewd bettor who was a hell of a lot better player than he let on, and Asia fiddled harder with his chips the better his cards were. The guy wouldn't last long with such an obvious tell. But it wasn't his job to point that out to the poor bastard.

Play was relatively slow as everyone worked the numbers and tried to pick up tells on their opponents. Oliver kept up his beach bum facade to the best of his ability, attributing his wins to awesome luck, dude. For the most part it worked; the other players underestimated him consistently.

By the end of play that night, a dozen players had been eliminated, and another dozen or so were short-stacked on chips and on the verge of elimination. He was up one hundred fifty thousand dollars and well pleased with the day's efforts, given how rusty he was. The hotel put on a free buffet for all the remaining players, and he piled his plate with salad and raw vegetables.

"Hey, handsome. What's your name?" A leggy California-blond type draped herself along his entire left side.

"Gun."

"Ooooh. That's an awesome name. Mine's Desirée. Desirée Moorhead."

Best. Prostitute. Name. Ever. He looked up from the serving tray of pasta. "Is that seriously your name?"

"Cross my heart and hope to die. It's on my birth certificate."

"God. I'm so sorry," he mumbled, moving on to the fruit and cheese trays.

"Can I be your dessert? I love to play with whipped cream. You can even eat my cherry."

Oliver grinned at the tanned blond. That was one of the worst come-on lines he'd ever heard. But she delivered it with such sincerity that it totally worked.

"Thanks, Desirée, but I think I'm just going to finish my meal and get some sleep."

"Some other time," she purred.

Not in this lifetime. But who was he to rain on her parade?

"What happened to the surfer breakfast?" a familiar voice asked from behind him.

"English. You still in the tournament?"

"Of course I am. You?"

He snorted. He was planning to win this thing, thank you very much.

"Are you already sitting with anyone?" Collin asked.

Jeez. What was this? A middle school cafeteria? "Nah. I'm not here with anyone. These aren't my friends."

"Mind if I join you? A redhead named Angeline seems to think I'm the most sexually deprived man on earth. I swear, she's stalking me."

Oliver grinned broadly. "The tournament director's paying for their services. You should take her up on her generous offer."

"She plays for the wrong team," Collin murmured low.

Hah. Nailed it. He glanced up quickly, catching Collin's gray gaze on him. Dude, that man was easy on the eyeballs. The Brit was square-jawed and clean-cut in a movie-star kind of way. His dark hair was thick and wavy, cut short on the sides, and painfully neat. The guy's suit was conservative, effectively hiding most of the wholly fuckable brawn beneath. But then, there was a lot more to Collin Callahan than met the eye.

Collin was astronomically not his type. He liked them a little dim, a lot casual, no challenge in the mental acuity department, and no strings attached. Just a fuck.

Not that he dared even contemplate getting involved with one of his competitors here. This was perhaps the biggest poker tournament of all time. No way was he going to risk his shot at taking home what was surely a massive prize just for a hot piece of ass. Still. Collin's was a damned tempting piece of ass.

"C'mon," he said reluctantly. "You can sit with me. Just understand people will judge you for hanging out with the likes of me."

They set their trays down and slid into a booth facing each other. "What's wrong with you?" Collin asked.

"Nothing. Well, nothing major. I do have the odd character flaw here and there."

"Oh yeah? Like what?"

"I'm told I'm stubborn."

"I can attest to that."

He rolled his eyes at Collin.

"What else?" Collin pressed.

He picked up a carrot stick and munched on it idly. "I'm also told I'm impatient and arrogant."

"Are you?"

"I'm impatient with stupidity, but I don't consider that a serious flaw. As for being arrogant, I'm not ashamed of being intelligent. Is that arrogance? I don't know."

"If it is, I'm right there with you. When I was a child, people tried to convince me it was more important to be liked and accepted by my peers than it was to do my best. I rejected that idea. Hence, I didn't have many friends. But at least I could have an actual conversation with the ones I had."

Oliver laughed. "I know. Right? Who wants stupid friends?"

They ate and traded small talk over everything but cards—video games, the weather, how gigantic the Rock of Gibraltar was in person.

And then Collin surprised him by asking frankly, "Why are you really here?"

"What do you mean?"

"You're not just here for the vacation to the Mediterranean coast to play some cards. You have an agenda of some kind."

Whoa. That was perceptive. Had he underestimated Collin? What else had he missed about the guy?

Maybe it was the bald honesty with which the question had been asked that prompted him to answer equally honestly, "I've been itching for years to prove that I'm the best poker player on earth. And now's my chance."

If he was truly arrogant, he might wonder if someone knew his fondest wish and had set this whole thing up to lure him in. A patently ridiculous thought, he knew. Still, it had been a hell of a piece of bait to dangle in front of him. But then, he supposed the idea of testing one's self against the best of the best would have been irresistible to most of the players here.

"Why haven't you just played a bunch of professional poker tournaments and proved you're the best that way?" Collin asked.

Oliver winced. In for a nickel, in for a dollar. "I'm not allowed to play poker pretty much anywhere." He added hastily as Collin's eyebrows sailed upward, "I've never cheated or ripped anyone off. I'm just too good. The casinos have to ban me or I'll take their customers for too much cash at the poker tables."

"Rough problem to have," Collin muttered.

"Actually, it does suck. There are a finite number of casinos on earth, and I can only play each of them once or twice before they kick me out. I could have made a good living at it. Instead, I…." How to describe essentially being homeless to this neat, organized man? "…can't," he finished lamely.

"Who are the other top players to watch out for?" Collin asked, glancing around the dining room.

Collin really didn't know? What the hell was he doing here, then, swimming with the big sharks? He was going to get eaten alive. Worry for the Brit shot through him, startling him. He'd never worried about the other pros he'd destroyed, and in some cases bankrupted, at the tables. They all knew the score. Knew it was nothing personal.

But this guy, this Englishman, was a lamb in the woods. Or keeping with the shark analogy, chum in the water. Either way, he was going to be gobbled right up.

"This tournament has attracted all the usual big-name players, but because banned players and hobbyists are also eligible, a fair number of folks have shown up who I've never seen before. Your best bet is to assume everyone here knows his or her shit."

"That's not very helpful," Collin responded, sounding disappointed.

"The best players will emerge in the next two or three days and start to pull ahead in the overall chip count. Random chance will gradually get overwhelmed by the mathematically superior decision-makers. Antonio Mastrianak, the bald guy over by the window, is a four-time world champ, and if I'm not mistaken will be the chip leader after today. He had a big-ass pile of chips in front of him when I walked past his table earlier."

Collin folded his linen napkin beside his plate. "So tell me, what do you do during your downtime to relax besides surf?"

His gaze shot to Collin's. Surely that wasn't a proposition. Not out of Mr. Stuffy Pants. "If I can't surf, I swim. If there's a hot guy around, and we're into each other…." He shrugged. There. That was as blatant an invitation as he could possibly throw down.

Collin shifted uncomfortably in his seat.

Oliver was feeling no little frustration himself. He leaned forward. "I can't read you, and it's making me nuts. Am I sensing 'I've got a hard-on and how am I going to stand up?' discomfort out of you, or 'Crap, I wish this guy would quit dropping hints' discomfort?"

Collin opened his mouth. Closed it. Opened it again. "Both."

Surprised, Oliver leaned back in his seat and nodded slowly. "Outstanding. I can work with that."

COLLIN WAS shocked at how forward Gun was being. He got that the guy was tense and looking to blow off some steam, and goodness knew he was wound tight himself. Trying to pass as a real poker player among the best of the best in the business was beyond nerve-racking.

He'd read every book he could get his hands on and could recite back nearly every word of them. His boss had even arranged for a retired professional poker player to give him hasty lessons. But the reality of an actual tournament was so much more daunting. He had yet to figure out the most efficient order in which to do the various mental calculations that were necessary before every single action, be it placing a bet or folding. Frankly, he'd gotten damned lucky today to only be down about fifty thousand dollars from his original one million.

Collin asked, "Would you mind if we went back to your room and talked a bit? I'd love to pick your brain about something. Or you could come to my room, 1086."

Gun looked genuinely surprised. But then those brilliant eyes of his lit up like blue fire, and Collin's dick leapt to attention, willing and ready to report for duty. Good grief. His own libido was dying to help him fail at this difficult assignment. He only wanted to talk, for God's sake! Well, he *wanted* to do more than talk, but he had no intention of doing more than that.

"Sure. You can come to mine and we can start by talking if that's what gets your engine going. But let's not be seen leaving the dining room together. People will be watching for betting alliances to form. And since the tournament rules didn't say anything about how team betting would be handled, I don't want to be the guy accused of doing it."

Collin nodded, surprised. He hadn't ever considered the concept of cheating by team betting. "Fair. You go first. I'll come up to your room in a bit."

He went back to his own room and watched a financial news channel on the telly until his hard-on finally calmed down. He put on tight Spandex trunks in lieu of his usual boxers, and slipped his trousers back on. Girded as best he could against an embarrassing display, he headed out.

When he got to the American's room, Gun offered him a beer out of the minifridge.

"No, thanks. I need to keep my head clear."

"Whatever floats your boat," Gun replied, taking an appreciative swig out of a brown longneck. He held up the bottle. "I had a drinking problem a few years back. Went cold turkey for three years, but I can finally enjoy a beer now without the need to have another, and another."

Alarm cut through him. "Seems like playing with fire to drink at all after having had a problem with alcohol."

"That's me. I live to play with fire."

"Still. Be careful, will you?"

Gun shot him a startled look. As if he wasn't accustomed to anyone else worrying about him or giving a damn if he fell back into a dangerous addiction. Collin sensed that he might have strayed into too personal territory and backed off, changing the subject abruptly.

"I have a question about how you play poker."

Gun threw up his hand. "Hey, dude. Pros don't talk shop, and certainly not in the middle of a tournament."

Crap. That made total sense. But he really, really needed someone's help. And he suspected every expert the Wild Cards might call to ask for advice was already here. He opted for a sliver of honesty. "You might have already noticed, but I'm not actually a professional poker player. I was sent here by my employer with orders to do my best."

Gun grinned around the end of his beer bottle. "Yeah, I noticed."

"What gave me away?"

"Pretty much everything." Gun asked, "So, your boss staked you to this thing? Why on earth would anybody put up a million bucks for an amateur to play here?"

Not a question he wanted to answer or had permission to answer. He just shrugged and hoped Gun would assume his boss was eccentric and had a lot of money to throw away. Rather than give Gun time to follow up, he said quickly, "Okay, so here's the thing I wanted to ask you. And I understand if you don't want to answer me. But maybe this isn't a trade secret or classified information. What order do you do the math in when you're working a hand?"

"What do you mean?"

"Do you calculate the odds on your own hand first, or do you start by working up the odds of what the other guys are holding? I assume you think about the odds of a certain card being turned over on the flop of the dealer's cards last."

"Well, yeah. The flop is the last thing to worry about. First thing to look at is how the other guys are betting. You have to get an idea of what's in their hands before you start looking at the possible hands your cards might make based on what you think they're holding."

"So, you read the other players first before you do any math."

"Sure. If they'll give you a hint. Some of the players here won't give you a read at all, so you have to watch the pattern of their betting over a few hours and get a feel for when they fold and when they play a hand."

"Yes, but pros bluff enough to make that difficult."

Gun shrugged. "Most pros think they bluff randomly, but human beings are creatures of habit. They fall into patterns whether they want to or not. Even a bluffing pattern can be read if you look for it. Dude, I could teach you all the numbers of the game, although that would take weeks or months, but the human psychology of poker—that beast takes years to master."

The good news: in Collin's line of work, reading and interpreting human psychology was a key part of the job. He'd been a human intelligence analyst—first for the British SAS and then for Wild Cards, Inc.—ever since he'd graduated from university. Patterns of behavior, he knew how to spot.

He confessed, however, "I have no idea how to bluff."

Gun frowned. "Sure you do."

"Excuse me?"

"How old were you when you came out?"

"I don't see how that has anything to do with—"

"You are out, aren't you?" Gun demanded in shock.

"Well, sort of."

"Explain."

This was really none of Gun's business. But Collin had been the one to initiate this whole conversation, so it wasn't like he could really take offense at where it went. He sighed. "In my own life, I'm out. My friends know. And at the job I have now, my employers know and don't care."

"But you've had a job in the past where you couldn't talk about it?"

"Correct." While the position of the British government was that sexual orientation could not be taken into account in the workplace, the reality wasn't always that simple. And his last boss had been quite the homophobe.

"What about your family?" Gun asked.

Mentally, he winced. But he answered evenly enough, "My family prefers to live in denial. We operate under the theory of they don't ask and I don't tell."

"Perfect."

He blinked at Gun's strange pleasure at what was a constant source of pain in his life. The guy must have read his pain on his face, for Gun said, "I'm not trying to be an asshole. Remember, we're talking about bluffing. Closeted people become extremely proficient liars by necessity. They have to *live* a lie."

Collin stared. He'd never thought of it in those terms before. But he knew exactly what Gun was talking about. He'd spent years pretending to be interested in women, lying at the office about dates he'd had with guys by changing the genders of his dates to be women in his stories.

Gun sat down on the edge of the bed and waved him down into the chair beside it. He stared as Gun planted his elbows on his knees and stared intently into Collin's eyes. *Concentrate, you idiot. This is not about sex. This is about your bloody job. A world-class poker player is gifting you with priceless insight.*

Gun said, "Think about how you held your face, your entire body, when you were passing as straight with your co-workers. How you checked your words and gestures—every little nuance of behavior—and considered what it would reveal before you followed through with it. Bluffing is pretty much the same. You have to focus intently on what you're doing."

Huh. He definitely knew what Gun was talking about. There had been a time in his life when he'd lived in that careful, secretive space all the time. Maybe that was why he excelled at his particular line of work. He could smell deception in the people he studied from a mile away because he was a practitioner of it himself. And just maybe it would make him a half-decent bluffer now that Gun had pointed it out. More to the point, he suddenly knew exactly what to look for in the other players seated at the table.

Gun was speaking again. "…trick, then, is to pick up on when other players are really focusing hard on their own physical actions."

Collin nodded eagerly. "So you use the concentration required to pull off a good bluff to reveal the bluff attempt."

"Exactly."

"Then I should concentrate on my actions that intently every hand. That way, when I do bluff, I won't give it away!" he exclaimed.

"Now you're catching on," Gun replied, grinning.

Lord, that man's smile was sexy. It stole the oxygen right out of Collin's lungs.

"How did you figure out the correlation between being closeted and bluffing?" Collin asked curiously. Gun struck him as the type who wouldn't have given a flying fuck what anyone thought when he'd figured out he preferred boys over girls.

"My old man can be a bit of a control freak. I had to play along with the idea of my being gay being merely a 'youthful rebellion.' At least until I left home and went to college. My father was embarrassed by my lifestyle choices."

Collin knew the bitterness in Gun's voice all too well from personal experience. At least they had that in common. "He does know it's not a choice, right?" he demanded.

Gun rolled his eyes, and they shared a look of commiseration. An awkward silence descended between them, and if he stayed here much longer, he was going to lean forward and kiss Gun.

A flash of guilt blinded him for a second as an image of Steve's face passed through his mind's eye. Of all people, Steve would want him to go on living. To find happiness. He knew that without a shadow of a doubt. But it was damned hard to let himself reach for happiness. He felt a deep obligation to grieve Steve properly, but no one had been able to tell him how long that would take. The grief counselor he'd spoken with had said he would know when the time was right to lay aside the worst of his grief. She'd said it would always be part of him, but it would eventually become a smaller part of him than the part that was ready to experience joy once more.

Was this that moment? Panicked that he might be misjudging it, he opted to flee rather than risk blowing it permanently with this magnetic man.

He took a deep breath and stood up. Gun rose as well, standing too close and several inches taller than him. Dear God, that man was attractive. His cock stirred, and he was abjectly grateful for the tight underwear containing it. He stepped around Gun, heading for the door and escape.

"Wait," Gun blurted. "Don't go."

Startled, Collin froze in the act of bolting from the room.

Gun pulled out a deck of cards from a suitcase lying in the corner and plopped down on one side of the king-sized bed. "Sit."

Even though it was spoken as a command, Collin heard the request in the word. For some reason, Gun didn't want to be alone. And that admission was completely disarming to him. Lord knew, he hated being alone too. He'd been so alone for all of the past year, ever since the accident. He knew better than anyone how awful and soul-crushing staring at the walls by oneself could be.

Quickly, Gun shuffled and dealt six pairs of cards faceup in an arc, reminiscent of a poker table, and five cards in front of himself, facedown.

Slowly Collin sat down beside him. Gun was making up reasons for him to stay? What did it mean? Mere loneliness? Or attraction, perhaps? Surely not. Gun was way above his league. Particularly in a place like this where skill at poker was the ruler everyone was measured by.

He listened intently as Gun rapidly explained how each imaginary player was likely to react given the cards in front of him. This was the thing the books and lessons had been missing—the synthesis of math and psychology. He leaned forward, studying the cards and running the numbers in his head from this fresh perspective that included behavioral factors.

"Okay, so you're hand number six," Gun said. "What will you do?"

He looked up and grinned. "I thought pros don't give away their trade secrets. I'm not going to tell you what I'd do." He *knew* what he would do in this case; he just wasn't going to share.

Gun laughed, and his entire face lit up with humor. The sound of it was infectious, and Collin's own grin widened.

Gun threw an arm over Collin's left shoulder. "God, I like you, and I have no idea why. You're so freaking proper and uptight. I just want to reach out and mess up your hair."

Their gazes met, and the laughter faded from their expressions. Gun's eyes were absolutely mesmerizing, an endless sea of sapphire he could lose himself in. "Thank you for the lesson," Collin managed to choke out past an inexplicable tightness in his throat.

"My pleasure," Gun mumbled back.

They leaned in a little closer to each other. "What's your real name?" Collin asked. "Surely, your parents didn't hate you enough to stick you with Gun."

Gun's mouth quirked up into a funny little half smile. "Oliver. Oliver Elliott."

"Pleased to meet you, Oliver."

"Likewise, Collin."

Oh my. They completed the short journey, and their lips brushed against each other's lightly. It was a chaste little peck, not at all what he was used to from his lovers, who usually fell on him voraciously and went straight for furtive sex without fanfare or foreplay.

The muscular arm fell away from his shoulder, and Collin straightened, clearing his throat.

Oliver murmured, "I'm sorry. I probably shouldn't have done that. But you're just so damned exasperating and irresistible."

He smiled ruefully. "Thank you, I think."

"Aww, man, I didn't mean it like that. You're pretty cool beneath all that starch and… wool."

"I'm not entirely British, you know."

"Get out!"

"My mother's English. Dad's American, so I'm a dual citizen. I was born in England but went to Princeton for university. I went back to England for graduate school and got a job in London. One thing led to another, and I've never been back to the States since."

Desperate to distract himself from the way his heart was pounding and those generous, warm lips that made him think dirty thoughts, Collin asked a little breathlessly, "Where are you from?"

"California. San Jose, originally. Stanford University. Lived in Las Vegas for a while when I was still playing poker, and then I went to Santa Cruz. Best surfing in California day in and day out. And Mavericks is only about an hour away."

"Mavericks?"

"Best big waves on the West Coast."

"Another surfing reference, right?"

"Give the man a gold star!"

God, he was tempted to lean forward and kiss all that laughter and sunshine in Gun's—Oliver's—face. Nobody'd warned him this mission would include a guy he couldn't keep his hands or mouth off of. It was supposed to be a routine in-and-out operation. Stick around a few days, just long enough to figure out what the deal with this tournament was, and then return to base. Which was why they'd sent in a desk jockey like him. Except he was mighty tempted to take his sweet time figuring out what was going on around here and prolong his time with Oliver.

"Do your close friends and family call you Ollie?"

"Not if they want to live. Like I told you, my nickname on the beach is Gun, and that's what everyone except my parents calls me. *They* tend to introduce me to people as their son, The Disappointment."

"From what I've seen, you're an impressive guy. Why would they be disappointed in anything about you?"

Oliver's gaze softened. In what felt like a moment of candor out of the surfer, he mumbled, "They wanted me to work in the family business, but I refused. They played the guilt card, claiming that they'd paid for my expensive education and they deserved to profit from it in return. When that didn't work, they cut me off financially. But I still refused to cave in to them. I'd rather be homeless than be their puppet."

Puppet was an interesting word choice. It spoke of strings that went far beyond simple familial duty. Collin's psychology-trained self red-flagged Oliver's family dynamic for later investigation and analysis.

"Have they accepted your independence yet?"

Oliver shrugged. "If by independence you mean not acknowledging my existence for years, then yes."

"Does that bother you?" Collin asked curiously.

Oliver frowned. Didn't answer right away. He was conflicted about being shunned by his family, then.

"What about your mother?" he tried. "You haven't mentioned her. Is she alive?"

Oliver snorted. "Oh, she's alive. She just chooses to live completely in my old man's shadow. Does whatever he wants whenever he wants it. She's the human version of a mouse."

Yikes. Plenty of resentment there. Probably related to her not protecting him from the worst of his father's abuses. He suspected some combination of physical and emotional abuse was in play, based on the violence of Oliver's dislike for his father.

Oliver dealt several more rounds of cards and quickly analyzed them while Collin paid fierce attention. He learned more about poker in those few minutes than from all the books he'd read. What struck him most, though, was how blinking fast Oliver ran the complex calculations of various odds. Collin was fast, but Oliver's mental speed was nothing short of stunning. The guy might look like a bum, but he had a brilliant mind beneath that scruffy exterior.

"What did you study at uni?" Collin finally asked.

Oliver shot him a crooked grin. "What else? Math." A pause. "I probably ought to disclose that I had a PhD in math by age nineteen. Did my postdoc work in probability. I was a full professor at Stanford by age twenty-four."

"Wow. That explains a lot about why casinos hate you." And maybe it explained a little about his own odd attraction to Oliver. He never could resist a brilliant mind. "If you don't mind my asking, why the whole beach bum persona? There's got to be more to it than pissing off your parents."

Oliver gathered up the cards and shuffled them idly. "That's a perceptive question."

"And that's not an answer."

"You have to understand. My father is a powerful man. Intense. Saying he pushed and pressured me is like saying a volcano is a little bit warm. I had to get away from not only him, but everything he stood for. I couldn't breathe anywhere near him."

Collin made a sympathetic noise. He knew plenty about suffocating families. His might have been well-meaning, but their failure to acknowledge who he was still stung. Having totally killed the mood by bringing up their shitty pasts, he rose to his feet. "Thanks for the poker lesson. I owe you one."

Oliver moved swiftly around the end of the bed, blocking his path to the door. "You owe me one *what*, Collin Callahan? What do you want from me?"

Collin stared, startled. Another revelatory choice of words. "I don't want anything from you. I'm merely expressing gratitude and willingness to reciprocate."

Oliver moved aside so he could pass. "Fuck. I'm sorry. It's just this tournament putting me on edge...."

"What about it is putting you on edge?"

"There's a vibe.... Something's wonky about it. Wonkier than the giant entry fee, no announced prize, and ultra private location."

Fascinating. Oliver felt it too, did he? Collin shrugged. "This definitely is a strange tournament. If nothing else, we'll know by the end of it who's the best of the best."

"That's the thing. I think there's more to it than that."

Collin tilted his head, considering Oliver closely. "Why?"

"Call it a hunch."

"A hunch? You're a mathematician. You rely on observable facts, not guesses or gut feels."

"I'm not just a math nerd. I've got layers, dude. I'm an onion."

Collin snorted in humor. "Right. I'll keep that in mind."

"Isn't this the part where you offer to peel me?"

Collin drew himself up to his full six-foot height. "I am classier and far more subtle than that when I make advances toward someone, I'll have you know."

"I dunno. You invited yourself up to my room. That's pretty damned forward where I come from."

Lord, he liked Oliver's quick wit. Even the rough edges were starting to grow on him. He had to get out of here fast, or else he was going to do something he *really* regretted. As he opened the door, he tossed out lightly, "The way I hear it, everyone is forward in California, Oliver."

"True dat, brah. True dat."

CHAPTER FOUR

OLIVER WAS sharp and the cards fell his way the next night. He went up almost a half million dollars and busted one guy from his table completely out of the tournament. When he checked the leaderboard at the end of play, he was pleased to see that Collin was still in the tournament and had actually pulled back to nearly even at a million in chips. Bright guy. Fast study. Must've taken his lessons from last night to heart today.

Another dozen or so players went out, their chips distributed among the other players as chip totals for the leaders started to climb.

The escorts were more aggressive in the restaurant tonight, but then the players were more aggressive at taking them up on their offers, too. Stress levels were climbing as the play intensified. That, and the players had figured out there was no charge for the services of the ladies and gentlemen. The players were availing themselves freely of the fringe benefits of this junket. Oliver gave it two more days until the pressure would climb enough to bring out the hard drinking and drugs.

And that was when the real pros would start to emerge. They would stay away from the booze and controlled substances, keep their minds clear, and take advantage of the idiots who muddied their brains with chemicals. To that end, he took note of who ate healthy and went to bed immediately and alone.

Speaking of which, he didn't see Collin in the buffet line. Was the guy avoiding him after that kiss last night? Dammit. He'd pushed too hard. Although why he was worried about moving too fast when he should be worrying about moving at all on the Brit, he didn't know.

Not only was something weird about this event, but something was definitely weird about Collin, too. The guy had no business being here. Who in the hell did he work for, anyway? And why would Collin's boss put up a million bucks to send an amateur to this event?

The obvious answer was that Collin worked for a foreign government. But Oliver had poked around on the internet last night and found no record of a Collin Callahan working for the British or US government, or any other government, for that matter. Of course, it was possible the guy was some sort of deep undercover operative or that Collin Callahan wasn't really his name. However, a spy probably would have come to this event a lot better prepared to pass as a real poker player. Which left him wondering, who was Collin and why was he here?

Oliver crashed in bed without coming up with any answers.

Of course, Collin showed up in his dreams wearing a tuxedo. He even ordered a martini shaken, not stirred, as he sat down beside him at a bar.

"You working, Double-Oh-Seven? Or are you just hanging out?"

"You tell me. I could be working...on you."

Hmm. Collin didn't strike him as the type to come on that strong. But you never knew with a Brit. Once the formal barriers came down, no telling how forward they would be. He tossed back his own whiskey, neat.

"Dance with me?" he offered.

They stood up, and he was wearing a matching tuxedo. Weird. He didn't even own a tie, let alone a suit.

"Looking good," Collin purred.

"Right back atcha."

They stepped into each other's arms, and the bar fell away, leaving them alone on a beach and wearing only baggy swim shorts. Collin's chest was smooth and muscular, strong without huge bulk. He ran his hands across the bulges of pecs and down the ridged abs to the bulge below.

Collin did the same, cupping his balls and lifting their weight.

They slipped their hands into each other's shorts, and he sucked in a breath as Collin's strong fist closed around his hard shaft. He did the same, measuring Collin's cock with approval. It was thick and long and hard, just the way he liked them. He slid his hand up and down the velvet-covered steel, loving the slide of flesh in his palm.

He groaned as Collin reciprocated, and his hips undulated in time with the pumping of Collin's hand.

The dream shifted again, and they were lying in a bed, facing each other, hand fucking each other slowly. Their hips strained against each other's hands, their erections pulsing, their balls pulling up tight against their bodies in anticipation of exploding.

But what totally captured him was the way Collin was staring into his eyes, deeply, darkly, with wonder and perhaps even awe.

Nobody'd ever looked at him like that. Like he was the greatest thing since chunky peanut butter. Like he mattered, really mattered to Collin. A rush of affection and appreciation for Collin surged through him, and the dream shifted yet again. He was on his back, his legs wrapped around Collin's ass, while Collin made slow, sexy love to him. His dick was caught between their bellies, and the sweet friction of Collin's thrusts into him rubbed his cock too.

Collin was big, and he grunted as the thrusts came harder and faster, loving the way Collin's gray eyes turned silver and then darkened to the color of a winter storm. Collin's thrusts became shorter and faster, and he gripped Collin more tightly with his legs, pulling him deeper inside, silently demanding more and harder.

Collin's entire body arched against his, and he met his lover halfway, letting out a shout of his own as his orgasm squirted between them, all over his belly. The smell of cum and sweat and the sea mingled as Collin smiled down at him....

Oliver woke up sweating bullets and so turned-on he could hardly breathe. Collin cast in the role of sexy secret agent was a good fit for the guy. He had that air of dark mystery about him.

Belatedly, he realized he was sprawled on top of the sheets, and sticky cum was, indeed, smeared across his belly. Huh. Last time he'd had a wet dream he was about thirteen and had barely figured out what sex was, let alone who he liked to have it with.

Oliver looked at his alarm clock. Nearly two in the afternoon. He didn't have to get up for another hour. But no way was he getting back to sleep after that smoking-hot dream. Might as well go down to the beach and take a swim. He showered quickly, then dried off and sprinkled baby powder over himself. It was the only way to put on a wet suit over damp skin. He pulled on his bright yellow surfing body suit and zipped it up.

A quick jog down to the beach, and he waded out until the water was chest deep. He jumped one last wave and then took off swimming.

He was careful this time to lift his head every minute or two and listen for Jet Skis or motorboats nearby. That had been a hell of a near miss the last time he'd been out in the water. Lucky for him he'd heard the Jet Ski coming and guessed the right direction of its approach when he'd surfaced to look for it. The water vehicle had been practically on top of him, looming over his head. He'd dived just in time and had actually felt the bottom of the craft rub against his back before the water blowing out the back end of the craft had caught him and tumbled him head over ass in the water.

Fortunately, he'd been tumbled enough times by big waves not to panic. He could hold his breath for a good long time, long enough to let the Jet Ski's turbulence settle, check the direction the bubbles were rising, and only then to head for the surface.

And there had been sweet Collin, floundering around looking for him, half-drowning himself. It really had been heroic of the guy to jump into the Med in winter to save him. In street clothes, no less. Foolish, but heroic.

He swam past the marina, past the gigantic yacht moored there, and paralleled the sandy flats that were the newly built, man-made beach on the east coast of Gibraltar. The developer who'd built El Rocca must have backfilled the rocky shore with entire shiploads of sand to create a beach that size. The cost of such an endeavor must be staggering. But then, land had to be incredibly valuable in this tiny British colony.

As he stroked onward, Oliver calculated the depth and volume of the concrete pilings that would be necessary to render the foundation of any building on this reclaimed land stable, taking into account erosion and the scouring action of water and sand. The numbers he came up with were daunting. But it wasn't like money was any object in a place like Gibraltar. The territory was both a banking haven and a playground for the rich and famous. It was a prosperous little place, clinging to the base of its famous rock. Space was the real commodity here, hence the extension of this stretch of coast into usable beachfront.

Curious, he looked back over his shoulder at roughly where he'd been swimming when that Jet Ski had nearly run him over. The prevailing direction of the swells and the lighting conditions out there were perfectly straightforward. The driver should totally have been able to see him. Weird. Asshole must've been distracted. Not paying attention to where he was going.

Ahead, he was surprised to see a cluster of men in dark business suits down by the water's edge. He recognized several of them as security men from the hotel, big and burly with military-style haircuts. They waved him away as he swam a little closer. Then they surprised him by physically closing ranks in a line on the beach. For all the world it looked as if they were trying to block him from seeing the object behind them on the beach. But he had excellent far vision, and they didn't wave him off soon enough. He'd gotten a brief but decent look at what they were clustered around.

A human corpse.

Holy shit. His smooth crawl stroke hitched. They obviously didn't want him to see that body. Maybe they wanted to keep it secret from the other players. Would they remove him from the tournament if they knew he'd seen the corpse?

Thinking fast, he raised one arm to wave back casually, like he thought the men were just waving a friendly hello to him. Then he put his head down in the water and swam with deliberately slow, relaxed strokes, casually pulling away from the group of men and the corpse and being sure to breathe on the side of his body facing away from shore. Meanwhile, his thoughts churned like mad. Surely, he was wrong....

No. He'd seen a dead body before. A surfer drowned a year or so back at Mavericks and had washed ashore the next day. That pale, bloated shape of seawater-soaked human flesh was unmistakable.

In that instant before he'd obeyed the men and turned away from the beach, he'd registered a plethora of details. He reviewed them as he swam, fixing them firmly in his memory for later retrieval.

First, he didn't see any police, which was strange as hell. Why wouldn't the tournament's staff call the police if they found a dead man? Second, it had looked like the security men were preparing to roll the corpse into a blue tarp stretched out on the sand. Surely, they should leave the body alone and not move it until the authorities arrived. Third, and most important, the security men's body language had been furtive. Secretive. It shouted that something fishy was going on regarding that corpse. *No shit, Sherlock.*

He swam back toward the El Rocca, his shoulder blades itching as if he was being watched. It was a struggle to resist the impulse to lift his face out of the water and look back over his shoulder, but he managed not to. He was careful to keep his stroke turnover down to a rhythmic, unconcerned pace as he returned to the resort.

He strode up the beach, unzipping the top of his wet suit. What was he supposed to do now? If he called the police, even anonymously, those men down the beach would know exactly who'd made the call. His wet suit was neon yellow trimmed with lime green and bright blue. Not exactly low-key. Besides, to his knowledge, he was the only poker player going out for ocean swims.

But he ought to tell someone....

Collin. The guy had to be with *some* sort of official agency. Who else would fork over such a large sum of cash just to get someone inside this event?

Intent on reaching Collin, he hurried inside the resort but immediately spied a surveillance camera sticking down from the ceiling in its black bubble. Dammit. He had to play this cool. He forced himself to relax, forced himself to slow down and saunter casually through the lobby, toweling off his hair as he went.

He really ought to call the police, risk to himself be damned. But by the time the police got out to that beach, that body would be gone, wrapped up and hauled away by the security men. He would look like a crank caller and potentially get in trouble with the law, assuming those thugs on the beach didn't make him disappear too.

One thing he knew for sure, now—this was not a friendly game of poker.

The people running this tournament had just covered up a death of some kind. But why? Who'd died? And *how*?

Just how dangerous was this event? He registered one more thing he knew now. This event was a test. Survival of the fittest. Literally.

Maybe rivals from warring drug cartels or crime syndicates had tangled with one another. God knew, the players came from all over the world, and more than a few had nefarious connections. He'd been approached by the mob more than once to handle money for them. He'd always had enough cash in his bank account to decline, but not all poker players had that luxury.

He went straight to Collin's room, still wearing his wet suit. He knocked, and Collin opened the door, fully dressed, shaved, and showered, if his damp hair and smooth cheeks were any indication. Talk about feeling underdressed all of a sudden.

"What are you doing here?" Collin asked in surprise. "I'm not really in the market for a hookup—"

"Good. Neither am I."

"Then what—"

"Inside," he muttered, pushing past Collin.

"What's going on?" Collin asked tersely.

Oliver grabbed a piece of hotel stationery off the desk and scribbled on it, "These hotel rooms may be bugged." While he showed it to Collin, he asked, "Do you have plans for our day off tomorrow? I thought I might do some sightseeing and wondered if you'd like to come along."

Collin looked shocked for an instant but recovered his composure fast enough that Oliver grew even more convinced his hunch about the man's real line of work had been correct. "I don't know," Collin answered evenly.

"Is it too much to ask of you to make up your mind?"

Collin laughed as he moved over toward his suitcase. "That's not why I'm hesitating. I wouldn't have the faintest idea what to look at. Why would anyone bother sightseeing? It's just a dinky little peninsula with a giant rock in the middle." As he spoke, he pulled out a black gadget that he plugged into his cell phone. He commenced passing it over the wall painting and lamp. Oh, man. Not only was the guy a secret agent or something spy-like, but he had cool spy gadgets!

Watching Collin sweep the room for bugs and realizing the conversation was patter for any possible surveillance devices, Oliver flopped down on the bed hard enough to make the springs squeak and said, "I suppose you're right. I'm just tired and wired after the last couple of days. Thought it might do me some good to get out and see the town." He asked casually, "How'd your cards drop last night?"

"Not bad. Yours?" Collin moved on to checking the television and furniture with his little gadget.

Oliver replied, "No complaints. We've got a sleeper at our table. Acts like a rich, dumb mark ripe for the picking, but he's actually a hell of a player. He's wiping out everyone else at the table, and I'm mostly staying out of his way while he takes them down."

Collin turned to face him grimly. "The room's clean. Wanna tell me why you thought it might be bugged?"

"Doesn't this whole tournament strike you as just a little bit sneaky and nefarious?" he asked. "Am I crazy for thinking the crookedness of this event might not stop at its setup?"

Collin looked thoughtful. "What makes you think it's sneaky?"

He shrugged. "Everything. The secretiveness of the invitations. The inclusion of banned players. The lack of overarching rules."

"I take your point. And yes, it all does seem a bit sketchy. But what do you mean about the crookedness not stopping at the setup? Have you seen or heard something about who's behind the whole thing?"

Oliver had a sick feeling in the pit of the stomach that he might know who was behind this tournament; and if he was right, the man wouldn't hesitate to bug—or kill—any players who got in his way.

Collin interrupted his speculation, asking, "What do you want to talk about so bad that it can't be overheard?"

Oliver spoke quietly, still nervous about possible ears and eyes in the walls. "Hear me out, okay? Don't think I'm crazy."

"I do not think you're crazy."

"I was out for a swim just now. Went north past the marina. I was swimming parallel to that stretch of man-made beach when I saw a dead body that looked like it had washed up on shore."

"Do you even know what human corpses look like?" Collin blurted.

"Actually, I do."

"Have you called the authorities?"

Oliver winced. "Here's the thing. The tournament's security team was there, and they waved me away before they thought I saw the corpse. I played dumb and swam away all casual, like I hadn't seen anything. There were no police present, and it looked as if they were getting ready to wrap up the corpse and move it."

Collin caught the implications of that immediately. "Why would they hide a fatality?"

"I have no idea. Gibraltar isn't the kind of place that's going to have frequent drownings, though."

"Drowning?"

"The body was bloated and waterlogged."

"Describe it," Collin ordered tersely.

"Umm, like the Stay Puft Marshmallow Man? You know. All white and puffy."

An exasperated huff. "Thanks for that mental image. What I meant was, did you see any details like hair color and length? How tall did the person look? Male or female?"

"Oh. Male. Bald. Maybe six feet tall. Probably paunchy even before the bloating."

"See? Now that's useful information." Collin thought for a moment. "Have the tables each player is assigned to this evening been posted yet?"

"Totally. Play resumes in less than an hour. You should be able to pull it up on your laptop," Oliver answered.

Collin sat down at his desk and signed in to the encrypted website for the tournament. Oliver leaned over his shoulder as the table assignments popped up. *Mistake.* Collin smelled better than a new car and hotter than an Italian underwear model. Meanwhile he probably smelled like salt water and rotting seaweed.

Oliver forced his attention back to the computer screen, a cursory glance immediately revealing a discrepancy to him. "We're down one extra player from yesterday," he announced.

"Which one?"

Oliver scanned the player list quickly. "Jesus. Antonio Mastrianak. The guy I pointed out to you in the restaurant who's the chip leader in the tournament. Correction: *was* the chip leader. And now that I think about it, he was a balding guy about six feet tall with a big beer belly."

Collin stared over his shoulder in alarm, and he stared back.

"Oliver, I'm starting to agree with your gut that something is definitely off about this whole tournament. Above and beyond the fact that no one knows who's running it or what prize we're playing for."

"Pull up the chip leaderboard," he murmured. "Let's see who's slid into Mastrianak's place as chip leader?"

Collin replied, "Surely you're not accusing a player of killing another player."

"People have done worse for money. Or whatever the hell it is we're playing for."

Collin looked sidelong at him, and Oliver's pulse leaped. He was still leaning down over Collin's shoulder, ostensibly looking at tonight's roster, and their faces were less than a foot apart. He ought to straighten up, ought to step back, ought to break the circuit of sizzling electricity flowing between them.

But damned if the memory of that smoking-hot dream of Collin as James Bond didn't roar back into his mind in all its vivid detail just then— the sexy slither of a bow tie from around Collin's neck, taut muscles revealed as starched cotton peeled away from Collin's physique, the slow dance of skin on skin. He'd practically been humping the bedpost by the time he woke up.

Collin's gaze dropped to his mouth, and Oliver's pulse notched up even more.

"Where would they take Mastrianak's body?" Collin murmured.

Oliver reluctantly forced his mind to the puzzle, intrigued with solving it in spite of all the snap, crackle, and pop arcing back and forth between them. "You're assuming they wouldn't put it on a boat and dump it at sea."

Collin shrugged. "Tricky currents around the Rock and through the mouth of the Mediterranean. Lots and *lots* of naval surveillance of everything and everyone who goes in and out of the Med. Hard to know where a dead body would drift. If you're looking to hide a death, you wouldn't take a chance with the body coming ashore again quickly."

Collin added, "And they weren't getting ready to bury it?"

"Didn't look like it. And it's not as if there's a whole lot of deep dirt on this rock to bury a body in, anyway. And that's assuming someone wouldn't notice you digging a grave and call the authorities."

"Good point."

He nodded. "Okay. If they're not dumping the body, then they have to take it somewhere. If not to a hospital or the police, they would have to bring the body into the hotel. Where in El Rocca would they stash a—I've got it! Surely the kitchen has some sort of walk-in refrigerator or freezer."

"It probably has both, and while that's disgusting, you're probably right."

Collin's voice was a sexy wash of whiskey and suede against his skin and sent shivers coursing down the back of his neck. It reminded him vividly of his dream from before, and his crotch rocket's engines rumbled to life.

Oliver swore mentally. Too much more of this and he could forget standing upright for a while. A roaring hard-on was growling in his blessedly tight wet suit, which would prevent the whole pokey-tent-pole problem, if not the horny bulge. However, there didn't seem to be a damned thing he could do to stop his attraction to this man when what he really ought to be more worried about were the implications of a dead poker player and whether or not his own life was in danger.

Collin spoke slowly, his stare never leaving Oliver's throat. "Why would somebody hide a drowning from local authorities?"

"To keep from drawing attention to the poker tournament?"

Collin shook his head thoughtfully in the negative. "It's known that there's a party going on here. No reason to hide an accidental drowning."

Accidental being the operative word. "But if it wasn't accidental—" Oliver broke off, appalled at where this line of reasoning led. He might suspect who was behind this tournament, but surely his main suspect would never stoop to outright murder.

Collin's grim gaze lifted to meet his. "If it wasn't accidental, we're only left with murder."

Fuck. Collin had gone to the same place he had. If the directors of this tournament were willing to hide bodies, odds were excellent that they knew something about the cause of death and had a reason to hide it. Which meant it was likely criminal in nature. Oliver's blood ran cold at the possibility. If he was right about who it was....

He didn't want to think about the ramifications. Surely, he was wrong. His father couldn't possibly have anything to do with this mess. But it stank of the sort of event his father would organize.

"Who would kill Antonio Mastrianak?" Oliver asked, desperation to be wrong coursing through him.

"Who had a motive?" Collin responded, his voice low and sexy.

Ay, chihuahua, he could eat that man all up. "Someone from Mastrianak's personal life who followed him here? An enemy or business deal gone bad, or an ex-wife, maybe?" he suggested, desperate to be wrong about his hunch. "How do you suppose he died?"

Collin frowned. "We'd have to look at the body to tell. He might have been killed and then dumped into the water. Or somebody could have held him under until he, in fact, drowned. He could've fallen overboard from a boat. Or he could've gone for a simple swim and had a heart attack. I'm not ready to definitively call it murder until there's an actual autopsy."

"There would have to be a body for one of those," he replied.

Collin added grimly, "And if there's a cover-up in place, his body may be long gone by now."

"A heart attack wouldn't prompt a cover-up, would it?" Oliver responded.

"Probably not."

Oliver took the next leap of logic. "At a minimum, the tournament's security team has to suspect foul play or be directly involved in foul play, or else they wouldn't hide the guy's death."

Collin nodded. "Given that Mastrianak has been here at the resort for at least the past four days and no outsiders are being let in, if there was foul play, we can logically deduce that someone in some way associated with the poker tournament did him in."

"Well, *that* certainly puts things in a different light," Oliver declared.

They stared at each other, him in dismay, and Collin in unhappy confirmation.

Oliver blurted, "Why aren't you more surprised?"

That elicited a short, humorless laugh out of Collin. "Not a lot about human beings surprises me anymore. I've seen the worst people can do."

Whoa. There was a ring of hard life experience in Collin's voice and the cynicism to show for it. "Where have you seen the worst of humans?" he asked quietly.

"My job."

Thank God. For a second there, he'd worried that Collin might have had a horribly violent or tragic past. But if it was his work, then he hadn't been the actual victim of the twistedness. Which, of course, begged the question of what sort of work Collin did, exactly. Aloud, Oliver asked, "What do you know about this tournament that you're not telling me?"

"I don't know anything. Other than how suspicious the whole setup is. Why include hustlers and banned players in a legitimate event? It makes no sense."

"Is that why you're here? To solve the riddle of why it's an open invite?" Even though he was no expert in being a superspy, that sounded like a flimsy cover story.

Collin, revealingly, said nothing. He merely smiled pleasantly, as if indulging Oliver's bizarre fantasies.

His dreaming image of Collin as a spy flashed through his head. His subconscious was not wrong in pegging this man as some sort of covert operator. Collin was lying. The guy *did* know something about this tournament that he wasn't sharing. And furthermore, he was obviously here to investigate it. Oliver tried again. "So, are you some kind of James Bond? Can I help?"

Collin's smile froze in place for just an instant. A person would have had to be staring right at him, and from nearly this close, and have spent a fair bit of time memorizing the guy's most minute facial expressions— the way a professional card shark would—to see it. But Collin froze. Which meant he'd nailed it on the head. The guy *was* a superspy.

Coolest gig *ever.*

"What are we going to do first?" Oliver asked eagerly.

"We're going to go downstairs and play poker like nothing happened. If you in any way reveal that you saw a body on the beach, or that you're upset, or that you know Mastrianak died, his hypothetical killer could come after you."

Collin had come to the same conclusion he had—a killer might have targeted a poker player. Possibly someone running the tournament or a staff member at the resort or, he allowed reluctantly, another card player.

Oh, man. Shit just got real. They could be trapped in a closed resort with a murderer, and one of them might be the next victim. Surely not.

Except the dismay and fear clenching deep down in his gut announced in no uncertain terms that Collin was exactly right. There was a killer among them.

COLLIN WAITED until Oliver had returned to his room to shower and get dressed for the tournament before he made a phone call to his boss at Wild Cards, Inc. "Hey, Pere. It's Collin. Looks like there may have been a murder here. Player named Antonio Mastrianak. Another player thought he saw Mastrianak's body wash up on the beach. But resort security waved him away before he could make a positive ID."

Pere swore. "This wasn't supposed to be a dangerous assignment. It's supposed to be purely a numbers game. No guns. No violence. You're a desk jockey, for Christ's sake!"

"Thanks for the vote of confidence, boss," he retorted.

"Aww, bollocks, I'm sorry. I have complete faith in you. But this was supposed to be a straight fraud investigation. No danger, no threats."

"Never fear," Collin responded. "I've got this."

"Don't do anything stupid or heroic, you hear? Promise me."

"I hear you," he replied evasively.

"Promise."

"Fine." A huff. "I promise. No stupid heroics." Which meant he wouldn't ever be mentioning his little stunt of diving into the Mediterranean to save Oliver from drowning.

"What else have you got for us, Collin?"

"I need you to find out who owns a yacht called *Erebus*. She's huge. Upwards of six hundred feet long and looks tricked out like mad.

There can't be many ships like her in the world. And while you're at it, I need a psychological workup on a guy named Oliver Elliott. Tell the analysts to pay attention to what's up between him and his father."

"Got it. Anything else?"

"No, sir. I'll be in touch when I can. It's time for me to head downstairs for the next round of play."

"How's the poker going?"

"I haven't bankrupted the Crown yet. I'm running about even, which puts me in the middle of the pack, at the moment."

"Brilliant! Good luck, Collin."

Yeah. Right. Luck. If only that had anything to do with what was going on around here.

Shockingly, he did get lucky during the round of play that night, hitting one great hand after another, which was probably the only reason he didn't bust out of the tournament. He was so distracted thinking about the dead man and who could have killed him that he barely paid any attention to the card play and bet much more recklessly than he should have. He actually came out nearly a million dollars ahead by the end of the night, putting him close to the two-million-chips mark.

Of course, the other distraction was Oliver himself. The guy was turning into a strange fixation for him. They couldn't be more unlike each other, and yet he found himself drawn to Oliver whether he wanted to be or not.

Why had Oliver come to him after seeing the dead man? Did he trust Collin, or was there a much deeper game afoot? Did Oliver suspect Collin of being a plant? Or was this a test of some kind? Was Oliver actually working for the shadowy, anonymous, tournament director?

Time was called on play, and his table had just finished a hand, so they sat back and relaxed while the other tables finished up their current hands. The Canadian across the table from Collin asked no one in particular, "So, what's the word on the prize for this shindig?"

While Collin listened alertly, the other players speculated, a few guessing that they were only playing for a hefty chunk of the pool of entry fees, while others guessed that a mansion, yacht, or some other exotic prize was at stake. Collin's personal opinion was that there would, indeed, be a cash prize, but that something other than a monetary item was also on the table. But what that could be, he still had no idea. He'd hoped some of the players would have an inkling, but this job wasn't going to be that easy, apparently.

The man beside Collin, probably one of the Albanian mobsters, commented in a heavy accent, "You play good tonight, no?"

He shrugged. "I was lucky."

"You will be biggest mover of day, I think."

Collin was startled. His intent was merely to stay in the tournament, not try to be competitive in it. He'd already noticed that the other players tended to go after those whom they saw as serious competition with an extra measure of aggressiveness. They didn't quite gang bet against the tournament leaders, but they definitely targeted the top players. The last thing he needed to do was draw the rabid dogs' attention.

The other tables wound up play, and the remaining hundred and fifty or so players adjourned. Using the general chaos for cover, he slipped away from the crowd heading toward the buffet and made his way down the hall toward the kitchen.

The space was bustling with activity as food was served up and carried out and carts of dirty plates were bussed back into the kitchen. Heart racing, he did his best to walk through the area as if he belonged there and headed straight to the big commercial freezer in the back. Pulling on the heavy door, he ducked inside, pulling it closed behind him. The lights were on inside the cavernous space, which was filled with metal shelving and stacked boxes.

He paused, breathing hard. In spite of his big claims to his boss, a steel-nerved field operative he was not. Crap, it was cold in here. It went straight to his bones and made him shiver in a matter of seconds. Or maybe that was the adrenaline screaming through his veins, giving him his own personal earthquake. Jesus, this was hard.

How did the regular Wild Cards operatives do it? They always sounded cool, calm, and collected when they called in from the field looking for information or assistance from HQ. If one of them were calling now, he would tell the agent to search the freezer fast and get out before hypothermia made him too stupid to complete the assignment safely.

Take your own advice, Einstein.

He eased forward. Two rows of chrome shelving stretched from floor to ceiling, loaded with frozen food. If he were hiding a body in here, where would he put it? Toward the back, maybe. The shelving stopped as he moved deeper into the frosty compartment, and a larger space opened out before him. A side of beef loomed in the ice fog, hanging from a meat hook. This was more like it.

A sound behind him made him dive for cover behind the beef, plastering himself against the frigid stainless steel wall. *Crap, crap, crap.* His entire body was cramping up from the piercing cold. Peering between the shelves and through the icy condensation hanging in the air, he spied a male figure gliding into the freezer stealthily. That was no kitchen worker fetching food!

No way could he slip out behind the guy and make an escape without being spotted. What to do? Panic ripped through him. In a second, the man would spot him. The words of his field instructor belatedly roared through his brain. The best defense was a good offense. Better to take charge of the situation than passively let someone else seize the upper hand. Right. Do something, then.

He waited until the man drew slightly ahead of him, and then he pounced, wrapping his arm around the intruder's throat, squeezing until the guy clawed ineffectually at his forearm.

"Who are you? What are you doing here?" Collin demanded. He released his arm just enough to let the man form sounds.

"Collin?" the figure croaked.

Shocked, he registered a hard, muscular back pressed against his torso, firm buttocks nestled against his groin, the scratch of beard stubble against his arm, and the saltwater smell of his prisoner's sun-bleached hair. He let go, and Oliver whirled around to face him.

"What the hell are you doing here?" Collin asked in disgust.

"Checking to see if Mastrianak's body is in here. What are you doing?"

"Same. I wanted to check for an obvious cause of death."

"Want me to stand guard while you look for the corpse?"

"Actually, that would be helpful," Collin answered.

"That's me. Mr. Helpful."

"Keep your voice down. The food in a freezer doesn't talk, and we wouldn't want to draw the wrong sort of attention."

"Oh. Right. Got it," Oliver whispered loudly.

Collin rolled his eyes and moved back to the side of beef. He searched the area nearby, and it only took a few seconds to find what had to be Mastrianak's remains. A rolled-up plastic tarp stood in the corner like a lumpy, rolled rug. Nylon cord tied around the whole bundle held the tarp in place. After taking a mental snapshot of the rope's knots and positioning, he reached for the top edge of the tarp and wrestled it down, revealing the dead man's face.

"Oh, man. That's gross!" Oliver exclaimed.

Collin about leapt out of his skin. "I thought you were standing watch."

"I figured you would want me to identify this body as the one I saw on the beach."

"Why?" he asked dryly. "Did you think there would be more than one dead man stored in here?"

Oliver flashed a grin. "Good point. Still. I'm here, and that does look like the corpse I glimpsed. What's that purple stuff around his throat?"

Collin glanced back at the corpse and pulled the tarp down a little more to fully reveal the livid line about an inch wide circling the dead man's neck. "Those are called ligature marks. It means this man was strangled to death, or strangled close to death, before he went into the water."

"Awesome," Oliver breathed.

"Why on earth would you say that?"

"We have our proof that he was murdered. Obviously, the tournament directors are up to no good if they're fishing murdered guys out of the drink and stashing the bodies." Oliver reached into his pocket and pulled out a cell phone.

"You're not going to tell someone about this, are you?" Collin blurted in alarm.

"Duh. Of course not. I'm taking pictures. Gotta collect evidence, right?"

Cripes. He should have thought of that. Oliver's unexpected appearance in the freezer had him more rattled than he'd realized. Or maybe he was a bigger chicken when it came to covert ops than he'd realized. Either way, he belatedly pulled out his own cell phone and snapped a series of pictures as well, including several close-ups of the ligature marks on the corpse's neck.

"Got some great pics," Oliver announced. "Do we need to take a few selfies with him to prove we found him and they're not just random pictures of some dead guy?"

Again, an excellent idea. Morbid, but logical.

Oliver snapped a few pictures of him standing beside Mastrianak, and then he passed his cell phone over to Collin. "Take a few of me with the old boy too, will ya?"

"That's bloody macabre!"

"I thought you said we should keep our voices down," Oliver chided.

Glaring, Collin just shook his head and pointed the camera at Oliver and the dead man. Oliver held up a peace sign behind the corpse's head at the last second before Collin clicked the picture. "Oh, for fuck's sake. Have a little respect for the dead."

"Why? Mastrianak's gone. This is just his meat. Besides, Antonio had a great sense of humor. He would think it was funny."

Not deigning to reply, Collin replaced the tarp and restored the ropes to their original position as best he could.

"Now what?" Oliver murmured.

"Now we have to sneak out of here undiscovered."

"What if we pull the fire alarm and slip out while everyone's evacuating?" Oliver suggested.

"Who would put a fire alarm inside a freezer?"

"Whoever built this one. I saw it on the way in."

Son of a bitch. "Well, okay, then."

Oliver murmured conspiratorially, "Should we go in separate directions? You know, to draw less attention to each other? And then we can rendezvous later in one of our rooms, all spooky-like."

The guy might act half-stoned most of the time, but that was a decent idea.

Collin muttered, "You go left and I'll go right. My room, in an hour."

"Be there or be square, man."

And clever Oliver was back to being Gun, the stoner beach bum.

CHAPTER FIVE

OLIVER WAS shocked at how nervous he felt standing at Collin's door. His belly was all aflutter as if he had a schoolboy crush. Weird. After all, he was no amateur when it came to hookups. He'd made them his stock-in-trade for most of his postpubescent life. But for some reason, this man was different. And not just because of the fuck-me-now British accent and those piercing gray eyes of his, or because of that sexy dream he'd had about the man last night. Especially not that.

Collin opened the door and smiled. Really smiled. With his eyes, his face, his whole demeanor. He was genuinely glad to see him.

Oliver's knees felt a little weak all of a sudden. Was he really that pathetic? Had his life been that deprived of love? One real smile of welcome and he was putty in Collin's hands? *Sheesh. Pull yourself together, dude.*

"You're late."

Oliver pulled out his cell phone and glanced at it. "By one minute!"

The corner of Collin's mouth quirked up. "I don't like to be kept waiting. I was worried."

"About me? Hey, no worries. I'm good, man."

Collin hustled him inside the room and closed the door behind him. "The tournament security guys, who might have been Mastrianak's stranglers, saw you out on that beach. You have to be careful. Lie low and don't attract attention to yourself."

"Kinda hard to do after I cracked the top ten on the player board." He held up his right hand for a high five, but Collin only frowned at it. He let his hand fall. "Party pooper," he mumbled.

"Congratulations, Oliver. That's spectacular, and I know it means a lot to you." But instead of looking happy for him, Collin winced as if anxious. Was he concerned that being top ten had just put him in the crosshairs of whoever could be knocking off the top players?

"What's the plan now?" Oliver asked, sobered by the concept of being a target for murder.

"I'll answer that only if you promise not to go running around anymore conducting amateur investigations on your own."

He frowned. "I was only trying to help."

"I appreciate it. But I'm a trained professional. Let me do the sneaky stuff."

"Hah! So you admit you're James Bond!"

"You never let up, do you?"

"Nope. I'm relentless."

Their stares met, and Oliver took the step forward that Collin was obviously hoping he would take. For whatever reason, Collin seemed unwilling to take the sexual initiative, but that was okay. Oliver had initiative enough for both of them. He reached out, speared his fingers into Collin's short, silky hair and tugged his head forward for the kiss they both wanted so bad.

Collin resisted, his gray eyes turbulent. "We shouldn't."

"You're right. And yet...." He leaned in a little closer.

"I can list a dozen reasons why this is a dreadful idea," Collin blurted.

"I can list two dozen." Oliver leaned so close that their breaths mingled.

"I... just... can't...."

"Ah, there's my repressed Englishman. Dude, you gotta learn to live a little. Loosen up."

"And you think you're the one to show me how?"

Oliver smiled wickedly. "I know I am."

Collin inhaled sharply, holding out for one last moment. And then he let go, leaned in the rest of the way, and all but inhaled Oliver. His mouth was warm and hungry and restless against Oliver's.

Once unchained from its uptight British leash, Collin's urgent desire was at least as intense as his, if not more so. Collin slid his fingers around the back of Oliver's head, grabbing his longish hair and pulling him in even deeper to the kiss. Their tongues clashed and teeth clicked, and there was nothing restrained or elegant about it. They were both voracious and held nothing back. This was no chaste kiss of getting-to-know-you. It was an I-wanna-fuck-you-wild kiss that promised raw lust and gnarly sex to follow.

Oliver grabbed Collin's shirt at the waist and tugged it free of his pants. He wanted skin and shoved his hands under the fine cotton in a frenetic search for it. *Ahh, better.* Collin's smooth flesh covering hard muscle slabbed over ribs, all of it laced with pounding blood, slid under Oliver's palms.

He hooked his fingertips into the muscular indentation of Collin's spine and pulled Collin's hips tight against his. The mutual bulges in their pants rubbed provocatively, and he groaned into Collin's mouth. A driving need to take him hard and deep spiked into Oliver. His gut tightened in anticipation—

A cell phone rang.

"Ignore it," Oliver muttered against Collin's mouth.

"Can't. Work."

Oliver actually ground his teeth in frustration as Collin stepped away, clothes askew, and fished out his phone. Oliver was too fucking horny to be amused that the ringtone was "God Save the Queen."

Collin listened to whatever was being said on the other end of the line in complete silence for a good thirty seconds. His expression passed through shocked to alarmed and then to grim as hell. "Understood. Will do."

Crap. That was a work voice. His temporary spell over Collin was broken. The Brit was back to being his usual repressed, no-nonsense self. Collin disconnected the call, pocketed his phone, and went to work tucking his shirt back into his pants.

Well, hell.

"Go ahead. Drop the bomb on me," Oliver said in resignation. "What's the big news that made you look like you've been sucking lemons?"

"Do you know Leon Tran?" Collin asked tersely.

"Yeah, sure. Everyone does. He's one of the leading money earners of all time on the professional poker circuit. Had some trouble with the Las Vegas casinos a few years back. Got himself banned from the World Series of Poker. He's in second or third place here right now."

"He fell out of a cable car en route to the top of the Rock of Gibraltar today. Broke his neck. He's dead."

A bucket of ice water in his face couldn't have stunned him any worse. Oliver stared at Collin in disbelief. "Someone *is* trying to knock off the top players! What the fuck? Do you suppose some player is knocking off the competition to make way for himself?"

"My boss thinks so, and I have to agree. Frankly, in light of this death, I have to wonder if the Jet Ski that nearly killed you was not an accident, either. You, too, are renowned as one of the top poker players on earth, as it turns out."

"I was at one time. But it's been years since I played."

"But does everyone else here know you haven't played in a while? Or do they just think you went underground, choosing to play only private games and illicit tournaments like this one?"

He stared at Collin, well and truly alarmed now. Then he shook himself. "This is real life. People don't just run around murdering the competition at a poker tournament. It's just a card game, for crying out loud."

"With literally millions of dollars on the table. And trust me, Oliver. Money brings out the meanness in everyone. The more money is involved, the meaner people get."

"You don't have to tell me that. I know up close and personal." And not just from poker. He'd grown up around his old man, after all. "Still, I'm just one of many good card players here. I don't think I'm that special. Mastrianak and Tran are—were—literally the best of the best."

"And yet, the day you got here, someone nearly ran you over."

"Surely the Jet Ski was an accident." But he even sounded halfhearted to himself in his denial.

Collin said soberly, "Are you positive about that? You have to admit, the timing is more than a little suspicious, especially in light of the other deaths."

A cold pit formed in Oliver's stomach. Him? Target of an assassination attempt? He was a surf bum who hadn't played poker in years. Any threat he might have once posed should have been long gone. But apparently, enough of his reputation lingered to provoke an attack on him. "How did your boss find out about Leon?"

"Leon Tran splatted in the middle of a busy street. Local news got hold of it."

"Maybe it was an accident," Oliver offered. "Or even a suicide."

"Would you kill yourself when you're one of the chip leaders in possibly the richest poker tournament of your life?"

Oliver shrugged. "No. But maybe he was depressed."

"A witness apparently told a reporter it looked as if he was pushed."

"That's easy enough to determine. But we'd need to get over to where he died and take a few measurements."

Collin frowned. "How? And why?"

"Simple trajectory motion problem. We measure the distance from the point of impact to the cable car door and calculate whether he would have been able to jump hard enough to land that far away or not."

"I'll bet you a hundred bucks he was pushed," Collin commented.

"That's not a bet I would take," Oliver responded. "It's a sucker bet."

Smiling, Collin shrugged. "It was worth a try." His smile faded as he looked around his room. His gaze lighted on the desk, and he grabbed a brochure off it and shoved it into Oliver's hand.

"What's this?" he asked.

"Map. We need a cover. We're going out sightseeing."

He snorted. "And we're obviously *not* taking the cable car."

Collin grinned broadly at him. "News coverage says it'll be shut down, anyway, until a thorough investigation is performed on how the door opened in midair."

Oliver was disoriented as they stepped out into a dark night. Right. While they played poker, the rest of the world slept. "When did this so-called accident of Leon's happen?"

"Within the past hour or two, apparently."

"This cable car thing is a twenty-four hour a day operation?" Oliver asked skeptically.

"Good question. Let's see if we can find out." Collin knocked on the window of a white minivan parked at the taxi stand, and a sleepy driver pushed the cap off his face. "We need to go to Gardner's Lane. Near where the cable car crosses it. By the way, are the cable cars running now?"

"No run at night," the driver replied in English with a heavy Spanish accent.

Oliver and Collin exchanged wordless glances as they slid into the back seat. Tran's death had been no accident, then. Suicide or murder. But which?

It took about fifteen minutes to wind around the north end of the Rock, parallel to the airport, and then head south along the west side of the peninsula to where Leon had died. The narrow, winding streets were deserted; but when they approached the scene of the incident, a mob of police cars lit the cobblestone street like a festive party. Collin slipped the driver a twenty-pound note to wait while they checked out the spot where Leon had died.

The police had outlined the corpse on the pavement with white chalk like some old-time police drama, but thankfully, Tran's body had already been removed from the scene. Only that ghostly outline remained. Oliver muttered, "I'm gonna pace off the distance to the cable line."

While Collin quizzed someone about what had happened as officiously as he could, Oliver counted off the paces until he stood directly under the steel cables snaking up into the darkness. He rejoined Collin, who was chatting up a fireman.

At a lull in the conversation, Oliver injected, "How high is the cable over the ground here?"

The local fireman looked up. "I'd guess it's about fifty feet at this spot. Most of the time, the car is closer to the slope of the Rock, but there's that cliff over there, and the ground falls away from the cable a bit extra right here."

Funny, that. As if someone knew exactly where to push Leon out to ensure he would hit the ground with sufficient force to die. Oliver made a sympathetic sound, already running the simple projectile motion calculation in his head. Collin must have done the same, for in a moment, his brows slammed together, and he threw Oliver a worried look.

Collin murmured to the fireman, "We'll let you get back to your work, then."

"Thank you, Inspector," the firefighter replied.

Oliver piled into the cab beside Collin. "Inspector?"

"Easier to get answers to my questions with an official title. That way I'm not mistaken for the press and people don't clam up."

"Lucky dog. You have the accent to pass for British."

"My dear sir. I am British."

"And there's that poker up your British ass."

They rode in silence the rest of the way back to the hotel. Pink and peach tinted the sky in the east beyond the still Mediterranean Sea as they climbed out of the taxi and he paid the driver more than he had given him to wait for them earlier.

When they got to Collin's room, Collin insisted on running his little black device over the walls and furnishings again before speaking. As he stowed the gadget, he murmured, "So. He was pushed."

"More like thrown by somebody chonking-strong to have traveled so far from the cable car."

"Chonking?"

"Chonky. As in chunky. Muscular. Bulky. Powerful—"

Collin threw up his hands. "I get it, already."

He stopped listing synonyms of the slang and fell silent.

"Two killers, then?" Collin said briskly.

"That would be my guess," Oliver answered. "Hard for one guy to wrestle with Tran and successfully launch him like that. But a couple guys could probably do it. Leo wasn't a big dude."

Collin sat down at his laptop and pulled up the poker tournament's website, specifically the leaderboard. "With Tran out of the way, one of the Albanians moves into the top ten."

"The tournament director is splitting up the top players every day so each of us sits at a different table. We don't have to go head-to-head yet and potentially weaken or eliminate one another," Oliver commented.

"Meaning what?"

"Now the Albanian guy is protected from having to play another top-ten guy."

"You think the Albanians are knocking out the competition?" Collin asked.

"It's as good a guess as any. They're mob connected, which means they are violent themselves or have easy access to violent people. Although honestly, any of the remaining players could be the murderous mastermind."

"Murderous mastermind?" Collin echoed, smirking.

"Hey. I got me a college edu-ma-cation. I know me them there big words."

Collin rolled his eyes.

God, he loved getting rises out of the man.

Collin said seriously, "We can't rule out the tournament directors or the resort staff as suspects. Although, I can't really see the resort staff caring about a few high-rolling poker players enough to knock them off."

Oliver commented, "Unless someone's paying them to kill players."

Collin added dryly, "Everyone's got a price at which they can be bought, after all."

Truth. It was a fact his father often exploited to his own advantage. He shrugged, then added, "Will the directors cancel the tournament?"

Collin answered grimly, "My boss thinks the director will have no problem with players eliminating each other as long as they keep the shenanigans off-site."

Oliver stared. "So this is what? Combat poker?"

"Something like that."

"That's sick."

Collin shrugged. "It would explain the inclusion of known criminals and players of questionable moral fiber. No offense intended."

"None taken. I'm banned for being smart, not a cheat."

Collin remarked, "I'll bet some thug is getting his ass chewed as we speak for not being more subtle about killing Tran and not hiding the body."

"No kidding. What do we do now?"

"If I were sitting back in England watching this from afar, I'd tell the operative on the ground to watch his back. And for God's sake, to stay out of the top ten."

Oliver stared at Collin in chagrin. Unfortunately, the advice made perfect sense.

Collin's eyes popped open in surprise. "Hey, man, I'm sorry—"

"No need to apologize for telling the truth. And besides, if you're right about the Jet Ski incident, I'm already targeted for elimination."

Collin moved quickly to stand in front of Oliver. "I'll do everything in my power to keep you safe."

"You can't watch me day and night."

"Why not? There's no rule against players spending time together."

"Yeah, but you could get hurt if you're too close to me the next time Jet Ski guy tries to kill me."

Collin answered quietly, "I'll take my chances."

Gratitude flowed through Oliver, but he had no words to express it. Instead, he stepped forward and wrapped Collin in a bone-crushing hug that said everything he could not.

Somehow, Collin's head got turned toward him, and his got turned, too, and their mouths brushed across each other. And then they latched on to each other desperately, kissing as if this was the last time they would ever see each other.

It was probably a terrible idea to fall into the sack because they were scared and looking for comfort. But damned if Oliver didn't want to. He had been quite the slut over the years, willing to sleep with anyone, anytime. After all, it was just sex. And if it felt good, why not do it if the other guy was willing?

But Collin wasn't his usual easy pickup. The guy was tense as hell about sex, practically closeted. Not to mention that whole honor and integrity thing Collin seemed stuck on. Not the kind of dude to crank the wank and walk away without looking back. *Like I would.* Hell, like he had a hundred times.

Oliver took a shaky step back. "Sorry about that. I didn't mean to derail the conversation about what we're going to do next."

Collin's gaze was clouded. Confused. Like the emotional whiplash of making out and then going back to talking shop was too much to process.

Oliver knew the damned feeling. Staring at the back of Collin's neck as he turned away to gaze out the window, Oliver couldn't help but notice the strong lines of tendon and corded muscle. God, he'd give anything to see those straining in the throes of pleasure. But instead they were tensed, probably in response to rejection.

He raised his hands. Started to take a step forward. Opened his mouth with an apology.

But before he could do any of that, Collin announced briskly, "You're right. We need to focus on work. And now, we need to figure out who's running this tournament and why."

Oliver's hands fell to his sides.

Collin sat down at the laptop and started typing rapidly. "Let's see how good El Rocca's security system really is."

Oliver blinked, startled. "Be careful. If they've got countermeasures in place, you could lead them to us."

Collin looked up from his screen at that. "Do you trust me?"

With his *life*? "I guess so." Even to his own ears, Oliver sounded doubtful. "Give me your key card. I'm going to run down to my room. I'll be back in a minute." He slipped out and headed down the hall.

Oliver grabbed a change of clothes, basic toiletries, and his own laptop computer, threw them in a backpack, and headed back upstairs. He paused in front of Collin's door. If he walked away right now, kept his head down, and made sure to stay just out of the top-ten players going forward, maybe he would be able to hang around until the end of the tournament and then take his shot at winning at the last minute so the killer wouldn't have a chance to take him out.

But if he stepped through that doorway, he would be going all in with Collin. He would be committing himself to helping Collin's investigation with the intent to rip this tournament open and expose its secrets to whomever Collin worked for.

What if his father was somehow mixed up in this mess? Did he dare tangle with his old man? He knew better than most just how formidable a foe George Elliott could be.

And in the meantime, two men were already dead, and he'd possibly been targeted for elimination as well. Did he dare expose himself to even more danger?

Did he dare try to survive in this jungle on his own?

He *ought* to go it alone, if for no other reason than to protect Collin from danger.

But Collin was so damned noble.

And so damned sexy.

But so damned naive.

And clearly out of his depth in a violent situation.

But he wanted Collin.

And shouldn't have him.

Fuck.

CHAPTER SIX

COLLIN LOOKED at his watch. He had approximately thirty hours before play began again. And he suspected he would need all that time to hack El Rocca's computer security system. Unlike if he'd been sitting back at HQ sipping a hot cup of English breakfast tea, if he screwed up here and got caught, he was probably a dead man.

Furthermore, Oliver was likely a dead man if he failed to get into the resort's computers and figure out what the hell was going on and who the hell was behind it all. No pressure there.

He vaguely heard Oliver return but was surprised when a laptop plunked down on the desk beside his and a chair dragged close. "What's your plan of attack?" Oliver asked.

"I beg your pardon?"

"You didn't think I became one of the top mathematicians of my generation without knowing a crap-ton about computer security algorithms, did you?"

"Oh! Right. Um, cool. I thought I'd make a run at some harmless admin system and then backdoor my way into the server."

"The reservation system, maybe?" Oliver suggested.

He shook his head. "Credit card numbers are stored in there. Encryption will be a bitch. I was thinking about going after the scheduling of housekeeping."

"That's pretty low-level stuff. You think you can climb into the main system from there?"

Collin shrugged. "Only one way to find out."

It was child's play to bust into the spreadsheet the housekeeping manager used to tell the maids which rooms had checked out, which ones were needed for early check-ins, and how many rooms had to be cleaned by what time. From there, Collin was shocked at how easy it was to jump into the housekeeping manager's desktop and clone it.

Now it was just a waiting game until the woman came in to work in an hour or two and typed in her username and password. Then he had to hope the resort didn't have some sort of tiered employee access system to data. Major corporations spent the time and money to set up tiered access, but the El Rocca was a small, private outfit. He hoped they hadn't hired a high-end computer security firm to set up their system.

In the meantime, Collin got to work setting up a few additional firewalls in his laptop just to be safe. Oliver looked on as he loaded the last one. "You think that's good enough. Collie?"

"Collie?"

"Hey, you wanted to call me Ollie."

"I've never had to kill anyone before, but I am not averse to doing so," Collin snapped.

"What kind of James Bond are you if you haven't killed anyone?"

"The smart kind who doesn't have to resort to brute force to accomplish one's mission."

"Let's hope it stays that way," Oliver muttered.

Indeed.

The housekeeping manager came on shift, and Collin's computer screen leapt to life. Username and password duly captured, he and Oliver went to work on the main prize: the resort's primary computer server. Not that they were competitive or anything, but they both worked like dogs, heads down, typing until their computers figuratively smoked.

It took a couple of hours, but Oliver sat back first, announcing, "There. Now I just have to let that run."

Collin had opted for a delicate, probing approach, searching for backdoors or system weaknesses gently enough not to trigger any alarms. He'd already run across a cache of child pornography bad enough to get one of the night managers jailed in any country. And someone in the security office was pirating pay-per-view movies off the resort's account. But so far, the El Rocca firewalls were holding. It was only a matter of time, though, before he found a chink in the armor.

"Okay," Collin announced a few minutes later. "My search is running autonomously. You hungry?"

Oliver grinned. "I'm always hungry. What have you got in mind?"

"I thought we might go to Old Town on the other side of the Rock. Grab a bite to eat. Do a little sightseeing."

"Sightseeing? With murderers on the loose?" Oliver squawked.

He shrugged. "There's safety in crowds and public spaces. And what would we normally do if we had a full day off? I don't know about you, but it would be more suspicious if I holed up in my room and never came out than if I went out and took a look around Gibraltar."

"Good point," Oliver said. "It would be unlike me to stay indoors or inactive for long."

They had the front desk call a taxi for them, and in a few minutes, they passed through the tunnel that dumped them out at Europa Point at the far southern tip of the Gibraltar peninsula jutting out into the nine-mile-wide Strait of Gibraltar. It was a clear, bright morning, and they could see Algeria, Morocco, Spain, the Atlantic Ocean, and the Mediterranean Sea simultaneously.

"Strategic little place, this Gibraltar," Oliver commented.

Collin made a sound of agreement. It was an interesting choice for an international gathering of the world's best poker players. He kept coming back to the question of why the tournament had been set up, though. What was so special about a bunch of people like Oliver?

Collin blurted, "Is it possible that the event's organizers are not trying to find the world's best poker player, but rather the world's best math-on-the-fly person?"

Oliver stared at him. "What for? Computers can outperform a human brain by orders of magnitude."

"Artificial Intelligence has yet to duplicate certain human brain functions. For example, intuitive analysis still requires a human brain."

"Intuitively analyzing *what*?"

Collin turned over the question, applying some of the exact same human analysis he was talking about. Computers still could not take intuitive leaps of logic like a living, breathing analyst could.

He spoke slowly. "Let's assume this is some sort of talent search. Why poker, and why this set of players? Obviously, they want a person who isn't hung up on morals or ethics. Otherwise they wouldn't have included hustlers and criminals in the player list."

Oliver snorted. "That doesn't narrow down the possibilities much. Since when are bankers or stock traders especially moral or ethical?"

Collin shrugged. "Where there's wealth, there's always greed."

"Poker players bring more than fast math to the table. Guts. Steely nerves. The ability to bluff. Reading fine nuance in human body language. Maybe those are the skills the tournament directors are measuring by using poker as this hypothetical test."

"Or all of the above," Collin replied.

"Okay, then. Following your logic—which I'm not entirely sure I buy, as an aside—who needs the same skill set as a professional poker player, and what would they use it for?"

Collin frowned. "Politicians. Negotiators. Decision-makers handling large sums of money."

Oliver added, "Military strategists. Entrepreneurs. Venture capitalists. Con men."

A vague shape was starting to form in Collin's mind, but the picture was far from complete. His gut said they were on the right track, though. This whole tournament could, in fact, be some sort of elaborate job interview.

They left Europa Point and headed for the city center, driving past the old bastion walls and plentiful boutiques bearing top designer names. Gibraltar was a popular cruise ship stop, and the high-end retail industry was ready and waiting to suck up tourist dollars. The seamless combination of southern European mountain town with traditional English village made for a charming, almost fairyland, feel to the place.

They walked the length of Main Street, a mostly pedestrian cobblestone affair that ended in Casemate Square, ringed by cafés whose customers spilled out onto the broad square at umbrella-covered tables. Collin led the way to a table inside a dimly lit coffee shop, where they sipped fresh-roasted coffee and pastries that made him seriously consider giving up any attempt to watch his waistline ever again.

They'd been people-watching and relaxing for perhaps a half hour when Oliver muttered, "Well, lookie there. It's the Albanians. And friends."

Collin looked out into the sunlit square. Sure enough, several of the Albanian poker players from the tournament and two tall, gorgeous women had just taken seats at a café. The usual Albanian bodyguards weren't present, however.

"Hey. That's Desirée Moorhead with the Albanians," Oliver announced.

"The blond?"

"Yup."

"The other one hit on me yesterday," Collin remarked. "Said her name is Cher."

Oliver snorted. "Cher what? Cher Chlamydia?"

Collin grinned. "I wonder where the rest of the Albanian mob is today. Don't they usually travel in a pack?"

Oliver shrugged. "Maybe the security thugs are getting laid back at the hotel while these guys wine and dine Desirée and Cher."

"Do you suppose the professional entertainment is reporting back to someone? Maybe Desirée and Cher are working the Albanians and not the other way around," Collin commented.

Oliver replied, "Good thing I'm hooking up with you, then. No juicy tidbits from me for the tournament staff."

Collin replied wryly, "Personally, I'm feeling a little left out. None of the male entertainers have hit on me."

Oliver tilted his head to study him intently. "You are objectively a very good-looking man. I think it's the repressed vibe you give off that's keeping them away from you." He tilted up his coffee cup to get the last few drops and set the cup down.

Collin said more confidently than he felt, "Their loss. Think of all the pillow-talk confessions they could have wrung out of me."

"How do you know I'm not a spy put in place to learn your deepest, darkest secrets?" Oliver teased.

"I might be more suspicious of that exact thing if I wasn't already convinced you're a target of whoever's trying to kill off the top players."

"Unless, of course, I'm the mastermind behind the deaths," Oliver quipped.

He said, "That Jet Ski came too bloody close to you for you to have been faking it. And besides, you had no way of knowing I would step outside just then and witness you nearly getting your head torn off."

Oliver reached across the table and squeezed Collin's hand briefly.

He was unused to public displays of affection and looked around quickly and furtively.

Oliver murmured, "It's okay. We're both adults. We can hold hands in public."

"Isn't this place Catholic?" he asked nervously.

"There's a heavy Spanish influence here, so yes, mostly. But this is the twenty-first century." Oliver leaned close to murmur, "The cootie police aren't going to jump out and arrest you for touching a boy."

"Wanker." He huffed and lifted his chin at the Albanians. "What about them? Will it cause you trouble in the tournament if we're seen hooking up?"

Oliver grinned, amused enough that it annoyed him a bit. To add insult to injury, he drawled in a fake British accent, "This, my dear Watson, is not hooking up. And frankly, I don't give a shit what the Albanians think. If they want to tag team me, it makes the math a little more complicated, but I'll still chew them up and spit them out at the poker table."

"Arrogant much?" Collin whispered, a little more turned-on by Oliver's confidence than he wanted to admit.

Oliver shrugged. "If you've got it, you've got it."

"A quintessentially American sentiment."

"You're just mad we won the war."

"What war?" Collin blurted.

Oliver gestured at the four British soldiers marching across the square in eighteenth-century redcoat uniforms in some sort of ceremony for the tourists. "You know what I see when I look at those guys?"

Collin bit. "What?"

"Losers."

Collin's jaw dropped in patriotic outrage. "You did not just say that."

"Loooo. Sers. Losers."

"When we get back to the room, mister, I'm going to make you regret saying that."

"Oh, yeah? You and what army? A bunch more losers?"

Collin couldn't help it. He laughed. Threw his head back and let go with it from the belly like he hadn't since before Steve died. God, it felt good to laugh like that again. For a while there, he'd thought he might never regain his ability to do it.

When his humor wound down, he said to Oliver, "Thanks. I needed that more than you know."

"Why's that?"

For the first time since the accident, he felt an urge to talk about it. "I had a longtime partner. He died a little over a year ago in a car accident."

"Oh my God," Oliver said softly. "I'm sorry."

"It was awful. It still is awful."

"It'll always be awful," Oliver said soberly. "But with time and distance, you'll get better at living with it."

"Wise words," Collin said in surprise. "Have you ever lost someone close to you?"

"I almost lost myself a few years back. Came close to killing myself a couple of times. It has been a long crawl back."

They shared gazes of mutual pain and understanding. Collin abruptly felt closer to this man than he had to anyone in a long time. And from a distance, he thought he felt Steve smiling at him. He knew without a shadow of a doubt that Steve would have wanted him to love again, to find happiness, to *live*. But this was the first moment he'd truly believed that in his heart. And maybe it was the first moment he'd given himself permission to do it.

"Whew," he mumbled. "First time I've talked about losing Steve and been able to see anything beyond him. You have no idea what a relief that is."

Oliver reached across the table silently and gave his hands a squeeze. "Actually, I do have an idea. I'll never forget the moment I decided killing myself wasn't the answer and that there was still a possibility of happiness waiting for me out there, somewhere, someday."

He squeezed Oliver's hands back. "I, for one, am delighted you're alive." He took a deep breath and released it long and slow. "Lord that feels good. It's as if I hadn't really relaxed since the crash."

"No kidding, dude. You've been wired tighter than my first pair of braces ever since I pulled you out of the Med."

"I pulled *you* out of the Med," he retorted indignantly.

"Hah. You're too easy to get a rise out of, man. You gotta learn to lock that shit down if you're gonna survive at the tables for much longer."

"What do you mean?"

"The amateurs are about done being knocked out. The big dogs are about all that's left standing. You should expect this crew to mess with your head, try to get to you, to needle you and irritate you. Hell, some of them will even insult you to your face to see if they can rattle you. The gloves are about to come off around here."

"Jesus. Given that two players are already dead, I'd hate to see what constitutes gloves off."

Oliver shrugged pragmatically. "Keep your head down, eh? Don't talk at the table, don't rise to any bait they throw at you. Just do your job. Watch the others, do the math, play your cards. That's it."

"Got it. And thanks again. It's more than decent of you to help me out like this."

Oliver replied, "It's not as if you have a chance of winning."

Stung, he did his damnedest not to respond to that comment. To give away none of the hurt or frustration of this man not perceiving him as an equal.

Oliver leaned over and slapped him on the upper arm. "Good job! See? I messed with you, and you didn't lose your cool. You're learning."

"That was a test?" he asked blankly.

"Of course. Anybody can win on a good day. There's only so much math in the game of poker. At some point, Lady Luck will assert herself. No telling who she'll smile upon."

That was a fatalistic attitude coming from as skilled a card player as Oliver. There was also no telling who Lady Luck would frown upon, either. Hopefully, next time, it wouldn't be fatal to Oliver or him.

The Albanians and the girls from the hotel wandered away. He and Oliver continued to sit, sipping coffee and making small talk, until Collin's cell phone beeped. "That's a notification from my computer. Time to head back to the salt mines."

They grabbed a taxi back to the El Rocca and split up, ostensibly heading for their own rooms. But Oliver would circle around using the stairwells to come to Collin's room inconspicuously.

The door latched behind Oliver just as Collin finished sweeping the room for surveillance devices. He nodded the all clear.

"What's up?" Oliver asked as Collin sat down at his laptop.

"My algorithm has found a sequence of vulnerable code. It's waiting for my approval to launch an exploit."

Oliver sat down at his own computer. "If we trip any alarms, they'll launch countermeasures. We'll have to move fast to avoid detection and identification."

"Then let's not trip any alarms."

Collin hit the Send button.

He held his breath for the next several minutes, but when his worm program didn't cause their laptops to blow up, he eventually relaxed. "It's a cautious protocol. It'll move slowly and enter the resort server by slow degrees. Like a good seduction."

Oliver grinned. "I dunno. Seduction's overrated. I tend to just go for it. Can't say as I've ever had any trouble getting what I want from who I want by being direct."

Collin grinned back. "Cocky much?"

"You have no idea." A pause. "Wanna find out?"

Collin shook his head. "That kind of come-on would never work on me."

Oliver rolled his desk chair over beside Collin's. "What would work on you?"

"That's for me to know and you to find out."

"Challenge accepted."

Collin looked up sharply from his laptop. "I beg your pardon?"

"You heard me. I'll bet you a hundred bucks I can get you into bed in, say, the next twenty-four hours."

Collin didn't know whether to cheer or gulp.

"C'mon, Collin. You're supposed to be a gambling man. So gamble a little already."

Except that was the problem. He hated taking risks. At the end of the day, he liked his life safe. Predictable. Boring. There was a reason he'd sat behind a desk all these years, dreaming of being a field operative but never acting on it.

He considered Oliver warily. He wasn't sure if he was ready for another relationship—

For fuck's sake, Oliver was only offering some sex. Not a lifetime commitment. He had to quit overthinking everything this man said. A bet, huh? If he won, he'd get a hundred bucks. If he lost, he'd get Oliver. No down side to that. He said slyly, "I'm worth a hell of a lot more than a hundred bucks, Shaggy."

"Shaggy?" Oliver asked.

"The American cartoon character. Scooby-Doo's human. You remind me of him."

"I'm allergic to dogs."

"It's the hair," Collin retorted. "And the surfer clothes."

Oliver very deliberately placed a knee on the chair beside Collin's right thigh and, staring deep into his eyes, bent down toward him. Collin gulped. Oh. Holy. Hell.

Oliver's hands landed on his shoulders. "Are you saying no to this?"

Collin opened his mouth, but his throat was so tight no sound came out. He clapped his mouth shut ineffectually.

"Mmm-hmm. That's what I thought." Oliver leaned down until their mouths were only a few inches apart. "In the name of rolling consent, I ask again. Are you saying no?"

Collin could only shake his head in the negative.

"Good. Now that we have the necessary preliminaries out of the way, kiss me, you fool."

Foolish, indeed. And yet, he was still going there, apparently. Collin tilted his chin up, and Oliver's mouth closed voraciously on his. Strong hands plunged into his hair, half lifting him out of the chair. Oliver stepped back toward the bed, dragging Collin with him, and gods below, he had no will to resist.

This was madness. He knew better than to mix work and pleasure, friend and lover. Staying free of emotional entanglements meant choosing his sex partners with a careful eye to men he would never see again. Never need to speak to. Never even cross accidental paths with. Oliver was none of those. At least not in the short term, and not in terms of the current assignment.

But when that muscle-slabbed, hard body pressed against his, all his self-discipline flew right out of his head, along with his good sense… and apparently the word *no*. He had no will to tear away from those strong arms. No will to speak the words that would return this insanity back to a platonic work relationship.

Oliver's hands shoved under Collin's polo shirt, lifting it over his head and tossing it aside.

"We shouldn't," he mumbled.

"I think we should."

"More accurately, I shouldn't."

"Why not?"

"Umm. Work—"

"Screw work."

"Steve is the last man I, umm—"

"Slept with? And you haven't had sex since? That's admirable of you. Noble, even. But would he want you to waste away without ever having this kind of pleasure again?"

"Absolutely not."

"So it's only your own guilt and hang-ups stopping us from having sex?"

He stared at Oliver. Was it really that simple? Had he made it a thousand times more complicated in his head because he didn't want to look at his own attitudes about himself being gay? Huh.

Was he really that ashamed of who he was? God knew, plenty of people around him had done their best to shame Collin, the boy, into being straight. And God also knew, he'd tried. Really tried to be straight. But no go.

This man, this moment, was his personal Rubicon. Once he crossed this bridge, there would be no going back to the person he'd been before.

He realized Oliver was studying his face, waiting and watching. He hated to think what the professional card shark was reading in his expression.

"What are you going to do?" Oliver murmured. "You want this. You're an adult, and you can have it, no harm no foul. Nobody will know but us, but you'll have to live with knowing that this is who you are."

"I've had sex with men before, thank you very much," he responded tartly.

"But the guilt and shame nearly killed you. Am I right?"

He stared at Oliver, dismayed at being such an open book to this man.

"What is there to be ashamed of? I want this, you want this, it'll feel good to both of us, we're not hurting anybody. Fuck the judgers who have an opinion about what you and I do behind closed doors. It's none of their business. Live and let live, dude."

It sounded so simple when Oliver laid it out like that. Hell, maybe it was that simple. Maybe he just needed to let go of caring what anybody else thought and focus on what he wanted.

He nodded once, a smile breaking across his face. "You're absolutely right. Let's do this."

"Hell yeah," Oliver crowed.

His belt buckle gave way to Oliver's efficient fingers, and then Collin's pants and briefs shimmied down his thighs. He would have kicked them free, would have reached for Oliver's clothing, but Oliver backed him up impatiently, pushing him until he tumbled onto the bed. Oliver's knee between his thighs, trapping his partially removed slacks beneath it, pinned Collin's legs down.

Collin's dick jutted up like a flagpole, loud and proud and ready to party. God, he felt exposed. Oliver grinned, and his fist closed around Collin's erection, giving it a light tug that nearly sent Collin over the edge right there.

"How do you like it, English?"

He gurgled something along the lines of "Wuhurmbuhgah."

Oliver laughed and drew his fist down Collin's shaft, pulling the skin tight across the tip of his cock. And then the bastard leaned down and gave it a slurp that made Collin's hips lurch up off the bed.

"If you don't tell me what you like, I'm going to do everything I've been imagining doing to you. And some of it's pretty twisted."

He managed a groan as Oliver's hot mouth closed on him again. Oh God. It was wet and tight and amazing, and he thrust up into the promise of dirty darkness, in spite of his best resolve not to.

"Top or bottom?" Oliver asked around the throbbing head of his cock.

"Uhhguhhuhyeah."

"Right. You get the bottom. Frontal or doggie?"

"Muhahwahdah."

"Doggie it is. Reach around, or do you want to be kept on the edge?"

Oh. My. God. The directness of this man was staggering. And exciting.

"Dude, in the total absence of feedback here, I'm going to assume consent for whatever I choose to do. You all right with that?"

Collin managed to nod and twist his fists in the bedspread, clenched there as Oliver's mouth and tight fist pushed him right to the verge of madness.

Oliver withdrew. "We need a safe word. How about 'God Save the Queen'?"

Collin couldn't help but be amused. He opened his mouth to agree. *Throat still not working.* He nodded breathlessly. Oliver was still fully dressed, but now, standing between Collin's spread knees and partially undone trousers, he reached for the button of his own jeans. Collin watched with unbridled anticipation as the zipper slid down one tooth at a time.

Yup. Commando. Oliver's cock sprang free of its confinement, and Collin stared at the size of it. Christ almighty. The beast was a deep rose color and jumped hungrily as Collin gaped at it.

"Can you take it?" Oliver asked. "Wouldn't want to tear you up."

Collin started as a groan slipped from his own throat. His asscheeks clenched and unclenched spasmodically as, suddenly, he wanted nothing more in the world than to be torn up by that magnificent cock. His own erection throbbed, and Oliver grinned, reaching down to smear Collin's precum all over the head of Collin's dick, rendering it slippery and so exquisitely stimulated he could sob.

"So here's the thing. I don't want you to come until I tell you to. Okay?"

Collin nodded cautiously, sensing more to the game than that.

"I'm going to get some lube out of my bag, and I need you to finish getting naked and get all the extra pillows out of the closet. We're going to need them."

All but whimpering in anticipation, he did as Oliver instructed. In a matter of seconds, he was facedown on the bed, his ass presented for Oliver's pleasure, and the hardest erection he'd had in a long time threatening to explode at any second. He clenched his teeth against coming right then and there.

Aw, jeez. Oliver's hand slid across his flank and the back of his thigh to cup his balls, which tightened instantly and almost painfully in response. The lube in his palm was warm and slippery, sliding all over Collin's junk in an erotic massage that did actually make him sob into the bedspread a little. All his fantasies with this man were coming true, one on top of the other. Too much. Too fast.

A tiny voice somewhere in the far recesses of his brain complained that this was a terrible idea and he shouldn't be doing it. But he couldn't remember why, and for the life of him couldn't work up the give-a-shit factor to care. *Shut up, little voice. It's high time I quit listening to you and let myself be happy again.*

Oliver knelt over him, his big, lanky, strong body spooning Collin's intimately. Lips and teeth closed on his right earlobe, and Collin turned his head, giving Oliver better access. A wet, warm tongue swirled into his ear, and he groaned.

"God, you're hot," Oliver muttered.

Said the pot to the boiling kettle. If he was hot, it was because Oliver made him this way. The snap of a condom announced that Oliver was a responsible lover. Oliver's hand intruded between their bodies, lubing up both of them, and then all thoughts whatsoever flew out of Collin's head as that impressive dick probed his ass. No matter how bad he wanted it or how well lubed he was, he still had to work hard to relax the appropriate muscles and accept Oliver's invasion. He'd done this plenty before but was by no means in practice. He panted, caught on the horns of pleasure and not-quite-pain as he slowly, deliciously, took Oliver into himself.

Oliver seemed to understand, though, and was perfectly still as Collin's body adjusted to the size of him. And then Oliver's slippery, lubed hand snuck around his hips and closed on Collin's raging erection, setting up a rhythm, pumping slow and steady, up and down Collin's shaft, like a piston gradually gathering speed and power. Images of steam engines flashed through his head. Black iron. Hot steel. Steam. Smoke. And those pistons. Always those pistons chugging away, transmuting fire into raging sexual magic.

Before he knew it or could stop it, Collin's hips were rocking into Oliver's fist, stroking his own erection, and moving his ass up and down on Oliver's dick. The twin sensations of penetrating and being penetrated were almost more than he could bear.

"You ready?" a deep, breathy voice muttered in his ear.

He'd been ready for this ever since he met Oliver. "Uh-huh," he managed.

Oliver's hips rocked forward, meeting his as he rocked back, and his entire being was filled to bursting with all that glorious man muscle and burning heat. His balls tightened, on the verge of explosion, but then Oliver's fingers closed into a vise at the base of his cock, shocking him into momentary stillness.

"Not until I tell you to," Oliver ordered darkly.

A shiver of delight rippled through Collin. Oliver rode him like an ocean wave, swerving up and down, side to side, as quick as a seal and strong as the ocean itself.

Oh God. It was so sexy to be taken like this that his entire body felt limp with joyous surrender. Oliver took him for real, then, pounding into him relentlessly, seating himself to the hilt time and again, flesh slapping on flesh, sweat sliding on sweat, rhythmic groans in his ear driving Collin completely out of his mind. To hell with fantasies. This reality was better by far than anything he could have ever imagined.

Oliver gripped Collin's hipbones in his big, strong hands, and Collin gave himself over to Oliver with abandon. It was messy and undisciplined and joyously free, totally unlike anything he'd ever experienced before. Who knew how repressed his sex with Steve had actually been? It had been sweet and respectful and lovely in its own way. But it had been nothing like this.

He loved how Oliver bent over his quivering, bucking body, absorbing his unschooled movements easily and reaching around with his other hand to milk his cock in rhythm with his primary plundering of Collin. Taken to the very edge of explosive release, that tight ring of Oliver's fingers held him tethered to the edge of the abyss, suspended between consciousness and little death, unable to pull back, unable to break free and fly. It was, in a word, magnificent.

Grabbing a pillow and plastering it to his face, Collin keened in desperate need to come. But… he'd… promised….

Oliver's hips increased in speed and urgency until they were going at it like wild animals, any sense of grace or restraint be damned. And then, without warning, Oliver let go of Collin's cock, pushed up onto his knees, and slammed into Collin with a shout of pleasure.

Collin exploded, a shout ripped from his own throat that devolved into an undulating cry as Oliver's orgasm went on and on. *And so did his.*

His arms gave out at the same time Oliver collapsed, the two of them pancaking onto the pile of pillows, gasping for breath.

"Can't. Move," Oliver panted.

"Don't. Move," Collin managed.

"Mind. Blown."

"Like. Wise." Collin sighed.

They lay in silence for several minutes, floating in and out of a semiconscious pleasure coma.

"You okay?" Oliver mumbled as he finally rolled onto his back beside Collin.

"Better than okay."

"I didn't hurt you?"

"No."

"Good. I don't want to have to wait while you heal to do that again."

Again. Suddenly that was his favorite word in the whole world.

Collin rolled onto his side and pulled the pillows out from under his hips. A long leg looped over his calves, and a muscular arm snaked around his waist. And all the glorious, muscular heat that was Oliver curved along his back from neck to heels.

As sanity gradually returned, his brain finally gained dominance over his body's pleasures. And a new word consumed his mind, flashing in bright lights and accompanied by jarring alarm bells.

Mistake.

CHAPTER SEVEN

OLIVER LOOKED around the poker hall with a frown. At least a dozen players had disappeared in the twenty-four-hour hiatus. Most of them had been hanging on near the bottom of the chip standings. Maybe they figured discreet withdrawal was better than risking death by continuing to swim in this particular shark tank. Smart guys.

Genius though he might be, common sense had never been his strong suit. A smoking-hot affair with a British secret agent being a case in point. But his dick started to get hard at the mere thought of Collin stripped of all that stiff, proper veneer, writhing beneath him like a wild thing.

Where were the Albanians? One of them had been in the top-ten chip leaders, and the others had been not too far behind when play was suspended. Oliver looked around carefully but didn't see any of them. Weird.

The only woman remaining in the tournament looked smug, her body language confident as she took her place at the same table with him. She was in the top twenty somewhere, but she'd come onto the poker scene after Oliver had left it. He'd heard she was smart, mentally tough, and a decent card player.

The round of play started, and he had to admit, she was good. Between the two of them, they decimated the other four players at the table, driving two of them out of the tournament outright and leaving the other two gasping on life support. He didn't set out to nuke the other players, but the cards fell his way and to do anything less than play them properly was against his personal moral code.

When play was called for the night, Oliver glanced around the room, casually, he hoped. Thank God. There was Collin sitting in front of a middling-size stack of chips. Interestingly enough, it looked like most of the top players hadn't advanced their causes much tonight. If anything, the top few players looked to have diminished their stacks.

Trying to duck the killer, perhaps? It made sense. Better to ride along in the middle of the pack, not call attention to oneself, and wait until the final tables of play to pounce on the remaining players.

The woman player, Stacy Kiern, moved up from number sixteen to number eight overall, and Oliver slid up from number nine to number five. Wow. He'd had a good night, but not that great. His suspicion that the other top players were sandbagging solidified.

He grabbed a quick sandwich out of the buffet line and headed straight back to his room as he and Collin had agreed to earlier. They couldn't afford to be seen as having formed too tight an alliance or else the other players would gang up on them.

But after eating, taking a shower, and stretching out on his bed to catch a nap, memory of the previous day in bed with Collin flashed into his head and would not get out, no matter how many differential equations he solved in his head. Fuck.

He grabbed his phone and texted Collin: *You up?*

An immediate *Yes*.

Lonely?

Missing you. Does that count?

Oliver smiled in spite of himself. He couldn't remember the last time someone had missed him. His parents had found him a gigantic and embarrassing inconvenience, and he'd been nearly a decade younger than everyone he ever went to school with. Then, when his peers were bombing around frat parties, trying not to flunk out of college, he was the professor doing the flunking. After he'd dropped out of real life and moved to the beach, he'd focused entirely on making no emotional connections at all. And, overachiever that he was, he'd succeeded spectacularly.

Until now. Until an uptight Brit jumped into the freezing Mediterranean to save him and nearly drowned. Silly, sweet Collin. The spy who was neither sneaky nor violent.

Oliver rolled out of bed and ran an impatient hand through his hair, which stuck out in every direction from his head. He really ought to clean himself up. Shave. Get some real clothes. He swore at his image in the bathroom mirror. Since when did he give a crap what he looked like? Since a neat, put-together British gentleman blasted into his life. Collin was miles classier than anyone he could possibly deserve.

Collin might have called him Shaggy in jest, but he'd always hated that character on the kid's cartoon. It was too early to find a barber open now. But he picked up a pair of small scissors and painstakingly trimmed his hair as best he could. He followed up with a close shave and donned his best shirt and least-wrinkled khaki pants. Maybe tomorrow he could buy a new suit or something. In the meantime, his lover was waiting for him.

Collin opened the door for him before his knuckles barely touched it. He slipped inside the room and into Collin's eagerly waiting arms. Something warm and delighted unfolded in his gut at being wanted like this. Even if it was pure lust and nothing more, he reveled in the fantasy of Collin giving an actual damn about him.

They didn't waste any time on preliminaries and got right down to the business of stripping each other's clothes off and tumbling into bed. They were hot and heavy, kissing and groping, figuring out what was going to go where, when Collin's laptop beeped suddenly. He lurched like a gunshot had just exploded in the room.

"What's up?" Oliver asked.

"We're inside the El Rocca server."

Collin disentangled himself from Oliver's arms and rolled out of bed. Oliver sat up, letting the sheets pool around his hips, swearing silently. The uptight workaholic had won out over the unrestrained lover without even a hint of a fight. He fought off a sense of rejection, telling himself that Collin's job was important, and choosing it first was no personal insult to him. But the insecure child hiding deep in his gut was hurt anyway.

Reluctantly, Oliver reached for maturity and told himself to engage with Collin on his own turf. He said, "Explain this to me. Why does a seaside resort have its own server anyway?"

Collin sat down naked at the desk. "Let's find out, shall we?"

Sighing and telling his hard-on to take a chill pill, Oliver went over to stand behind Collin and kibitz on the hack. "What are you going to target now that you're in?"

"I was thinking I'd go for emails and the security camera feeds."

"Why don't you pass the security cameras over to my laptop, and I'll check those out while you sort through emails," Oliver offered.

In short order, the two of them were seated side-by-side without a stitch of clothing, typing away at their laptops like a couple of total geeks. But then Oliver found security films of the poker tournament, and his attention was arrested by the footage.

"Somebody using hotel computers is closely monitoring the play of the poker tournament," he announced.

"Of course they are."

"I'm not talking general surveillance to make sure no one's cheating or stealing chips. I'm talking they're watching hold cards and how people are betting."

"How in the hell can they see our hold cards?" Collin blurted.

"Cameras in the poker tables. Television coverage of major poker tournaments uses them. Every position has a tiny camera mounted at table height so when a player tips up their cards to peek at them, the cameras, and the viewing audience, see them too."

"Oh, right. I watched a bunch of poker on the telly when I was preparing to come here."

"Seriously? You learned to be as good a player as you are from the television?"

"I read a bunch of books and talked to a couple of retired professional players too."

Oliver shook his head, frankly amazed. "Damn, you're a natural at this gig. You should think about learning how to play for real. You could make serious bank if you put some time and effort into it."

"No, thanks. I'll take my nice, boring desk job and my quiet, boring life over all these thrills and chills."

"You? Boring? Hah! You forget I've had sex with you."

A pink tinge climbed Collin's chest, taking over his face, but he studiously avoided looking over at Oliver. He looked back at his own laptop lest he lose control and jump Collin where he sat, all naked and geeky and fuckable.

Oliver frowned, noticing something strange about the camera feeds from the tables. "This is weird. The images from the hold card feeds are obscured, like they may be filming through fabric."

"They who?"

"That's a damned good question."

"Guesses?" Collin asked.

"I can't imagine the El Rocca staff gives a flip about poker, which means the tournament director set up the surveillance."

"Why?" Collin responded. "This isn't ever going to be televised, is it?"

"No. And enough of the players here are banned from television-based tournament play that I can't imagine the director plans to sell coverage of this event later, even to a private network or pay-per-view outfit."

He frowned at Collin, who frowned back.

Collin suggested, "Are they feeding betting information to one or more of the players?"

"Possible. But why call a tournament at all in that case? Everyone has already paid the money to play. It's not as if the tournament director needs a particular individual to win this thing. Spying on the cards makes no sense."

"Unless," Collin said slowly, "we were right, and this actually is an elaborate job interview of some kind. The director could be watching how everyone plays as part of learning all he or she can about us."

"To what end?"

"It's a good way to find out how much nerve a person has. When they're bluffing. What their tells are. How reckless or cautious they are overall."

"Maybe." He paused doubtfully. "Still. Who would go to such lengths just to interview someone? It must be a hell of a job. Any progress on those emails?"

"Whoever's on that giant yacht in the marina is pirating the hotel's Wi-Fi."

Oliver laughed. "Dude's sitting in a yacht worth hundreds of millions, and he's pilfering the Wi-Fi from El Rocca?"

"Yup."

"Figures. Can you tell who it is?"

Collin frowned. "The main user on the yacht goes by a code name. Zephyr. Most of the recipients of Zephyr's emails have Greek names of one kind or another. Some are gods, some are mythological figures. My guess is that it's an organized group of some kind. A private social media group, if nothing else. But, given how circumspect they're being about revealing their identities, I have to surmise we're looking at a secret organization of some kind."

"Ooh. Like SPECTRE?"

"From the James Bond movies?"

"Yeah. You're James Bond and they're the bad guys."

"Who does that make you? Pussy Galore?"

Oliver snorted with laughter. "That's one I've never been accused of. But if I get to fuck James Bond, I'm down with being called that."

"Let me keep reading emails," Collin said more seriously. "Maybe I'll find a clue to the yacht owner's identity."

Oliver reviewed the list of players remaining in the tournament. None of them appeared to be Greek, let alone tycoons who could have set up this tournament for their own personal entertainment. "Is there anything in the emails that might identify the organizers of this tournament or their reasons for doing it?"

"Not that I've found."

Perplexed, Oliver kept browsing through the camera feeds around the hotel. Nothing exceptional leaped out at him.

"Check this out," Collin said abruptly a little while later.

Oliver leaned over and read an email that seemed to be setting up some sort of board of directors meeting to conduct a job interview of a new candidate. "What's the big deal? Somebody's getting hired."

"Look at the date and location."

He read, *T.R. Two weeks from now*. That could be anywhere.

"T.R. The Rock, maybe. El Rocca," Collin supplied.

"That's a rather thin guess. T.R. could be someone's initials or a reference to a place of business as easily as it could be what you suggest."

"How long will the rest of the poker tournament take?" Collin asked.

"Normally I'd say a few days. But this one's taking an inordinately long time. Players are being exceptionally cautious, and the minimum bets are very low relative to the amount of money on the tables."

"So, a couple of weeks?" Collin pressed.

"Yeah. Probably."

Collin scrolled down through several more messages and inhaled sharply. "Zephyr sent this last night. Check it out."

Oliver leaned over to read the message.

"Blood sport proceeding about as expected. The Albanians appear to have been eliminated, although no bodies. Too bad. I had high hopes for at least one of them. Our weapon is performing as expected. Should make the final table if another attempt doesn't take him out."

"'Our weapon'? Who do you suppose that is?" Oliver asked.

Collin looked up at him grimly. "These guys seem prone to giving code names to one another. It makes sense they'd give code names to their targets as well. If you're asking my opinion as an analyst, I'd have to say they're talking about you. Weapon. Gun. You're called Gun in the poker community."

Oliver stared. "*Another* attempt? As in an assassination attempt? On me?"

"The Jet Ski," Collin bit out. "We have our confirmation that it was a murder attempt."

"By whom?" he blurted.

"No idea. Have you found any security footage of the beach in the El Rocca feeds?" Collin responded. The man's voice was inordinately terse, even for Collin. A warm fuzzy feeling blossomed in his belly at how coldly furious Collin seemed at the idea of someone trying to kill him.

"I don't have the beach feed, but I do have the feed at the marina." He saw where Collin was going with his line of questioning. Was there film footage of the attack on him? He scrolled back through the archives of the past week to the afternoon before the tournament when he'd gone swimming. "You said the Jet Ski came from the direction of the marina, right? What time was it, exactly?"

"It was about three thirty when I stepped out to enjoy the sun," Collin supplied.

Using the time stamps on the video feed, he fast forwarded to three twenty-five and hit Play. The marina was quiet, with no movement. But then a Jet Ski roared out from behind the massive yacht, *Erebus*, and zoomed out of the picture frame. Oliver paused the feed and rewound it a few seconds. Using stop frames, he captured a still image of a blurry Jet Ski. He couldn't make out anything of the driver other than a black blob on the vehicle.

Collin, however, dug around in his suitcase and came up with a magnifying glass with a built-in light of some kind around its edge. He leaned forward, studying the laptop screen intently through it.

"Why are you using a magnifying glass?"

"Blowing up an image on screen fuzzes out the edges of it as it starts to pixelate. The magnifying glass enlarges the existing image with less fuzzing." A pause, then Collin murmured, "Slight figure. Female, if I had to guess. Caucasian." Another pause. "Advance one more frame."

He passed Oliver the magnifying glass. "Have a look at this." Collin jabbed at the screen as Oliver peered at the figure that leapt into view. Now that Collin mentioned it, that did indeed look like a woman in the wet suit. He'd seen a whole lot of male and female surfers in neoprene body suits over the years, and those curves were definitely female.

Collin advanced the video by one frame and muttered, "Look right there. A lock of hair escapes the wet suit hood. We advance a few more frames, and we see the hair get wet and plaster back to her wet suit hood. She's a blond."

"So are half the women at this hotel," Oliver retorted. "Hell, Desirée Moorhead is a blond. Maybe she tried to kill me."

"Possible," Collin replied absently.

Oliver stared. Seriously? Air-whistling-between-her-ears Desirée? His impression of her had been that the girl couldn't plot her way out of a paper bag, let alone plan and execute a murder. Had his read on her been dead wrong? The idea shook his confidence badly. He'd always prided himself on being an astute observer of people.

Collin used a small plastic ruler to measure the length of the Jet Skier's thigh from hip to knee. He did a quick calculation on a piece of scrap paper and then announced, "The skier is five foot six to five foot eight."

Wow. Collin was good at photo analysis. Really good. Which jived with his unspoken job as a spy or someone who worked with spies. Oliver commented, "That's the height of most of the female blonds at the hotel, including Desirée."

"You think homicidal hookers are killing off the players?" Collin asked incredulously.

Oliver grimaced. "Now that I think about it, it's very possible. Though if they are, they've hidden their abilities well."

Collin rolled his eyes. "I have to admit the women I've met here have not come across as rocket scientists. But then, at first glance, you don't come across as the brilliant mathematician you are, either."

Oliver smiled a little at the backhanded compliment. Not that Collin was wrong, of course. He went out of his way to come across as a dumb surfer, especially when he was playing poker. "If—and that's a big if—the escorts are involved, maybe by luring players into murder traps, I'd wager they have someone telling them what to do. Which means we're looking at a large-scale conspiracy and not a lone killer."

Collin stared at him for several long seconds, finally saying in a reluctant voice, "I have to concur."

Oliver sighed. "And here I was so sure the Albanian mob was behind the deaths and disappearances."

Silence fell between them. At length Collin asked, "Can we check that marina feed to see if anyone recognizable comes and goes from the *Erebus*? I'd love to know who's aboard."

Oliver shrugged. "It could take a while. We've got days' worth of film to go through."

"If we send that to my—" Collin broke off. He continued carefully, "—to my associates, they can help us look through all the film and all the hotel's emails. We need more manpower than just the two of us looking through all this data during our down time."

"And who might these associates of yours be, exactly?" Oliver asked.

A pause stretched out while Collin undoubtedly measured the level of trust between them. Oliver could hear the thoughts tumbling around in his lover's brain. Did Collin trust him enough to reveal more about his true reasons for being here? Maybe to reveal a real name or an employer?

Did hot sex equate to trust or not? He knew the answer to that one through bitter experience of his own. Oliver sighed and said, "I get it. You still don't trust me enough to tell me the whole truth."

Collin replied, "What I need you to do is leave this tournament before you get hurt or worse."

Oliver jolted. He hadn't seen that one coming. "Why would I leave? I'm sitting in fifth place, and lots of the top players are sandbagging. It's possible that if I merely play my best, I'll win the whole thing."

"Or die," Collin retorted.

It wasn't as if his life was any great shakes. It wouldn't be that huge a loss if he kicked the bucket. "Why should I leave?" Oliver demanded.

"Can't you just take me at my word that more players will likely die before this is over with?"

"You mean you want me to trust you?" Oliver asked ironically. "Sort of like me asking you to trust me enough to tell me who you work for?"

The pause was longer this time, colored by frustration. Oliver totally knew the feeling.

Eventually, Collin glanced up at him candidly. "I work for a company called Wild Cards, Incorporated. And no, we're not a bunch of card players. We're a private security firm."

"Who are you here to provide security for?" Oliver blurted.

"We're not at liberty to reveal any information about our clients. Sorry."

Oliver frowned. "No offense, but you don't act like much of a bodyguard. How does your playing in a poker tournament protect someone? I'm the only person you're spending any time with, and God knows nobody hired you to protect me. And I certainly didn't hire you."

Collin shrugged. "I'm not here to protect anybody. Security firms do more than just provide bodyguards. I've been hired to find out who's running this event and what the winner's prize will be."

"Okay, so let's send your company all this data and then get some sleep. You and I have poker to play in a few hours. And it's not getting any easier to stay afloat at the gaming tables."

Collin glanced at the camera feeds on Oliver's laptop. "I know how it could get easier for us. We have access to all the play so far. We could study the other players."

"That's cheating!" Oliver exclaimed.

"In case you hadn't noticed, other players are being *murdered*. That email called this tournament a blood sport, for God's sake. I don't think a little garden-variety cheating is out of line in this particular venue."

It went against everything he believed in. His father was the kind of man who wouldn't hesitate to cheat, lie, or steal to get ahead. Hence, he'd made it his mission in life to be scrupulously honest.

"How far are you willing to go in the name of winning, Oliver?"

He stared at Collin in utter frustration. "I get that what you're suggesting makes sense. But I can't tell you how much I hate the idea."

"On a personal level, that's encouraging to hear. I applaud your sense of ethics and morality. Furthermore, I happen to agree with it. But people are dying. And you could be next."

"Are you telling me you're willing to break all the rules to protect me?"

Collin shrugged, refusing to answer.

But the answer was plain as day in his eyes. He *was* willing to do anything, including blowing up his own code of ethics. *To protect him.* In his entire life nobody, *ever*, had been willing to compromise themselves for him.

Collin said soberly, "I don't think we have any choice but to use every tool at our disposal to stay alive and to stay in the tournament. If we don't figure out what the hell is going on and who's behind it—fast—more people will die."

"And possibly me," he added.

"I swear I'll do everything in my power to keep you safe. Up to and including dying myself to protect you. Please believe me."

Oliver smiled gently. "You risked your life to save me before you ever met me. Of course I believe you'd do the same now that we're close."

Collin said quietly, "In my mind, we're more than close." He added in a rush, "I don't expect you to return my feelings, and I don't have any long-term expectations of you. But you're important to me. More than you know."

Whoa. Him? Important to this achingly cool and sophisticated man? Gratitude washed over him.

"We're agreed, then. Cheating sucks, but we gotta ride the wave."

Collin nodded. "This is not the first step down a moral slippery slope. Rather, it is a onetime necessity precipitated by crisis."

Oliver replied dryly, "That's what I said."

Collin ducked his head and said ruefully, "Clearly, if I'm going to be with you, I must learn to speak surfer."

"Hang ten, brah."

"Umm, right."

Oliver turned his attention to the hold card video feeds. As distasteful as this was, their lives might depend on how prepared they were to get down and dirty.

Particularly if his father was behind this whole tournament. Unfortunately, this fiasco had all the hallmarks of a George Elliott scheme. His father played with other people's lives as if they were pawns on his personal chessboard. He manipulated and ruined people without a second thought. Honestly, he'd long wondered if his father was some kind of sociopath. But if George was having players killed, he'd obviously kicked over into being a full-blown psychopath.

If only he knew what the bastard was trying to accomplish. Then maybe he could thwart his old man. But until he did know what the deep game was, like it or not, he had no choice but to play this his father's way. They had to join the blood sport if he and Collin planned to survive.

Chapter Eight

Collin woke slowly, disoriented. Something was strange about where he was. Gibraltar. Poker tournament. And then it hit him. *He was not alone in bed.* An arm was thrown across his stomach and a leg trapped one of his. *Oliver.*

Smiling lazily, he reveled in waking up with his lover. It had been his favorite part of his relationship with Steve: that feeling of belonging to another person and having them belong to him. They'd always maintained their own apartments for appearances' sake, and they'd been cautious about being seen too often staying over at each other's places. But a couple of times a month, they'd risked spending the night together and having a lazy morning wake-up like this.

It felt wholly right to wake up with Oliver the same way he used to with Steve. It was also nice being able to remember a good moment with Steve fondly and not have it overwhelmed by profound sadness. Maybe he was finally beginning to get the distance from his loss and grief that the counselor had assured him would come one day.

It wasn't that he would ever stop loving Steve or stop missing him. But the grief counselor swore that he would make room in his life for a new love and for happiness when the time was right.

Turned out it hadn't been the right time he'd been waiting for. It had been the right *man* he'd been waiting for. He felt settled, way down in his gut where he hid his deepest feelings.

Oliver stirred beside him, smiling lazily. And it melted his bloody heart.

"We've got a while before play begins," Collin murmured. "Any idea how we should spend the afternoon?"

"I'm going to teach you how to play poker."

"I know how."

"No. How to really play."

"Why?"

"I need you to be here with me until the end," Oliver answered. "If you bust out of the tournament, they'll cart you off to the airport within the hour. And I need James Bond here to look out for me."

"What you *need* is to leave. We both know this tournament isn't what it seems, and players are being allowed to *kill* each other in the name of winning."

"Which makes it all the more important that both of us stick around till the end of this madness to have each other's backs while we find out exactly what's going on," Oliver retorted.

"I am not willing to risk your life just to get answers," Collin declared.

"I'm okay with dying."

Collin sat up sharply. "Why do you value your life so little? You have a great deal to offer the world. Minds like yours don't grow on trees."

"Surfers like me do. And that's all I am now."

"You're in the top five of what's potentially the best group of poker players ever assembled. That's pretty rarified air, my friend."

Oliver shrugged. "Eventually computers will learn to read body language and outplay every human on earth."

"Yeah, and you'll be the guy programming and teaching that computer."

Oliver shook his head in the negative. "Artificial intelligence is not my gig. Makes me hinky to think about computers who can replace humans. I like my flesh and blood real, warm, and horny." And with that pronouncement, Oliver fell on top of him, and they wrestled, laughing, until the bedclothes were everywhere, and they were out of breath.

"The maid's going to think we had a hell of a good time in here."

"Let's not disappoint her, then," Oliver murmured.

An element of frustration underlay their lovemaking this morning. He still wanted Oliver to leave the tournament, and Oliver was adamant that he wanted to stay, regardless of the risk. Collin was the intelligence professional, dammit. He knew an unacceptable risk when he saw one, and the amateur surfer dude did not.

"Earth to Collin, come in."

Collin started. "What?"

"Where did you go just then?"

"I was trying to figure out how to force you to quit this tournament if you won't do it voluntarily."

"Not happening, buddy. That ship has sailed, so you can get over it."

Collin opened his mouth to argue, but Oliver cut him off. "How about instead you stick around the tournament till the end so you can protect me?"

"I'm no world-class poker player!" Collin protested.

"You could be. You have all the brains and observation skills it takes." Oliver climbed out of bed naked and went to the desk to rummage in his duffel bag, which already was vomiting its contents all over the far corner of the room. How one man could make that big a mess so fast, Collin had no idea. Oliver was a veritable hurricane of clutter. Although he secretly admired Oliver's confidence and freedom of spirit to make messes. Steve always said he could afford to loosen up a bit. Maybe he should try to be more like Oliver.

Oliver plopped down on the bed, shuffling a deck of cards. He skipped straightening the bedspread before he sat down as well. And the world didn't end. *Small victories, my man.*

"We can't play strip poker because we're already naked," Collin remarked.

"Winner tops, loser bottoms."

Collin grinned. "What's the incentive for me to win, then?"

Oliver laughed as he shuffled. "Fine. Other way around."

Collin listened closely as Oliver dealt and talked his way through a dozen faceup hands and how he would analyze each player's cards based on various bets his opponents might make. The math was relatively straightforward, particularly after he'd been playing so much poker for the past week.

"With me so far?" Oliver asked.

"Yup."

"Okay. Now let's talk about bluffing and what it does to the probability calculations...."

Some of the math he just had to take at face value because they didn't have blackboards and weeks for Oliver to go through the lengthy derivations and proofs to make Collin understand how Oliver had arrived at his various formulas.

Oliver dealt another hand, and this time had Collin talk his way through the math.

"You're going to end up on the bottom yet," Oliver declared.

Gee. Darn.

The tutorial shifted to betting strategy, and they entered into a spirited discussion of caution versus bold risk-taking. No surprise, Collin was of the school that card players should play the numbers. Trust the odds and work the statistical calculations slow and steady.

"But it's called gambling for a reason," Oliver argued. "Every now and then you have to trust your gut and take a chance on a hand."

"But why?"

"Because luck is the one variable that cannot be accounted for. The very best players get intuitions from time to time, and they know when to listen to those and act on them."

Collin knew the feeling well. Intelligence analysts had to do the same, particularly with threat assessments. Sometimes the facts didn't bear out a risk, but his gut feeling was strong enough that he would make a call anyway. Sort of like going to bed with Oliver. There was no logical reason whatsoever for him to have taken a chance on this guy, but there'd been something about him....

"Okay. I'm going to deal a hand facedown. Play it without doing any math. Fast," Oliver instructed.

"But—"

"Just play. Don't think."

"But I think about everything," he protested as the cards went down across the sheets.

"I noticed," Oliver retorted.

In spite of the order not to, Collin did some fast, basic calculations in his head as he bet the next few hands. They went disastrously. Had there been real money on the bedspread, he'd have lost it all.

"Stop thinking," Oliver ordered more sternly. "Just play."

Frowning, Collin tried again. And again, the hands went disastrously. He consistently zigged when he should have zagged.

"Oh, for crying out loud," Oliver complained after yet another awful hand for Collin. "Am I going to have to take you out cliff diving or bungee jumping to loosen you up?"

Alarm blossomed in Collin's gut at the thought of doing either. The zip-lining he'd had to do in his field operations training had been bad enough.

"Christ. You look like you're having a stroke. Breathe, buddy."

"I would rather engage in activities that are slightly less death-defying," Collin managed to squeeze out past the panic in his belly.

"How about something like surfing? Have you ever tried that?" Oliver asked.

"Not much surfing in rural England, sorry."

"Next day off from the tournament I'm taking you surfing."

"So you *are* trying to kill me after all," Collin exclaimed. "I knew you were the murderer!"

"That's me. Professor Plum with the candlestick in the library."

"What is it about the candlestick that so fascinates people?" Collin groused. "Why don't people ever use the rope or the knife when they make Clue references?"

Oliver tilted his head. "Because the candlestick is something you'd pick up in the heat of the moment. It connotes passion. Spur-of-the-moment rage. It's more exciting than a dry, premeditated murder with a recognizable weapon."

"Do you suppose that's why our killer or killers are using escorts as bait?"

"Has anyone ever told you that you overthink everything?"

Collin smiled crookedly. "Maybe once or twice."

"I know how to loosen you up." Cards and covers went flying, and Oliver tackled him without warning. And oh, how Collin let him. Oliver was like an oversized puppy this morning, eager and playful. And Collin could not help absorbing some of his infectious joy.

They'd made silly, inelegant love and were breathing hard, lying side-by-side staring at the ceiling, when Collin's cell phone rang, jarring him out of the moment. That was the Wild Cards ring.

He flung his arm out to the nightstand, groping blindly for his phone. "Yes. Hello. Callahan here."

"It's Pere. We've been looking at the emails and camera feeds you sent us. We've got an image of a man on the deck of the *Erebus*. We've spotted him several times aboard the yacht, leading us to believe he's staying aboard and may be the owner, or at least the primary guest. But we've only got one image good enough that it can be enhanced."

Wild Cards HQ had some of the best image enhancement technology in the business. He knew; he'd been part of the team that developed it. Collin rolled out of bed and moved over to the window, staring down at the massive ship berthed down the beach.

His boss continued, "We were able to make a positive identification. The man is named George Elliott."

Collin's entire body went stiff. *No way.* "You're positive?"

"Absolutely."

It was impossible. Except the Wild Cards staff couldn't be mistaken. They'd built all kinds of safeguards and caveats into the facial recognition software. If there was the slightest question about a facial match, the computer would spit out the odds of the match being accurate. More often than not, the program spit out a set of odds and not a positive ID. Fuck. He bit back a sound of surprise and denial. George Elliott was Oliver's father's name. Surely, this was the same man.

Pere was speaking. "...West Coast mogul. Made his fortune investing in films and then in real estate. Finances went offshore about twenty years ago. No one knows what he does with his money now. Rumors of involvement in several shady international consortiums have surfaced from time to time but have never been confirmed. His son is playing in the tournament."

Hell, his son was playing in Collin's bed.

Pere continued, "You asked about him two days ago, if you'll recall. The team's worked up a profile on the son."

Collin chose his next words carefully. "Have you got any more on that?"

"Interesting character, young Oliver. Left home very young to go to Stanford. Math whiz. Dropped out of sight about five years ago after a reported mental breakdown. Our psychologist thinks it was more likely just a youthful rebellion with a solid dose of screw-over-mommy-and-daddy. Recent rumors have him going to work for his father, perhaps as a financial analyst—which is an elliptical way of saying the son may be in cahoots with the father in whatever shady enterprises Elliott's got himself embroiled in. God knows, the son would be dangerous as hell as a criminal mastermind. We tracked down two of his old professors at Stanford. They both said he's the smartest math student they've ever seen."

Smart enough to be hoodwinking him? Smart enough to be working on the sly for the directors of this tournament? Spying on the spy? Surely not. *Fuck*.

OLIVER SPENT the afternoon watching the secret tapes of other players and their hold cards. It was cheating, which made him feel surprisingly guilty. At least he knew he hadn't inherited his sire's completely amoral business instincts. That was a relief. George Elliott was widely known to be a barracuda who would not hesitate to destroy anyone or anything in the name of making a few more bucks.

His therapist had given it a name: sociopathy. His father had no emotional or moral compass to speak of. He used ambition as his only guide and demolished anyone or anything that got in between him and his goals. Turned out a fair number of CEO types were sociopaths to one degree or another. That kind of brutal, unfeeling focus apparently helped a person get to the top of the heap.

The therapist also said the best thing Oliver could have done was get away from the bastard as soon as possible. He'd been lucky that his talent for math had gotten him out of the house at barely fourteen years of age. Still. His old man had left plenty of scars on him.

Given that his opponents were killing each other, Oliver supposed he shouldn't feel too guilty about studying the tapes. Still. This whole tournament was an ugly business. The name of the game here was to win at all costs. *All* costs. It left a nasty taste in his mouth. Nasty enough that he didn't care anymore about finding out if he was the best poker player on earth or not. Nasty enough that it reminded him of his father.

He'd been pretending ever since he'd gotten that all-expense-paid email invite to this event that it didn't smack of George Elliott. His father had always worshipped minds that were quicker than his, particularly in mathematical and computer fields. He'd been massively proud of young Oliver's talents...at least until he'd started rebelling against Daddy Dearest. George took huge pleasure in having power over brilliant people. It made him feel intellectually superior, Oliver supposed. Whatever.

He wanted nothing to do with his old man, regardless of what made the bastard tick. He had no proof that his father was involved with this tournament, but he also had no proof that George wasn't. This was exactly the kind of gathering of minds his father would most relish.

Which worried the hell out of him. What would George plan for a group like this? For surely he would have some dastardly endgame. Even if someone else was behind this fiasco, asking himself what his father would do should give him a decent predictive model to work from.

One thing he did know: he had no intention of abandoning Collin to these thugs and hustlers. The guy would get eaten alive. Collin was far too decent and trusting to run with this crowd.

He consoled himself with the thought that he was cheating to protect Collin, not to advance his own success in this damned tournament. In fact, whenever Oliver ran across something interesting or revealing about one of the remaining players in the play tapes, he shared it with Collin. After all, the object was for one or both of them to stay in the game long enough to find out who was running it and why. And sharing the stolen information about how the other players really bet made him feel a tiny bit less guilty about having it.

Collin had been uncharacteristically quiet since that phone call had come in. Like he was preoccupied with something at work. Should Oliver push to know what it was, or leave it alone? Hard to tell with Collin. Sometimes, he was an open book, and at others, he held his metaphorical cards very close to the chest. The guy might be uptight, but Oliver guessed that was not how he wanted to live his life. The trick was to get him out of his head enough to let down his hair and relax more. Easier said than done, though.

Collin had taken a break from staring at emails on the El Rocca server and was in the shower—and Oliver was seriously considering joining him—when Collin's laptop beeped to indicate an incoming email. He should leave it alone. It was private, right?

But hell, he was cheating at cards; why not cheat a little at love? He'd already jumped off the ethical cliff, after all. Collin's laptop was open. All he had to do was lean over and touch the mouse pad to wake up the screen. He'd seen Collin type in his password enough times to know it by heart.

He leaned. He touched. He typed.

The sender was Pere at WCI. That would be Wild Cards, Inc. A work email, then.

He justified reading it by reasoning that if there were an emergency, he could tell Collin about it right away. And besides, they were working together. Right? Admitting to himself that this was not his finest hour, he nonetheless glanced at the body of the email.

The name Elliott jumped out at him, and that was when he seriously started reading. Holy shit. This was a *complete* dossier on *him*. What the hell? Collin had people digging into the most intimate details of his past? Why? Fury at the invasion of his privacy ripped through him. Suddenly he was feeling a lot less guilty about snooping on Collin's fucking laptop.

When the report devolved into a lengthy psychological analysis of his daddy issues, his fury boiled over. He surged up out of his seat, grabbed his wet suit, and barged out of the room. He was going surfing. And he fucking well wasn't taking Collin along like he'd promised.

He stormed down to the hotel's porters and waited impatiently while they retrieved his surfboard out of the luggage storage room. Fortunately most of the cabs in Gibraltar were minivans, and he was able to stuff his board in one. It was a pain in the ass walking across the windswept runway at the airport that also marked the Gibraltar border, carrying his surfboard. It acted like a fucking sail and caught the wind like nobody's business, but he was so mad he barely noticed.

Once on the Spanish side of the border, he grabbed another cab, and sat back, brooding, while the cabbie drove down the coast to Tarifa.

The surf was made up mostly of bunny waves today. But they were enough to work off the worst of his anger. He zipped up his wet suit, picked up his board, and jogged out into the Atlantic Ocean. He took his cue from the dozen other surfers working one particular section of the beach. The locals would know where the best waves were generated.

He caught a few swells and got the feel of the curls, and then it was on. He attacked the waves like they were enemies in need of conquering. It took a while, but the rhythm of the sea, the paddling, and the exhilarating sensation of being flung along by Mother Nature gradually soothed the worst of his fury.

Why should he be pissed off at Collin for doing to him exactly what he was doing to the other players in the tournament? It wasn't as if anything in that profile of him and his father was a big secret. Anyone was free to draw whatever half-assed psychological conclusions they cared to from the public details of his life. Still, it stung to have his lover poking around behind his back. If he wanted to know the details, why hadn't Collin just asked him outright about his old man?

Maybe he'd been too angry to notice before, but he'd paddled out to the farthest point where swells were forming and had just stood up on his board when he felt a strange vibration pass through his feet. It felt almost electronic in nature. What was up with that?

Shrugging it off, he surfed in to shore and paddled out again. This time he noticed the pulsing vibration clearly as he lay on the board. What the fuck? He rolled off the board and ran his hand along the smooth finish of the board's underside. Nada. He did feel a small ridge in the epoxy resin coating that would need sanding out and refinishing soon, but nothing to explain the odd vibration. Was it coming from the water?

Next time in to shore, he called over to another surfer to ask in his unreliable Spanish if there were ever earthquakes in this area. The guy looked at him like he was smoking dope, so he took that as a no.

His third time paddling out to pick up a swell, something bumped the bottom of his board. He frowned. He'd felt a bump like that once before. It had been a mako shark off the coast of Hawaii investigating his board's edibility.

Another bump. Harder this time.

He yanked all his limbs out of the water and, sitting on his heels, stared down into the murky water all around him. He couldn't see a damned thing. But that had definitely been a shark testing his board.

Best bet with a shark was to get the hell away from it. A small swell was rolling his way, not one he'd usually surf, but it was big enough to push him in toward shore. He would take it. He jumped to his feet, picked up the wave, and carefully rode it, milking all the forward speed he could coax out of it.

All of a sudden, his board lurched violently, yanked right out from under his feet. He registered his ankle tether going slack just as his face hit the water. He popped up immediately and flattened out his body into a rigid length, body surfing for his life. Whatever had hit his board had cleanly severed his steel-fiber reinforced ankle tether. And only one thing in the water approaching from below was capable of that.

A shark.

Thankfully the swell he'd been riding grew as it hit the shallower water and pushed him forward with even more speed.

"Hey man! You lost your board!" one of the other surfers shouted.

"Shark!" he shouted back.

The word sent all the surfers to their feet on their boards, frantically riding whatever wave they could catch to shore. Surfers ran ashore all along the beach. Several came over to him, and one picked up the end of the ankle tether that should have been attached to his surfboard.

"Clean cut, dude. Shark bite."

Oliver nodded, winded. "Any sign of my board?"

The surfers around him scanned the beach. One said in an Australian accent, "Red-and-white board with yellow racing stripes?"

"That's it."

"Just washing ashore now. I'll fetch it for you, mate."

He caught his breath after the frantic swim for shore as the guy jogged down the beach to his abandoned board. But his breath accelerated again as the guy laid Oliver's board down beside him in the sand. A huge, semicircular bite had been taken out of the side of the board right where Oliver normally stood on it.

The white polystyrene core of the board was plainly visible, along with several wires sticking out of the foam. Frowning, he leaned over to examine them more closely. What on God's green earth were wires doing embedded in the foam of his board? Except, as he examined them, he concluded that they weren't embedded as much as they'd been poked into the board's core after its manufacture. He pulled out his ankle knife and dug farther into the foam core, but whatever the wires had been attached to had apparently been in the part of the board the shark had eaten.

"Are shark bites common in this area?" he asked no one in particular.

"Not at all," the Aussie replied.

Quickly, Oliver described the strange vibrations he'd felt just before the shark attacked him, but the surfers all stared as if he'd lost his mind. He *knew* he'd felt those vibrations!

As the other surfers drifted off, losing interest in the crazy guy, the Aussie stuck around. Oliver looked up at him ruefully. "Do you think I'm crazy too?"

"Nope. I happen to be a marine biologist in my real life, and I've been working on a team doing research into using radio signals to attract and repel sharks. If you had to describe the vibrations you felt, would you say it felt like low rumbling or something at a high, fast frequency, like, say, a dentist's drill?"

He frowned, thinking back to earlier. "Nope. Definite low rumbling. Almost a pulsing, like a heavy metal song playing in the next car over. Why?"

"That's the optimal type of frequency for attracting sharks."

"Where did you say you do this research?" Oliver asked curiously.

"We're based over in Gibraltar."

"What kind of radios are you guys using to generate these signals?"

"They're pretty simple, just a small transmitter with a bunch of wires attached that send the signal out into the water."

Son of a bitch. "Do you guys keep track of the radios, by any chance? You know, count them and account for them routinely?"

"Nah. They only cost a few dollars apiece. We've got a big box of them in the lab."

And he would lay odds the research team was down at least one radio. Either that, or he was having paranoid delusions. Somebody could easily have tampered with his board in the past week, while it had been sitting in the luggage closet at El Rocca. That someone could have planted a shark-attracting radio in the core of his surfboard and then repaired the hole, which would explain the ridge he'd felt on the bottom of it before.

It was a far-fetched conspiracy theory. Borderline paranoid, even. But was it any more far-fetched than poker players murdering each other? Or homicidal hookers? He was well-known in the poker community as a surfer. And the bellman had commented that his surfboard was the only one in the luggage closet this morning when he'd started to describe it.

Temptation to head straight for the airport and take the first flight out of Gibraltar was high as he rode back toward the resort and its homicidal guests. The only thing that made him walk across that broad expanse of runway and hail a cab for El Rocca was Collin. Smart though the guy might be, and nosy as he might be about other peoples' private lives, he was not up to taking on the worst of the worst in the gambling world alone.

As disappointed as he was at Collin for going behind his back, he couldn't abandon the lamb to the lions.

CHAPTER NINE

COLLIN STEPPED out of the bathroom, a smile on his lips. But it faded as he saw he was alone in his hotel room. Perplexed, he looked around for a note or something to explain where Oliver had disappeared to. And then he realized the neoprene wet suit that had been hanging in the closet was gone. Ah. He'd gone surfing. Relieved not to have been included in that outing, Collin finished dressing and sat back down at his computer.

A message had come in from Wild Cards, Inc. in his absence. It was the final psychological analysis of Oliver and his father. No surprise, the elder Elliott was a control freak who'd bullied his only son mercilessly until Oliver finally revolted. All in all, he was proud of Oliver for getting out from under his old man's thumb.

He continued reviewing video footage from the hotel's security cameras and made a number of interesting connections between various players meeting surreptitiously with other players, presumably to form secret alliances going forward in the tournament. He wrote down the pairings to show to Oliver later. They could compare the list against the players they were assigned to play with.

He'd been at it for a couple hours when the door burst open behind Collin, and he smiled, turning to greet his lover. But the words died on his lips as a pair of burly men in dark suits loomed in the doorway.

"Hotel security. You need to come with us, Mr. Callahan. Now."

Shocked, he stood up. As he did so, he surreptitiously hit the shutdown button on his laptop.

"Bring the computer too."

Uh-oh. Well, at least if they try turning it back on without the codes, it will trigger the automatic wipe.

As he scooped up his laptop, he shoved aside a stack of notes, conveniently covering up Oliver's laptop that still sat on the desk.

Thinking fast, he followed the hotel security men out of the room. His hack must have been discovered and tracked back to him. If one of Wild Cards' field operatives were to call him at HQ in a similar situation, what would his advice be? Claim to merely be engaging in a little snooping in an effort to get ahead in the tournament. Admit to the lesser crime—watching the secret tapes of other players playing—and distract his accusers from the larger crimes of reading private emails and watching the security camera feeds from the entire resort. Oh, and stay calm.

Easier said than done.

He was startled when the men led him out of the elevator on the ground floor and headed toward the rear exit of the resort. They weren't going to take him somewhere and kill him, were they? Frantically he made a point of turning his face up toward every security camera they passed, to make sure a clear shot of him was left behind for Oliver to find. He prayed it wasn't the only trail he left behind.

Should he fight? Run? Thing was, this might be an exceptionally revealing moment in his investigation. He might be en route to the person behind this whole crazy, dangerous game. His curiosity won out over his raw, unadulterated terror. Reminding himself that he was an amateur field operator and his fear would be exaggerated out here on his first mission, he pushed through it and went along with the security types.

The men slogged out onto the sand of the beach in their dress shoes, and Collin frowned, confused. Where were these guys taking him? If he didn't know better, he would say they were heading for the marina. Sure enough, they crossed the sand and stepped up onto the wooden pier. He watched as one of the men punched a security code into a number pad and opened a steel-barred gate onto the dock itself.

Were they planning to take him out to sea to dump his body? He knew all too well how fast hypothermia would claim him if these two didn't strangle him first.

There had to be a spot between a couple of boats where he could make a break for it, dive into the water, and then duck behind a boat for cover. Then what? Hang out in the water until he was too cold to swim for shore? Or make a swim for freedom that would take him the entire length of the broad beach to rocks barely visible in the distance before he could safely climb out of the water without being seen and shot?

Maybe he could make his way into a boat unseen, hot-wire the engine, and make a getaway. That was probably his best bet. He eyed a cluster of small craft and gathered himself to jump off the—

One of the men reached out to take his upper arm in a ham-sized fist. "Mr. Elliott wants to talk to you."

Oliver was out here on the dock? Confused, he looked around. Oliver hadn't said anything about having access to a boat. And then his brain kicked in. The *other* Elliott wanted to talk to him. The one on the bigass yacht. Crap.

Although, part of him was deeply interested to meet Oliver's father for himself. To judge the accuracy of the assessments from the Wild Cards analysts. And maybe to see if he could spot any part of the father in the son.

Momentarily derailed from his escape plan, he realized with a start that they had passed by the cluster of likely boats for his escape. The only vessel moored ahead of them now was the gigantic yacht, *Erebus*.

Two more burly men, these dressed in matching navy blue polo shirts and khaki slacks, met him at the gangplank , took his laptop from him, and ushered him aboard the *Erebus*, leaving behind the hotel security men. Interesting.

"This way, Mr. Callahan."

To say the yacht was luxurious didn't begin to do it justice. Highly varnished wood inlays lined the hallways, plush carpeting silenced his footsteps, and glass sparkled everywhere. Murano glass, cut crystal, and shining prisms throwing rainbows of light surrounded him. He was led to an office that Collin estimated was only halfway to the top deck. It was spacious and bright, with floor-to-ceiling tinted windows. The décor was Italianate, all whites and golds with incredibly intricate workmanship everywhere he looked—from the etched mirrors to the painted ceiling frescoes to the carved crystal desk accessories. The room dripped of limitless wealth.

Okay, color him intimidated.

He sat down in the delicate chair in front of the empty desk and gave himself a silent pep talk. The stuff in here was just stuff. And it was clearly calculated to impress visitors. He gave the decorator credit for having achieved their goal, and then he set aside his initial reaction.

He'd been brought to a beautiful office whose owner would likely take umbrage with blood being sprayed all over the place or the smells of death being released in here. That was good news at least.

The owner of the desk, presumably George Elliott, took his sweet time showing up. If the intent was to scare him, it had the opposite effect of giving him time to collect his wits and regain his equilibrium. When the door behind him finally opened, he intentionally did not crane his head around to look at whoever entered. Instead, he continued to gaze out to sea through the picture windows.

A large man stepped into his field of vision and sat down at the desk. Collin's first impression was that the delicate décor emphatically did not suit its gruff-looking owner.

Collin focused on the man's face and experienced an unpleasant jolt of recognition. This was undoubtedly Oliver's father. Same nose. Same brow. Same stubborn chin. But the eyes were completely different. Oliver's were bright and mischievous, ready to laugh. Curious. This man's were… mean.

"Mr. Callahan," the man said accusingly, obviously trying to throw him off-balance.

Collin snorted mentally. Two could play that game. "Mr. Elliott," he replied casually.

George Elliott looked up sharply, his expression irritated. Thought he would shake in his shoes at merely being in the great man's presence or something?

"You've been a naughty boy, Mr. Callahan."

Going on the attack, was he? Collin had participated in training numerous Wild Cards operatives in various interrogation techniques and how to resist them all. "Indeed, I have," he agreed readily.

"Which infraction would you be referring to, specifically?" Elliott demanded.

He shrugged. "You're the one who had your guys drag me aboard your boat. Obviously you have one in particular you want to talk about. So talk." There. Collin had squarely taken the initiative away from Elliott.

His opponent scowled darkly. Although there were striking physical similarities between father and son, Collin took note of the differences as well. Oliver must take his coloring from his mother, for George had dark eyes, dark, thick hair, and the bronze complexion of his Greek heritage. Oliver was fair-skinned and light-haired, and his brilliantly blue eyes definitely didn't come from George. His features were more finely drawn than this man's heavier ones too.

Silence stretched out between them as George glared and Collin stared back impassively. Ah, the uncomfortable silence gambit. See if

Collin would blurt out something in order to break the rising tension. That would be a solid no. It could get as awkward in here as ol' George could stand.

The silence went on for upward of a full minute. Collin never looked away from his host and possible captor, never flinched, never let his face register anything other than bland disinterest. God bless Oliver for teaching him the fine art of giving away nothing at the poker table. Who knew it would come in so handy in this way?

It was a fascinating exercise watching the various emotions and thoughts flicker across Elliott's face. The guy was good, but not anywhere near as accomplished as his poker-playing son at hiding his interior thoughts and feelings. It didn't hurt, either, that Collin had spent most of the past two weeks studying professional poker players, all of whom were excellent at disguising their thoughts and not revealing anything about their cards.

Collin occupied himself by reviewing everything he knew about George Elliott from the Wild Cards dossier. It was hard to believe this formidable man in front of him had a small penis and insecurity about his masculinity, but the source of that particular detail had been rated as impeccable. Must have been a former mistress or paid escort who'd informed on him.

Finally, Elliott broke the silence. "My men tell me you broke into El Rocca's computer and stole certain videos you shouldn't have."

Computer. Videos. The word choices signaled someone not particularly tech savvy. "That's correct," he answered.

Elliott seemed startled by his ready admission. "Why? What were you trying to accomplish?"

"I'm here to win the tournament. Isn't that why everybody's here?" He was happy to answer a question with a question. The tactic often threw off inexperienced interrogators.

"How did breaking into the computer help you win?"

There it was. The genuine curiosity of a man who'd been derailed from his original line of questioning. A good interrogator never asked a question he didn't already know the answer to. Or at least most of the answer.

Collin leaned back in his chair and tucked his thumbs in his pants pockets, letting his arms hang loosely, signaling with his body language that he was entirely comfortable having this conversation. It wasn't how he felt at all, of course.

"Being able to study how my opponents play when they've got various hold-card combinations is invaluable in helping me spot their tells, in knowing when they bluff and how they give away their bluffs. I've shot up in the rankings as a result." Truth be told, it was Oliver's tutoring that had allowed him to move up in the chip standings, but George didn't need to know that.

"I should throw you out of the tournament for cheating."

Should. The key word there. The guy *wasn't* planning to toss him out. Which meant Elliott probably also wasn't planning to kill him. A huge weight lifted off Collin's chest.

Collin asked gently, "But isn't cheating the point of this tournament?"

"I beg your pardon?" Elliott demanded.

Didn't like being transparent to anyone, and certainly not to some upstart unknown, apparently. Collin leaned forward, idly fiddling with a crystal inkwell on the desk, turning it sideways before withdrawing his hand. It was an invasion of Elliott's territory to do so. Collin started a mental clock on how long it would take the guy to put the inkwell back.

Three. Four. Five. Five seconds for the man to reach out and turn the inkwell back to its original position. Control issues. A tendency toward obsessive-compulsiveness.

"What do you mean, cheating is the point?" Elliott demanded, rather like a man who knew he'd lost control of this conversation.

Collin shrugged. "You tell me. You're the one who invited hustlers and criminals to your game. Obviously, you expected them to behave badly. Compared to the homicidal behavior of some of your players, my garden-variety hack to look at footage of game play is a very minor infraction, wouldn't you agree?"

"Yes. I do. And that's why I'm going to let you continue in the tournament. For a price."

Collin let his right eyebrow rise questioningly.

"As you may know, my son is playing in this tournament as well."

Interesting. Elliott didn't know that Oliver was Collin's lover, then.

"I have big plans for him," George announced.

Oh, Lord. The man thought he was going to get Oliver back under his thumb, and somehow this tournament was the mechanism by which he planned to do it. That was hilarious. Had the man met, or even spoken with, his son any time in the past decade or so? Or did George fancy Oliver to be the heir to whatever throne he imagined himself perched upon?

Granted, if George owned this massive yacht, the wealth Oliver stood to inherit sooner or later was mind-boggling. But boggling enough for Oliver to consider playing ball with his old man to get all of this?

His gut said no. At his core, Oliver was an ethical guy. Either that, or his own ability to read a human being had gone completely to hell.

George shocked him out of his thoughts with, "I want you to help him win."

Rather than readily agree to what was a no-brainer for him, Collin went on the offense instead. "What's the prize for winning?"

"Why do you care? If my son wins, it won't matter to you."

"Before I agree to forgo my own shot at the prize, I want to know what you're asking me to give up."

"That's not how this works. You help Oliver win, and I let you live."

Collin let one corner of his mouth turn up into a smile, signaling his disdain for Elliott's threat, while he quickly considered how to respond. Unfortunately, the man had regained the upper hand in this conversational chess game.

He was saved from answering, however, by the office door bursting open behind him.

"What the hell are you doing, Dad?" a familiar voice demanded from behind Collin.

Collin's head did swivel around this time.

George blurted, "What the hell are you doing here?"

Collin's mind leapt into hyperdrive, bombarding him with questions. Oliver must have seen George Elliott's goons drag him aboard the ship and come racing down here. To rescue Collin? If so, that was insanely sweet of him, particularly given how openly he despised his father.

"I gather you've met my old man."

"Indeed, I have. We were just discussing my extracurricular activities watching stolen security footage of my fellow players at work."

"Were you now?" Oliver asked cautiously. Oliver seemed to have taken the hint that Collin had the situation under control and made no further comment.

"Nice boat your father has," Collin prompted, curious to gauge Oliver's reaction in front of his father.

A shrug. "I guess."

Thank goodness. He hadn't read Oliver wrong. The guy had zero interest in his father's wealth.

George demanded, "How did you get aboard?"

Oliver shot back, "It turns out flashing the Elliott name opens doors around here."

Intriguing. The friction between these two was palpable and held a bitter edge. A toxic edge, even.

"When did you buy a goddamned freighter, Pops?"

"If you'd spoken to me anytime in the past five years, you'd know when," George shot back.

Oliver responded dryly, "That would involve me giving a flying fuck."

"Quit swearing. You know it upsets your mother."

"And she's where in this room?" Oliver demanded.

Why the reference to the mother? George was a control freak who would exert power over his spouse. All the reports painted Phyllis Elliott as a classic mousy, submissive wife. George had spoken like his wife would see this conversation. Via surveillance camera, maybe? Or perhaps later he would show the footage of this meeting to the bereaved mother who missed her son. There was some important family dynamic he was missing, here.

Collin's gut red-flagged the mother as a dangerous topic. He frowned infinitesimally at Oliver, hoping he would catch the hint to tread lightly with wherever George was trying to take this conversation.

"So. Are you kicking him out of the tournament?" Oliver demanded baldly of his father, lifting his chin toward Collin.

So much for the treading-lightly hint getting through. Not long on subtlety was Oliver. Collin sighed. At least Oliver had changed the subject.

"No. I've given him a stern warning, though. And I'm giving you the same warning. No shenanigans out of you, boy. Do your job and win the damned tournament."

So. This tournament was a giant setup after all, to establish Oliver as top dog in the poker world. But why? What did George have to gain out of enhancing his son's reputation? It would only matter if Oliver was planning to go to work for his father in the near future and they wanted competitors to be intimidated by Oliver's prowess at... at what? Bluffing? Mental math? At manipulating odds?

"What if I refuse?" Oliver asked.

"Just because you're my son doesn't mean I won't throw you out of this event on your ear."

"God knows, you've thrown me out before."

"Watch your mouth."

Collin rose to his feet. "Thank you for your hospitality, Mr. Elliott. I'll consider your offer carefully. And in the meantime, your son and I have a poker tournament to prepare for." He moved toward Oliver and smoothly took his elbow on the way by, turning him toward the door.

"Say goodbye, Gun," Collin ordered. He used the casual moniker on the assumption that it would be the name a casual acquaintance from the poker world would use.

"Goodbye, Gun," Oliver snarled.

"Don't be surly. Your father was nothing but polite to me."

"Surly? Me?" Oliver exclaimed as Collin all but shoved him through the office door.

"Yes. And childish."

"Childish?"

"Immature too."

"What the actual fuck—" Oliver started as Collin all but shoved him down the hallway toward the gangplank.

"Keep arguing and keep walking," Collin muttered under his breath without moving his lips. He added louder, "No wonder your father threw you out. You're a brat."

"I am not! You're the asshole here. What the hell are you doing hauling me off my own father's yacht?"

"I'm taking you back to the poker tournament, and I'm sincerely hoping one of my fellow players kicks your ass."

"Well, fuck you too."

They cleared the yacht and made it to the dock. Collin stretched out his stride, forcing Oliver to hustle to stay beside him. Which was a feat, given the length and power of Oliver's legs. Punching in the code the guards had used to get him in, Collin opened the gate before one of the hotel security guards loitering on the beach could reach it from the other side.

"We don't need an escort back to the hotel, boys," Collin snapped at the pair of men. "Go find yourselves a few of the girls, or guys if that's how you swing, and take a long lunch break, eh?"

Startled by his verbal assertiveness, the men fell back, giving him and Oliver wide berth.

"Umm, really. What the actual fuck?" Oliver muttered.

"My hack was discovered. Your old man said he would let me stay in the tournament if I help you win it."

Oliver burst out laughing beside him. "Oh my God, that's rich. Does he know we're—"

"I don't think so. And we need to keep it that way," Collin bit out. "My life, and very possibly yours, depend on him not finding out. And given the degree of surveillance we now know to be in place, that means we have to stop seeing each other, at least publically."

Oliver stopped to stare at him. Collin's heart wailed in anguish, but this was his only choice. The best way to keep Oliver safe was to minimize being associated with each other, even if it meant cutting ties with him. Now.

Give up his lover and they both lived. Keep seeing Oliver and forfeit his life. More important, if he was reading George correctly, keep seeing Oliver and forfeit Oliver's life, too.

Collin said forcefully, "I'm not kidding. You and I can't be seen together."

"You're going to give in to him? Just like that?"

"Not just like that. I can't lose you, dammit. If it's a choice between your life and not seeing you for a while, I choose the latter."

He turned and walked away. Swear to God, it was the hardest thing he'd ever done. He'd thought burying Steve had been hell on earth, but this was it. Right here. Finding a man who was possibly his perfect match, his perfect counterpoint, his perfect challenge in every way, and having to walk away from that man, potentially forever… pure hell.

Chapter Ten

OLIVER SCOWLED at his fellow players as he sat down at the table. Everybody in this fucking resort was in his Rolodex of hate right now. He was pissed off at his father for interfering in his life, more pissed off at Collin for letting the bastard interfere, and most pissed off at himself for breaking his own cardinal rule and having feelings for Collin Callahan. He *knew* better than to let anyone inside his fortress of emotional solitude.

He peeked at his hold cards, and they sucked. He didn't care. He bet aggressively, completely faking out the other five players at his table and raking in a big pot. Stupid fuckers. Although exactly who he was mentally referring to, he wasn't certain.

Another hand. This time spectacular cards, and he bet wildly again. This time the other players were suspicious of his uncharacteristic betting and called every bet he made. The flop fell his way, he showed the table his winning hand, and raked in another huge pot. Hah. Assholes.

His anger settled down a bit after the two quick wins, but he played from a state of cold, calculating fury the entire night, taking pleasure in busting out one after another of the players at the table, forcing them into reckless and foolish bets in the face of his ferocious play. By the time play was called for the night, he'd eliminated every other player at his table. He counted his massive pile of chips, handed them in to the floor boss, and headed for the exit.

A hand on his arm made him turn sharply.

"What the hell are you doing?" Collin bit out. "Everyone here will be out to kill you after that show you just put on."

"Why do you care? We're not seeing each other right now, remember?"

"I didn't say we were on a break. Just that we can't be seen together. I care about you and your safety, you idiot."

"Stay away from me if you can," Oliver snapped.

Collin's hand fell off his elbow, and Oliver stalked down the hall toward the bar. He hated this. Fuck his father. Fuck them all.

COLLIN WINCED as the big electronic leaderboard at one end of the ballroom was updated shortly after the end of play. Oliver had vaulted all the way into first place, and everyone in the room was buzzing about how he'd utterly destroyed his competitors. War stories about what a hell of a player Gun Elliott had been a few years back flew around Collin. The consensus was that Gun had found his mojo again and was now the player to beat.

Which was to say, the player to kill, if George Elliott wasn't the person engineering the killings. Thing was, George didn't seem interested in advancing his son's interests unfairly over those of anyone else here. Yes, he wanted Oliver to win, but he hadn't been willing to help his son cheat, for example. If it wasn't George and his cronies orchestrating the murders, that left one of the players as the murderous mastermind.

He gazed around the dining room where most of the players were still eating. Which one of them was willing to kill to win this thing? Which one had the resources? Using a paper napkin from under his soft drink, he jotted down the names of everyone there, and the names of the other players who'd opted out of a meal after play. He would send the list to the Wild Cards when he got back to his room and ask for emergency background checks on everyone. There had to be a tell somewhere in someone's background as to who had the means and motive to kill off the competition.

What the hell was he supposed to do? He needed to keep a close eye on Oliver, but if they couldn't be around each other, how was he going to keep the stubborn jerk alive? The guy had turned and stormed away the second Collin said they had to stay apart.

Didn't Oliver get that both of their lives depended on keeping Oliver safe and in the game? It was the only reason George hadn't already killed Collin or at least kicked him out of the tournament. Surely, Oliver understood that George Elliott would squash Collin like a bug if anything happened to his son.

C'mon, Oliver. Think it through. See the logic.

Collin frowned. Maybe that same logic could work as an excuse to stay close to Oliver. He could claim to be protecting Oliver on behalf of George.

Yes. It could work.

And he was desperate enough to be around Oliver, even if the guy was furious with the whole world right now, to give it a try. Especially if Oliver was going to react the way he did to the recommendation to stay apart.

Collin was pathetic.

He was okay with being pathetic if it gave him a reprieve and he could continue to be in the same space, breathe the same air as Oliver, without increasing the risk.

Hurrying back to his own room, he scooped up Oliver's laptop, which was still sitting on his desk, and headed to Oliver's room. As he expected, Oliver was cautious to find Collin at his door. And as Collin also expected, Oliver was drinking.

"Whaddiya want?" he demanded.

"Let me in and I'll tell you."

Oliver stepped back, gesturing with a glass half-full of ice and amber liquid. Going for hard liquor tonight? He surmised this was aimed at his father. Illuminating.

Collin sighed. "You left your laptop in my room."

Oliver snatched it out of his hands and tossed it onto the sofa. "Thanks. Now scram."

"Look, Oliver. Your father gave me no choice. I'm on his radar now and he'll be watching me. If he suspects that you and I are together as a couple, I got the distinct impression he would be extremely unhappy about that. Does he even know you're gay?"

"How can he not? I've fucked every dude between LA and San Francisco who would have me in the past few years. I don't delude myself that I successfully hid from him. He has undoubtedly had surveillance on me and gotten reports on my antics."

"Which means he likely already suspects me of being your lover." Collin added sarcastically, "That's great."

"I get that I'm not worth taking a chance on."

Collin took a fast step forward and shoved Oliver back against the wall, his forearm planted across Oliver's chest. "Cut the bullshit. I'd die for you and not regret doing so. But it's *your* life I'm worried about, you colossal twat!"

"My life? My old man wouldn't kill me—"

"Yes. Yes, he would. I happen to think your father is a psychopath with violent tendencies. My analysis, and that of my colleagues, is that he wouldn't hesitate to kill you if you displeased or embarrassed him enough."

Some of the tension drained out of Oliver's body beneath Collin's arm. "You figured that out, huh? He's pretty good at hiding his sociopathic tendencies."

Collin snorted. "He doesn't just have tendencies. He's a full-blown sociopath. Which means he's capable of doing absolutely anything if he's properly triggered."

"Well, then, he should be thrilled to death after tonight's round of play."

Collin glared into Oliver's turbulent eyes. "Yeah, and now you've got a big fat target on your back. All the other players are going to be gunning for you now. Figuratively and literally."

"Bring 'em on."

Collin sincerely hoped that was the whiskey talking. Otherwise Oliver's odds of surviving the next week or two had just plummeted. What the hell was he supposed to do if the guy actually had a death wish?

"Don't you die on me," Collin ground out.

"Why do you care?"

Was *that* what was making Oliver so surly? The man thought Collin didn't like him? Hell, he was halfway in love with Oliver.

"Tell me one thing, Oliver. Are you working with your father?" He stared into Oliver's bright blue eyes, using every bit of his training and years of experience to look for the slightest sign of a lie in his answer.

For his part, Oliver froze, staring back at Collin. "Is that what you think?"

"No, it's not what I think!" he exploded. "I'm trying to do my job here, and it requires me to ask that of you once."

"Fuck no. I would never work for or with my father. I loathe him and everything he stands for. Your turn to answer my question. Why do you care if I die or not?"

"Because I have feelings for you, obviously."

"Promise?"

"On a stack of Bibles," Collin replied.

"If you want to get out of the middle of the Elliott feud," Oliver commented lightly, "now's your chance. Run. Be free."

"Get your head out of your ass and look at me, Oliver. I'm not going anywhere."

He shoved his chest up against Oliver's aggressively. Oliver stared at him in minor shock. Which made sense. He wasn't usually this aggressive. But it was high time the guy got shocked out of his self-involved shell.

"Collin, what the hell are you—"

"Shut up and kiss me." Collin grabbed Oliver's face in his hands and kissed the hell out of him.

Oliver stiffened, resisting. And then all of a sudden Oliver kissed him back with every bit as much passion. Clothing went flying, and they surged onto the bed in a heated rush. Collin was firmly in charge today, pushing Oliver to respond, forcing the mathematician to acknowledge actual feelings, showing the surfer bum that he was so much more than a dropout from life, wrapping the lonely child in unconditional love and acceptance. He pinned Oliver to the mattress, using his weight and strength to subdue him when he would have reversed their positions.

"Today I'm making love to you," Collin declared. "It's your turn to relax and let it happen."

"But—"

"Deal with it. I'm showing you how I feel today, and you can just get over it."

Laughing a little, Oliver subsided against the pillows. "Well, then. I knew there was a spine in there, somewhere."

"It's always been there. You just haven't pissed me off enough to make me show it."

"How did I piss you off? You're the one who said we couldn't see each other."

"And you went and had a tantrum and put yourself in first place." He nibbled Oliver's corded neck. "I only want...." He bit down on Oliver's ear hard enough to make him swear a little. "To save...." He bit Oliver's shoulder hard enough to leave teeth marks and made Oliver rumble with laughter. "Your. Fucking. Life."

"Fucking being the operative word," Oliver said with a chuckle.

Collin reached down past Oliver's stone-hard erection to cup his balls. They were already tight and heavy, ready for action. Not to be outdone, Oliver gripped his cock as well, stroking it rhythmically, as if he would milk it dry.

Collin's back arched into the intense pleasure, and he shoved Oliver's knees wide, grateful for the man's athleticism and flexibility. Propped on an elbow planted beside Oliver's ear, he reached down to sheathe Oliver's dick in thin latex and smear the whole with plenty of gel. And then they were belly to belly. He pushed onto Oliver's cock, taking it into the heat and tightness of his body.

He relished how Oliver's lips pulled away from his teeth in a rictus of pleasure-pain and then settled into a smile of delight as Collin started to move around him. Oliver's blue eyes glazed over with pleasure, and his own cock jumped against Oliver's abdomen. Collin angled his body to take Oliver deep, deep inside him.

The sex was slippery and horny and wholly delicious. Oliver started groaning in the back of his throat, and Collin wrapped his legs around Oliver's hips, urging him onward, matching him with thrusts of his own hips. With every collision of flesh, he tried to show Oliver how much he cared about him. He silently declared Oliver important, worthy, and magnificent. He stared into Oliver's eyes and tried to let him see every bit of the hopes and dreams he harbored for the brilliant man who'd temporarily lost his way in the world but had rescued Collin right back when Collin tried to rescue him.

Their bodies pumped together faster and faster, the tension building higher and higher until it became unbearable for both of them. Collin's entire being gathered itself, paused for an endless moment of perfect anticipation, and then he exploded, emptying his heart and soul for Oliver. Oliver came as well, surging into him one last time with a shout of release.

They stilled gradually, their breathing ragged.

Oliver stared at him in wonder. "How did you find me?"

Collin did not mistake the question Oliver was truly asking. He answered seriously, "You were always there, Oliver. All you needed was for someone to see you. The real you."

Oliver breathed on a long, slow sigh. "Thanks. I may actually owe you my life."

The terrible tension coiled in Collin's gut ever since the interview with George Elliott unwound a little. "Promise me you'll do everything in your power to stay alive."

"Only if you'll promise me the same."

"Of course," he lied. He didn't stand a chance of winning this tournament from hell, but Oliver did. His primary mission had just shifted from finding out the prize to making sure Oliver was the one to collect it.

"To that end," Collin continued aloud, "I checked your laptop before I brought it to you, and you're still inside the hotel's mainframe. They didn't find your incursion. Which means we still have access to the play tapes of the other players."

Oliver grinned up at him. "Why, Mr. Callahan. Are you suggesting that we cheat?"

"Indeed I am. We'll have to be careful, of course. But between the two of us, we ought to be able to spot any weaknesses your remaining opponents have."

"Our opponents," Oliver declared. "You have to make it to the final table too."

Collin smiled politely and said nothing.

"Okay, so how do we do this without tipping off my old man?" Oliver declared, jumping out of bed and heading for the shower.

Collin sat up, enjoying the sight of Oliver's tight bum and muscular thighs. "You're staying in the room for this rest day. Put a Do Not Disturb sign on the door and don't let anyone in here. That way nobody can bug the room in your absence. I'm going out to buy a bunch of food, and then the two of us are holing up in here and not coming out except to play."

Oliver's head poked out the bathroom door. "That sounds fun, but won't my father realize we're together?"

"Not if he doesn't know I'm coming and going from this room."

"How are you going to pull that off?"

"I already wrote a small virus that's going to cause the hotel's cameras inexplicable glitches for the next few weeks. At the top of every hour, the surveillance cameras in the hallway outside your room will freeze on whatever image they're currently showing for two minutes," Collin replied. Odds were that most of the time, the cameras would be freezing on a still picture of an empty hallway. He expected that 90 percent or more of the camera glitches wouldn't even be discovered.

Only if a person were caught in a frame at the exact second the camera froze would the security people even become aware of it. It was the sort of gremlin that should drive the security team crazy before they solved it.

"So, we'll have a short window of time in which to come and go unseen," Oliver breathed. "Nice."

"Speaking of which, we're coming up on the hour in a few minutes."

Collin washed up and threw on his clothes hastily. He waited until the top of the hour, let himself out of the room, and strode quickly down the hallway to the elevator. As the seconds ticked by, his tension increased. He was on the verge of bolting for the stairwell when the elevator opened, and he hurried inside. Man, that had been close. He should have programmed two or three more minutes into the camera failure. Except even two minutes had been pushing it.

He went downstairs and grabbed a bite to eat as the buffet was winding down, then returned to his room alone. He napped for a few hours until the sun came up and Gibraltar's businesses opened for the new day. It sucked sleeping without Oliver's vibrant warmth beside him, but better a cold bed than a dead lover.

Safely buried in the middle of the pack of remaining players, he highly doubted he was perceived as a threat to any of the others. Using that anonymity, he took a taxi to a market and grabbed enough snacks, fruits, and premade sandwiches to see him and Oliver through today's break in play and tomorrow morning and afternoon. No sense risking anyone poisoning them.

While he waited for a cab to pick him up from the market, he made a quick call to Wild Cards, Inc. He reported briefly that he'd met George Elliott, and that the profile of the man was spot-on. Then he asked, "Any news from your end?"

"Yes, in fact," Martin Wylde answered. Martin was co-owner of Wild Cards, Inc., along with Pere. "We got the analysis back of the ligature marks on the corpse in the El Rocca freezer. Pathologist thinks the marks were made by something about the width, shape, and texture of a necktie. Additionally, based on the bruise evidence, the cloth was knotted and tightened from the front."

"It takes a fair bit of strength to strangle a man his size to death. Mastrianak would have fought back if he could," Collin mused, thinking out loud. "Which means he was either unconscious or physically restrained at the time of his strangulation. Could it have been sex play? Erotic asphyxiation gone wrong?"

"Maybe."

"The day the Albanians went missing, I spotted a couple of them with two of the female escorts from the resort. I've been kicking around the idea of a team of homicidal hookers working at El Rocca."

Martin chuckled. "Oh, that's rich."

Collin commented, "We think the driver of the Jet Ski that almost killed Oliver was a woman, too. Thing is, we've met some of these escorts. It's our opinion that someone's directing them."

"Do the escorts appear particularly chummy with or deferential to any of the players?"

"They're chummy with everyone, Martin. They're paid to be friendly. But I get what you're asking, and no, they don't seem particularly familiar with or deferential to any single player, at least not in public."

"We'll take another look at the security feeds you sent us and see if we can find anything on the escorts and who might be pulling their strings," Martin said.

"My primary hack into the mainframe was discovered. I'm done sending you resort emails. However, there's a second hack. I'll continue streaming the video feeds to you from it."

"Oh really? And how did this other hack happen?"

"Oliver Elliott's not only good with math. He's also good with computers."

"You're working with him? Is that a good idea?"

Clearly, Martin thought it was a lousy idea.

"It's a long story. He's an outstanding poker player and he's been giving me hints and tips. We struck up a friendship and have been watching each other's backs. I wouldn't have gotten this far in the tournament or in my investigation without him."

"Is he trustworthy, given who his father is and given that George Elliott appears to be involved with running this tournament?"

"My instincts and professional analysis say Oliver can be trusted."

Martin was silent for a long time. For his part, Collin held his breath, hoping against hope that his boss didn't pull him off this job on the spot. At length, Martin said heavily, "You two be careful. Neither of you can afford to antagonize his father."

"Roger that. Gotta go. My ride's here."

He carried the groceries to his room to wait for the camera outage. He'd set up a glitch every hour on his own floor as well. In theory, he should be able to slip out of his room and into Oliver's completely unseen. To pass the time, he swept his room for bugs. The maid had come in to clean his room while he'd been out, and he couldn't be too careful.

No huge surprise, he got a hit. Just one, attached to the underside of the room's telephone, audio only. He left it in place, relieved that it was only a hastily placed bug and not a full-room surveillance package he'd found.

He arrived at Oliver's door slightly out of breath and with only a few seconds to spare. "It's me," he muttered urgently through the panel.

The door cracked open and a hand grabbed his arm, dragging him into the darkened room. "Where the fuck have you been?" Oliver demanded angrily.

Aww, Mr. Grumpy Pants had missed him. He wrapped Oliver in a hug, pressing his lips to Oliver's ear. Collin breathed, "Have you left your room at all since I left last night?"

"No. Why?"

"I found a bug in my room just now."

"Jesus," Oliver muttered. "This place is a mind fuck."

Collin sighed. "Unfortunately, I'm going to have to go back to my room now and then to make it sound like I'm living there, but we should be able to work around my visits back to my place."

"Excellent. While you were gone, I watched some more play tapes. I found a few things I want to show you."

He followed Oliver to the desk and watched with deep interest as various tells became obvious when they compared hold cards to expressions, movements, and bets by the other players.

Collin asked, "Have you spotted any anomalies in how anyone's betting? Meaning bets that don't fit how many chips they have or based on how their stacks compare to the other players at the table."

"You mean besides you?"

Collin blinked. "I beg your pardon?"

"You bet inappropriately about five percent of the time. It's throwing off your competitors, which is a good thing. You're keeping them off-balance. I can show you how to capitalize on that uncertainty."

They fell into a rhythm of watching tapes, snacking, napping, and Collin racing back to his room now and then to flush the toilet or slam a drawer. During one visit, he took a shower in his room and even ordered room service. He threw the food off the balcony into the bushes below in case it was drugged or poisoned and set the empty dishes outside his door, making sure to glance in the general direction of the hallway surveillance cameras as he did so.

But at the top of the next hour, he rejoined Oliver, and they resumed poring over the video footage as if their lives depended on it.

Oh, wait. They did.

CHAPTER ELEVEN

CARD PLAY the next night was uneventful, other than the other players ribbing Oliver about how he'd managed to stay alive through the latest break in play. It hadn't escaped anyone that the chip leaders were disappearing at an alarming rate.

"Hey, you know me," he replied jauntily to his fellow players. "I'm a slippery dude."

The only remaining woman player, Stacy Kiern, huffed from the next table over. "What's your deal, Gun? You talk a big line and play the party boy, but you don't take any of the girls back to your room."

He grinned and preened for her. "I need to get my beauty sleep if I'm going to look good for you, darlin'."

She rolled her eyes, and he teased, "When are you going to quit blowing me off and accept my declaration of true love?"

"Bring it on, buster."

"Roses are red, violets are blue, take pity on me 'cuz I can't live without yewww," he recited melodramatically.

Stacy swore at him robustly as the other players guffawed, and they were all saved from further poetic butchery by the bell signaling start of play.

Oliver kept an eye on Collin, who was seated at the next table with Stacy. He appeared to be having a good night, and his chip pile grew steadily throughout the evening. No one wanted to take over the number-one position on the chip list, and Oliver was not surprised to find himself still on top at the end of play.

Collin had moved up in the standings into thirtieth place, which was a hell of a showing for an amateur. But then, Collin was frighteningly smart and already had the tools to be a great poker player. He just had to learn how to put them all together. And the guy was learning *fast*.

After tonight, the field was down to one hundred and five players. The next night's play should bring the total down to the magic one hundred, when the rules allegedly would change.

Collin returned to his own room, and Oliver trudged back to his, shocked at how much he missed Collin every minute they were separated. He was not surprised to see that the hairs, threads, and bits of paper he'd placed in doorjambs and drawers the way Collin had shown him to had all fallen.

His father had obviously ordered his room searched in spite of the Do Not Disturb sign on the door. The bastard never had respected any boundaries between them. But then, he was beyond respecting his father's boundaries too.

Oliver dared not underestimate George or his cronies. He'd known vaguely as a kid that his family was involved with certain shadowy elements—guests who came and went in the middle of the night, secret meetings while he was told to stay in his room, financial assets that his father's legitimate business couldn't account for.

But now he had to seriously ask himself if his father was some sort of underworld kingpin. All the signs were there. Even the intensifying psychopathic tendencies.

Was his mother okay? She'd always been in the background, a pale moon orbiting the sun of her big, aggressive husband. She'd barely spoken to Oliver, as if she had no idea what to say to him. The feeling had been mutual. He'd never had a clue what to say to her, either.

The family's longtime housekeeper, a grandmotherly sort named Eugenia, had been more of a parent to him than his own biological mother had ever been. He'd long suspected his mother was hooked on some sort of sedatives or sleeping pills. And honestly, he couldn't blame her. He would be eager to check out of reality if his spouse were George Elliott too.

Oliver looked at his watch. He'd surreptitiously slipped Collin a note during a break in play earlier, dropping it in his lap as he walked by, inviting Collin to meet him in the gym's sauna two hours after play ended. He'd felt stupid doing it. He wasn't in fifth grade anymore, for crying out loud. But Collin was increasingly paranoid about surveillance in their rooms and refused to have sex anywhere he thought they might be overheard. And right now, he could seriously use the stress relief. He suspected Collin felt the same way.

He stripped down in the locker room, wrapped a towel around his hips, and headed for the sauna, praying that Collin would be there. He wasn't. Oliver sulked in the heat and had just dumped a ladle of water over the hot rocks to create a blast of steam when the sauna door opened. He looked up hopefully.

"Is there room in here for me?" Collin asked.

He'd come. "Shut the door and lock it behind you," Oliver answered in relief more intense than he cared to admit.

"More steam. It fogs up the glass in the door," Collin muttered as he dropped his towel and moved forward.

In moments, Collin's body was drenched in sweat, and it was arguably the sexiest thing Oliver had ever seen. They came together, slippery and strong, making more creative use of the tiered benches than Oliver expected their builder had imagined. The sex was hard and fast at first, but as the heat sapped their breath, it slowed to a more languid, lazy pace. Finally, when they were both sated, exhausted, and lying limply on the benches, they got around to talking.

Collin said, "I got a call from my boss. They think Stacy Kiern may be running the homicidal hookers. They've spotted her talking surreptitiously to several of the escorts."

"Huh. I hear she's a real ballbuster."

Collin replied, "I can say from personal experience that she's a hell of a poker player."

Oliver added, "I expect her to end up at the final table for sure."

"Just be careful around her, eh?"

"Is there any way to deflect her and her girls away from killing me?" Oliver asked.

Collin winced. "Your spectacular move to the top of the leaderboard has cemented you as target numero uno around here. The best bet for you is probably to knock her out of the tournament."

"Assuming I can get seated at the same table with her," Oliver replied. "First time I am, I'll see what I can do. But there's only so much I can control at a table. The rest of it comes down to the cards."

"Channel whatever was going on in your head the night you wiped out everyone else at your table and vaulted to the top of the leaderboard."

"I was royally pissed off at you. At the whole world, to be honest."

"Duly noted. I'll be sure to infuriate you right before you sit down to play against Stacy."

"Please don't. I wasn't in a good headspace when I thought you didn't want to be with me anymore."

"If you thought we'd basically broken up…which we hadn't… does that mean we're officially… something?"

His gaze met Collin's through the steam. A slow smile spread across his face, and he was immensely relieved to see a matching smile spread across Collin's features. "Yeah," he said quietly. "I guess we are officially something."

Collin sat up and he did the same, opening his arms. Collin hugged him so tight and so long he started to have a little trouble breathing. And he loved every second of it. Of Collin.

Whoa.

Love was one of those adult words he tended to run screaming from. But the only direction he wanted to run these days was toward exactly where he was now. Wrapped up in the arms of his lover. His friend. His partner in crime. His Collin.

How fucked-up was it that he'd had to get mixed up in this disaster of a poker-murder-fest, orchestrated by his father no less, to find the best thing that had ever happened to him?

His life had plenty of irony baked into it, but finding Collin in this place took the cake.

WHEN THE table assignments were posted for that night's play, it turned out Collin would be seated with Stacy Kiern in that night's play and not him.

Collin left to go catch some shut-eye in his room, but Oliver barely slept all day. Instead he spent the time poring through every bit of video on Stacy's play. She was very, very good. He picked up a few small hints he could pass to Collin, but that was it.

As the remaining players filed into the ballroom, he fell in beside Collin and muttered, "Watch for her to twirl her hair on bluffs. Sometimes she chews the inside of her cheek when she's got a hot hand. Bluffs about one hand in ten, folds middling cards about half the time."

That was all he had time for before Collin nodded infinitesimally and peeled away to his own table. It was a dangerous gambit for Collin to go after Stacy directly. If she figured out he was targeting her, she might very well turn her cadre of homicidal hookers on him too. Assuming she was the brains behind the escort-killers.

As far as he could tell, Collin had managed to fly below her radar prior to now. And Oliver bloody well intended to keep it that way. Even if he had to draw all the homicidal attention to himself to protect Collin.

As if the fates were taunting him intentionally, Oliver ended up seated with his back to Collin and Stacy's table. He couldn't even keep an eye on them from afar. Nervous as hell, he peeked at his first cards. Here went nothing.

IT WAS not in Collin's nature to provoke killers into coming after him. But when the alternative was Oliver being the target of said killer, it turned out Collin had balls of stainless steel.

The trick was to time his attacks on Stacy when she was showing tells of a mediocre hand or an outright bluff *and* when he had decent cards to work with. Patience would be the name of the game tonight. He might only get two or three hands all night where everything lined up, but when they came, he had to jump on them.

Judiciously, he dropped a comment early on about what an honor it was to play with someone of her fame and success. Might as well cast himself as an amateur sycophant in her mind. He accentuated his erratic play early, the way Oliver had suggested he do intentionally. He went down a couple hundred thousand chips, but that was the plan. Make Stacy think he was ripe for the kill.

And then a hand came down where he was staring at a pair of pocket aces—his down cards—and Stacy reached up to twirl her hair and then pulled her hand back down to her cards. He'd picked up on an additional tell to her bluffing. Her pulse accelerated very slightly, and a faint flush climbed her neck. The lighting had to be just right, and a person had to have been watching her pulse for a while to see the change. But this was his moment. Now to lure her into a big bet.

Blessedly, one of the other players came out betting aggressively, which allowed Collin to hang around in the hand, merely matching bets and raises as Stacy focused on driving the other guy out of the hand. The river card—the fourth out of the five dealer's cards—turned, and it was an ace. Along with the pair of eights the dealer had already revealed, Collin now was sitting on a full house, aces over eights. There were no flush or straight possibilities in the dealer's turn cards, which meant he almost certainly had Stacy beat. Time to move in for the kill.

He made a wild bet, easily twice what it should have been if he'd been sitting on a great hand and been trying to milk Stacy for more chips out of her stack.

She frowned, staring him down while she tried to figure out what the hell he was thinking. He let one corner of his mouth quirk up in a self-deprecating smile as if to apologize for being such a pain in the ass to a big pro like her. It tipped the scales, and she not only matched his bet but raised it substantially.

It was his turn to stare and scowl, as if flummoxed by her response and unsure how to respond. His stack was bigger than hers by a bit, and he pushed the entire pile forward. "All in," he declared.

It was a ballsy bet. If she matched it, pushing in all her chips as well, whichever one of them lost the hand would be out of the tournament. The mountain of chips in the middle of the table was huge, though, and had to be tempting as hell to her. Particularly if she thought she had him beat. He figured she had a full house with eights over one of the other small cards in the dealer's hand forming the smaller pair. God only knew what she thought he was holding in his hand.

The pause while she considered her move stretched out until finally one of the other players groused, "C'mon, Stacy. Grow a pair or fold."

Collin could have kissed the guy. It was the exact right thing to say to push the woman into matching his bet.

She snapped, "It's my bet, asshole," then paused just long enough to make it clear that matching his bet had been her decision and had nothing to do with the nudge from the other player. "All in." She pushed her whole stack of chips forward.

Play at the surrounding tables stopped as other players craned to see the action at their table. All-in bets were unheard of at this point in the tournament, with everyone being so cautious about not climbing too high or falling too low in the standings.

The final card turned, a five of spades of no use to either of them.

Stacy flipped over her cards triumphantly. "Full house. Eights over sixes."

He let her have the moment, nodding and murmuring, "Nice cards." He turned over his cards and laid them down on the table. "Aces over eights."

A gasp went up all around them. Stacy pushed back from the table, swearing up a blue streak. "This isn't over," she snarled.

He looked up at her, met her furious stare with a cold one of his own, and said icily, "It's not over for me, but it is for you."

She whirled and made a noisy exit from the room. Collin collected the massive pile of chips the dealer had pushed his way and began the lengthy process of counting and stacking them. He felt the stares of dozens of people upon him, reassessing him cagily. Crap. He'd just given away the fact that he was no lucky amateur bumbling along without having any clue what he was doing. He'd just entered the big leagues.

If they'd correctly pegged Stacy as murder mastermind, the good news was he'd just put the elimination-by-death spotlight firmly on himself and stolen it away from Oliver.

A bunch of players came over when play ended to congratulate him for knocking out Stacy Kiern. Apparently, she was a highly respected, and even feared, player, and everyone was glad not to have to go up against her. He couldn't have done it without Oliver. Not only had Oliver given him specific hints on how to read Stacy, but he'd also honed Collin's amateur game into something resembling a real poker professional's.

The leaderboard was updated, and he was stunned to see his name at number eleven overall in the chip standings. He'd had no intention of vaulting to such prominence. He'd only wanted to eliminate a threat to Oliver.

He ate from the buffet on the assumption that his food could not be poisoned if he ate from the communal pot, as it were. Several of the other players invited him to sit with them, and he was happy to oblige, falling back into his bumbling amateur shtick, expressing amazement and honor at getting to play with the likes of them.

The talk was all about having finally arrived at the magic one hundred players. In point of fact, they were down to ninety-four players after tonight's play. Everyone expected the minimum bets to go up significantly and for the pace of play to increase sharply. The players seemed happy about that. This two-week marathon had taken its toll on everyone's patience and concentration, apparently. He knew the feeling.

He stepped into a public restroom after the meal to wash his hands. The lobster that had been served tonight was messy, and he had butter all over his fingers. He'd been in the empty bathroom for about thirty seconds when someone slipped in and disappeared into a stall. The door was closed for about ten seconds, and then in the mirror he spied a masked figure surging out toward him.

He spun and ducked, lashing out with his foot and connecting hard with his attacker's knee. The guy grunted and swore in Spanish as Collin attacked aggressively, his elbows and fists jabbing in a fast flurry. His years of martial arts training took over, and he attacked, not stopping to think about anything. A fist connected hard with his jaw, and then something sharp and searing hot slashed his side.

He got in a punishing punch that broke his attacker's nose with a loud crunch, and the guy staggered back, blood spouting everywhere. His knuckles ached like crazy, but it was worth it to watch the attacker, hand over his masked face, turn and flee, with Collin in hot pursuit. But only a few steps beyond the bathroom door, the stitch in his side became so excruciating he was forced to stop, gripping his waist.

Hot wetness under his hand made him look down, startled. A bright red stain was spreading fast through his shirt. He'd been cut.

Swearing under his breath, he made for the elevator and punched in Oliver's floor. Holding his side as best he could, he hurried down the hall and banged on Oliver's door.

"What the hell are you doing here? It's not the top of the hour—"

He barged past and pushed into the room, heading straight for the bathroom. "I've been stabbed. Or at least sliced."

"What the hell?" Oliver exclaimed.

Collin stripped off his shirt and mopped at the six-inch long cut that was bleeding freely. "Thank God. Looks like a surface wound. But it's deep enough to need stitches."

"Christ, that's a lot of blood!" Oliver exclaimed in alarm.

"I promise you, I'm not dying. I've seen much worse than this." He didn't add that he'd only seen such wounds by remote camera feed and that his training in trauma medicine was entirely theoretical. "I need you to clean the wound, slow the bleeding, and stitch it closed. I would do it myself, but it's in an awkward place, and I can't reach it."

Truth be told, he had no idea if he could stitch his own skin without passing out. He'd seen field operatives do it before. Most stayed conscious. But a few did not.

"You're fucking kidding me."

"Oliver, I need your help."

"You need a hospital!"

"And advertise to the other players that I'm hurt and vulnerable?"

Oliver pulled a face at him. "I still think you should see a doctor."

"And yet you're all I've got. We'll need a mini bottle of vodka and the hotel's sewing kit from the nightstand. I'll talk you through it."

Oliver hustled around the room, getting all the supplies Collin listed.

Meanwhile, he lay down on the bed with a bunch of towels under him and another one pressed hard over the wound. "It's a slice-style cut, so it's all about getting the wound closed in order to stop the bleeding."

"This is so gross."

"Emergency field medicine. Just do it," he ground out.

Oliver pulled a face, but with determination soaked the thread and needle in vodka. "Ready?" he asked grimly.

"Do it." Collin gritted his teeth together, bracing himself. But nothing could have prepared him for the breathtaking agony as Oliver poured vodka over the open wound. He cried out in spite of his resolve not to and frantically grabbed for a washcloth to stuff it in his mouth. He clamped down on the dry terry cloth in fiery, blinding pain.

Oliver leaned down over his side and commenced sewing. The first pierce of the needle through his flesh felt like a hot volcano erupting against his side, and he panted in a valiant effort to maintain consciousness. But the idea of being sewed on like a quilt was too much for him. It wasn't the pain that did him in. It was the mental image of a needle and thread piercing his skin that knocked him out.

The next thing he knew, he was blinking up at Oliver, who stared worriedly at him. "Welcome back, Collin. Don't pass out on me again, okay? You scared the hell out of me, and I don't know what to do next."

"How long was I out?"

"Couple minutes. Long enough for me to, umm, sew you together. And by the way, that's the grossest thing I've ever experienced…and I've seen a surfer get his lower leg bitten off by a shark. Please don't ever ask me to do anything like that again."

Now that he studied Oliver more closely, the guy's face was a sickly gray color and covered in a fine sheen of perspiration. "Don't you pass out on me," he blurted in alarm. "I'm in no condition to catch you when you go down."

"I'd better sit down, then." Oliver perched on the edge of the bed and looked ready to puke. The guy could use some distraction, and fast.

"Is it still bleeding?" Collin asked quickly, for lack of anything else to say. The pain was back, but now it was more of a sharp ache underlying the searing heat from before.

"It's seeping."

Collin pressed down hard on his side with the heel of his palm, which hurt like hell. But the pain cleared his head like nobody's business. He considered their next medical move. "Let's go ahead and bandage it. I'm not likely to pass out while you do that. I may swear a bit, though."

"Swearing I can handle. But, um, what are we bandaging it with?"

Dammit. All the field operatives he usually worked with carried first aid kits in their gear. "I guess you'll have to go down to the front desk and claim an injury. Get antibiotic cream, some gauze pads, and tape. And see if they have some sort of long elastic bandage like you might use on a sprained ankle. I'm going to need to keep pressure on this cut for a while."

"Collin, I'm not a total moron. I know what it takes to bandage a wound."

He smiled up crookedly. "Sorry. I can be a bit of a micromanager when I'm under stress."

"You don't say."

It took upward of a half hour for Oliver to go downstairs, come back with a first aid kit, and bandage the wound.

While he was gone, Collin rather more slowly than normal checked Oliver's room for bugs. He found one under the telephone and another behind a painting on the wall. He sat down and wrote a note to Oliver, telling him where the bugs were.

When Oliver returned, Collin groused about how long it had taken to get a stupid bandage while he showed him the note. Oliver nodded and Collin burned it in the bathroom sink, then rinsed it away.

It was another ordeal to sit through having cream smeared on the cut and getting taped up, but at the end of it, Collin had a reasonably repaired side and an even more gray-faced Oliver, who looked on the actual verge of passing out.

Collin stood up carefully and borrowed a clean shirt from Oliver. "Lie down. Elevate your feet over your head. Get some sleep if you can. I have to go back to my room to get some rest myself." Their gazes met in mutual understanding. The hallway cameras would have recorded Collin coming in here, and the bugs had recorded Oliver helping him with the wound. Collin had to go back to his room to maintain the ruse of them just being friends.

"What you need to do is quit the damned tournament and go home," Oliver declared forcefully. "I'll win the thing, and when I do, I promise to tell you what the mystery prize is."

"In case you hadn't noticed, I'm holding my own very nicely, thank you very much."

"You're not a professional, and you're not a crook. This crowd is too rough for you."

"And you are a crook?" Collin shot back.

"I've played with these guys before. I know how they roll."

Collin leaned in close and whispered under the noise of him picking up a pad of hotel stationery and rustling the paper, "In case you forgot, my job is to study guys exactly like these and predict their actions. I likely know them better than you do."

Oliver dropped his voice to bare breath of sound, but it still vibrated with frustration. "Then you know they won't hesitate to kill you if they find out who you really work for and what you're doing here. My father or Stacy Kiern or whoever sent that attacker after you, will try again. And I can't—I won't—stand around and watch you be killed."

His voice sounded a little ragged. The catch in it made Collin's heart flip-flop. Oliver really did care about his safety. Well, hell.

"I feel the same way about you, Oliver."

"And that's sweet of you, Collin. I never thought I'd meet a guy like you and have you actually think I'm not a total asshole."

Oliver pointed at the bug behind the painting and said dramatically, "Don't come to my room again. You had the right idea before. We need to stay away from each other for both of our sakes. The other players mustn't think we've formed some sort of alliance or they'll come after us. I refuse to watch you die, and I'm determined to win this tournament on my own. We *are* done, Collin. It's over between us. No more poker buddies, no more hints and tips about the other players. You're on your own."

Collin might have freaked out anyway, even knowing Oliver was talking for the bugs, at the conviction resonating in his voice. But thankfully, Oliver made a heart with his fingers and pointed at him while he delivered his diatribe.

As it was, Collin did freak out for a second at the idea of Oliver actually loving him. It dawned on him belatedly that the heart symbol with his fingers was probably the only nonverbal signal Oliver could think of to show him that he didn't mean the bitter words he was speaking aloud.

Damn. For a second there, his pulse had leapt with exuberance he hadn't felt in a long, *long* time. Which begged the question of what his feelings were for Oliver. Clearly they were running stronger than he'd consciously realized.

"The tournament will be over soon," Collin soothed. "We can talk then. I'd love to pick your brain. Learn more about poker from you. You may be banned from every casino on earth, but I'm not. My pro career is just getting started."

He flashed heart fingers back at Oliver along with a crooked smile.

Oliver stepped forward, flashed his middle finger at the painting on the wall, and wrapped him up in a short hard hug that made him gasp with pain, even though Oliver's arms were around his shoulders. Oliver let him go immediately with an apologetic look.

He laid his hand on Oliver's cheek in forgiveness and affection. They traded rueful smiles and he stepped back.

"Thanks for helping me out with my cut. I was an idiot to let it happen. I won't bother you again."

Oliver looked pained as he reached for the door handle. *Same, my dude. Same.* He purely hated having to leave him alone like this. He mouthed over his shoulder, "Lock the door."

Oliver nodded glumly.

Collin took a tiny sliver of comfort in Oliver's pain at their separation. At least he wasn't the only one in this relationship who hated them being apart.

He opened the door and looked back into the room in time to see Oliver mouth, "Don't die." The guy looked genuinely scared as he formed the words.

He flashed a quick thumbs-up and then slipped into the hall.

He understood Oliver's terror at losing him. He felt the exact same way about Oliver.

But he'd learned a hard lesson in the past year that stood him in good stead now. He couldn't let his fear of losing Oliver stop him from loving the man. Life was too short, too unpredictable. Losing Steve had taught him that he had to grab happiness whenever it came along and hold it close to his heart for as long as he could.

He was fiercely glad he'd known Steve and that they'd had a few years together. No matter how painful Steve's death had been, his life was better for having loved the guy for a little while. It had taught him that love was possible for him. And when a man like Oliver had come along, he knew both the risks and rewards—and he knew they were worth going for.

But as he let himself out of the room, Collin had to wonder what would really happen after the tournament ended. When the drama and danger had passed and life settled back down to a rather more normal existence, would their relationship survive the banality of the day-to-day grind?

Would Oliver go back to his big waves and meaningless existence, or would he come out of retirement and travel the world, playing cards wherever he could get permission to play? Either way, a boring intelligence analyst who sat at a desk all day long in England didn't fit into the picture. More than just his side ached as he trudged dejectedly back to his room.

The two of them just couldn't seem to catch a break.

CHAPTER TWELVE

OLIVER WAS startled the next afternoon when he and the other players filed into the ballroom to play. Only four tables were set up with six seats at each. What the hell? Obviously, this had something to do with the rules change that had been announced at the beginning of the tournament. The ninety-plus remaining players milled around in consternation. Numerous players sidled up to him and muttered, "Any idea what's up?"

He gave them all the same answer. "Nope."

The tournament emcee spoke into a wireless microphone. "As some of you have surmised, this is not just a simple poker tournament, and what all of you are playing for is not merely money or luxury prizes, although those will certainly come with the package. Indeed, all of you have been auditioning, as it were. The winner of the tournament will be offered an exclusive opportunity to earn wealth, prestige, and power beyond your wildest imaginings. It will, literally, transform your life."

An interested buzz broke out, and the emcee waited patiently for it to subside. When it had, he continued. "As you may recall, I said at the beginning of the tournament that the rules would change after we got down to one hundred players. And, indeed, they will. The organizers of this tournament are looking for someone bold and courageous who prefers to run at the front of the pack. We are aware that, for various reasons, many of you have chosen to lag behind the leaders intentionally. For those of you who have done that, we are not interested in your caution and willingness to perform at less than your best for the sake of blending in. Therefore, the bottom seventy players are dismissed. You may pack your bags and leave. Two buses are waiting in front of El Rocca to take you to the airport."

An outraged outburst accompanied this bombshell. Voices shouted that they'd intentionally been staying out of the top ranks because someone had been trying to *kill* them. The emcee was unmoved. But then, he was only a mouthpiece for whoever was running this circus.

Oliver had to give his old man credit. This was an unexpected twist, and frankly, kind of brilliant.

Twenty-four players would duke it out for the prize, huh? The tournament should wrap up in no more than a day or two, then. The remaining players would get down to serious business now and start playing full-out, going for each other's throats.

Sure, most professional poker players spouted a big line about how all they could do was play the cards they were dealt. The game was nothing personal. Just math. But that was a lie. Poker players were barracudas at heart, and they went for the jugular of their opponents.

Thankfully, he and Collin were seated at different tables. He was relieved not to have to go head -to-head against him yet. He knew the guy's poker game so well by now that he would have a hard time not wiping the guy out without even trying. Of course, he allowed, that might go the other way, too. It was possible Collin knew his game well enough by now to read him like an open book also.

Oliver scoped out the other five players who sat down beside him and was not surprised to see them measuring him carefully. The carnage he'd wrought to get to the top of the chip leaderboard had clearly made them all cautious of him. Which he could use to his advantage, of course.

Interestingly enough, by cutting off the bottom seventy players, the tournament directors had actually gotten rid of a number of the best card players in the bunch. Which would make his job easier—

He cautioned himself about getting cocky. These were still some of the best poker players in the world. Turning his baseball cap around backward, he sprawled sloppily in his seat. Putting on his best stoned-surfer drawl, he said, "Whacked, man, all those players getting cut like that."

Brows twitched around the table.

He grinned stupidly. "I've been lucky as shit so far with the cards. I sure hope it holds up. Think about all the chicks who'll wanna lay me if I win me some real bank."

"Have you been enjoying the girls here?" a Japanese player asked in careful English from across the table.

He shrugged. "They're not bad. But I'm talking about the serious talent. The chicks from Eastern Europe who look hot as hell and will do anything—and I mean anything—you can imagine. They'll go for stuff that's twisted as shit, man."

Being a male himself, he knew that every player at the table immediately veered off into thinking about the most twisted thing they could think of to do with or to someone else. He kept up a patter of sexual games he'd always wanted to try as the dealer got set up and the chips were delivered to the tables. He counted his chips sloppily and had to start over twice, even though in his mind he'd added them up with quick efficiency the first time.

The cards were dealt and play began. What was it Collin had said to him? Channel whatever he'd done that night he wiped out the whole table? Right, then.

Channeling a lifetime of fury at his father, and reaching for his rage last night at whoever had attacked Collin and sent him to his door bleeding and in pain, he looked at his first set of hold cards. No more pussyfooting around. It was time to crush his opponents.

And crush them he did, all the while rambling on about Lady Luck having the serious hots for him and how he wanted to do her.

COLLIN SAT quietly as play began. He highly doubted anyone at his table took him seriously. Someone always got lucky and performed well above his or her skill level for a while, according to Oliver. And at this tournament, that player was Collin. Which was fine with him. He lay low, did the math, and watched his opponents carefully, verifying the quirks and tells he and Oliver had discovered from the play tapes. About halfway through the session, he finally started seriously betting, interspersing bluffs and legitimate hands.

Nobody at the table had any idea what to make of him. Collin would like to think he wasn't giving away any decent tells, and the failure of the other players to read him suggested he might be right. He made a point of thinking about Oliver from time to time, allowing his worry to come through. The players would misinterpret his emotions as being directed at the cards, which suited his purposes perfectly.

At other times, he practiced meditation and self-calming techniques the Wild Cards operatives were taught to deal with stress in the field. His side hurt, and he allowed himself to wince and shift uncomfortably in his chair with that, too. Anything to send confusing signals to the other players.

When play ended, he was second in chips at his table, and the two bottom players had busted out. Not a bad showing for an amateur.

His side actually did hurt like hell, and he headed straight back to his room, popped a bunch of painkillers, and crashed.

And so it went for the next night's play as well. The field was winnowed down to twelve players, and the third day, only two tables sat in the middle of the now cavernously empty ballroom. The space was dark except for spotlights shining down on the two tables. A haze of smoke danced in the beams of light, and the mood was grim as the twelve remaining players filed into the room.

They were all exhausted, and they were all ready for this tournament to be over. Him more than most. He just wanted Oliver and himself to get out of this mess alive and then sit down for a long, serious talk after it was all said and done.

He'd had a lot of time to himself between these last rounds of play when all the players had been asked to stay in their rooms and order room service, and he'd arrived at several conclusions. He wanted a long-term relationship with Oliver. He wanted Oliver to consider pursuing a new career, something that made use of his brilliant mind and helped mankind. He was willing to leave his job, if necessary, to be with Oliver. And he really needed to know if Oliver returned his feelings.

Yet again, he and Oliver were seated at different tables tonight. How they'd managed to avoid competing head-to-head for all this time, he had no idea. Maybe it was luck or, more likely, George Elliott had a hand in keeping them apart. Either way, he was grateful as hell for it.

Oliver had smiled distantly and merely lifted his chin casually when Collin had smiled tentatively and wished him luck on the way into the room. He knew it was only an act, but it still freaked him out a little to have Oliver acting so aloofly toward him. As he took his seat, he gave himself a stern lecture not to let emotion get the best of him. He and Oliver were fine. But panic still perched like a nervous sparrow in Collin's breast, ready to fly at a moment's notice.

Play began, and over the next few hours, the two short-stacked players at Collin's table were eliminated by other players. Meanwhile, Oliver—still on a vicious tear, from what Collin overheard between concentrating on his own cards—obliterated four players at his table. The field was now down to six.

The emcee called an end to play early and told everyone to get a good night's sleep before resuming single-table play tomorrow. There would be no more days off to recuperate. From here on out, it would be a marathon to the end.

Oliver was still in first place, although two of the other players weren't far behind him in chip totals. Then there was a good-sized gap in chip countdown to Collin and the other two players.

Tomorrow, he and Oliver would finally play against each other.

As they filed out of the ballroom, Collin grimly considered his options. He could bust out of the tournament intentionally, throwing all his chips to Oliver. Otherwise, he would need to reverse his luck strongly to survive the next night's play. He would have to go for broke, play courageously, and hope the cards fell his way.

Undecided on how to approach play and desperate to talk with Oliver about it, he snuck out of the hotel at the top of the hour for a walk on the beach to clear his head and think. He walked away from the marina, away from the suffocating opulence of George Elliott's yacht and the threat it represented.

The air was damp and chilly beside the sea, the sand wet and heavy beneath his shoes. He moved down by the water where the waves had pounded the sand flat and hard enough to walk on, heading for a rocky outcropping that looked like scree calved off the face of the looming Rock of Gibraltar. As he neared it, he saw the rocks were actually boulders the size of cars, piled haphazardly. Only a narrow strip of sand separated the rocks from the water, and he hesitated to go past it and then get trapped by a change in the winds that might drive the water up onto the rocks.

What the hell. What was life without taking a few risks? Funny how much of Oliver's philosophy of life had rubbed off on him in the three weeks they'd known each other. Although it seemed like much longer than that. The stress of this bizarre tournament had warped time wildly in his mind.

He rounded the point and was startled to see that the beach ended abruptly a dozen yards ahead of him in a sheer cliff. He turned around to head back when a dark shape rose up out of the water only a few yards offshore. It was a big man in a wet suit and mask. Fuck! Collin looked around frantically for a stick of driftwood or a rock, anything to defend himself with as the swimmer came ashore purposefully, striding directly toward him.

He backed up the tiny strip of beach until his shoulder blades touched cold rock, rough through his shirt, reviewing his self-defense training quickly. Watch the body mass, keep hands and weapons outside of his own arms at all costs. Stay vertical. Accept injuries as part of staying alive—

"What the hell are you doing out here?" the swimmer demanded.

Oh, bloody hell. Oliver. Collin almost peed himself in his relief.

"What happened to your neon yellow wet suit?" he demanded.

Oliver stalked forward threateningly. "You didn't answer my question. What are you doing out here? We're all supposed to stay in our rooms."

"You're not in your room."

"My father's running the damned tournament so I can win it. What's he gonna do if I want to take a swim and work off some stress? Kick me out at this late date? I could stroll right through the lobby, flipping off every camera and every security guard, and they wouldn't do anything to me. I'm the boss's kid. I get a free pass."

Collin grunted. The guy had a point.

"You didn't answer my question. What are you doing out here?"

"Taking a walk. Clearing my head."

"What the hell do you need to clear your head for?"

"I don't know how to play tomorrow. I'm trying to figure it out."

"I don't want to talk about poker. I want to talk about why you're exposing yourself to another attack by being out here alone like this?"

"I'll have you know, I successfully fought off my attacker in that bathroom. He might have cut me, but I broke his nose and made him run. I can take care of myself, thank you very much."

"And what if they send a couple of big thugs after you? Or next time your attacker is armed with a gun and not just a knife?"

He flared up, irritated at Oliver's irritation. "What about you? You're alone and exposing yourself to an attack. Not to mention, it's the middle of the damned night, and you shouldn't ever swim alone in an open body of water like the Med. If something happened to you, there'd be no one to rescue you."

"Like you tried to rescue me the first time we met? Yeah, that went great. I ended up having to haul you to shore."

"At least I tried to help you."

They stood glaring at each other, breathing hard. Collin was the first to break. He said in surprise, "Are we fighting because you're so worried about my safety that you're freaking out?"

Oliver frowned. "Yeah. I guess so. Is that why you're fighting with me?"

"Absolutely."

"Huh." A pause. "Cool."

Collin had to laugh. "You have the greatest gift for understatement of anyone I've ever met."

"Thanks, I think?"

They laughed together and Collin leaned back against the rocks, half sitting on a small outcropping. "Actually, I'm glad you're here. What am I supposed to do during play tomorrow?"

Oliver slogged up the beach and leaned on the rock wall beside him. "What do you mean?"

"Should I sandbag early and pass all my chips to you? Should I try to play more aggressively and move up in the chip standings? Should I lie low and let the other players around me duke it out and take each other down?"

Oliver sighed. "Depends on your end goal."

"I want you to stay alive."

"Then you need to stick around to protect me. Play aggressively when your cards are good and stay out of the way when the guys in second and third place go after the three of you at the bottom of the chip count."

"How can I help you win?"

"I don't care about winning. I only want both of us to walk out of this alive."

"Don't you want to know what your father is planning to give away as the prize?"

"You think I give a damn about the power or money or whatever the hell we're playing for?"

"I know I'm curious. And it is why I was sent here. To find out what we've all been playing—and dying—for."

"Really? You're still worried about doing your job? You should be a hell of a lot more worried about staying alive." Oliver's voice rose a little.

"You sure as hell don't seem to be worrying about your safety," Collin shot back.

"Are. You. Fucking. Kidding. Me." Oliver pushed away from the cliff, and with each word, Oliver leaned in closer, bringing them nose to nose. Even in the faint starlight, Oliver's eyes sparked with real irritation.

"My father won't kill me. But he sure as shootin' will take you out if you cross him."

"Oh, he'd kill you too if you cross him. You give your father far too much credit for human emotions."

"He has plenty of emotions," Oliver retorted.

"Yeah. Self-interest, self-aggrandizement, and greed. He doesn't feel things like love or family loyalty. I've done extensive studies of the sociopathic mind and you have not—"

"You're seriously going to split hairs with me?" Oliver demanded. "Here? Now?"

"You need to understand what you're up against—"

Oliver cut him off, grabbed him by both shoulders, and kissed him forcefully. "I grew up with the man, you moron. I know exactly what I'm up against."

Collin kissed Oliver back, their teeth colliding and tongues clashing. "I think he has evolved since you last interacted with him—"

"You're a goddamned idiot if you think I want to talk about my old man right now," Oliver ground out as he ripped Collin's sweater over his head.

"Says the pot to the stupid kettle," Collin retorted as he yanked down the long zipper on the front of Oliver's wet suit. Yup. Commando underneath the black neoprene. He reached hungrily for Oliver's flesh, cool to the touch, but with fire pulsing beneath the skin.

Collin's shirt fell away, and at the same time Oliver sucked Collin's tonsils from his throat, he went to work on Collin's belt buckle and trousers.

The night air was a shock against Collin's naked body, but then Oliver's body slammed into his, shoving him back against the rock.

Oliver bit his neck, and he raked his fingernails down Oliver's back hard enough to be painful. "Asshole," Collin muttered.

"Jerk."

"Bastard."

"Fuckwad."

"Fuck me." Collin gasped the words as Oliver's fist closed around his dick, forcing him in a matter of seconds to the point of riotous explosion. Collin's hips rocked forward violently, and Oliver grabbed him and turned him around, shoving him down to his hands and knees. Collin grabbed fistfuls of wet sand as Oliver spooned his body on top of Collin's.

"If you die, I'll hate you forever," Oliver growled hoarsely.

And then Oliver was plunging into him, all heat and restless motion, surging deeper and deeper until Collin couldn't string thoughts together. Oliver surged up onto his knees, one hand grasping the back of Collin's neck, and the other reaching between them to cup Collin's balls.

Collin keened in pleasure as Oliver's cock stroked him hard and fast, turning him into a hot mess of lust and longing. He threw his head back and shouted his pleasure as Oliver slammed into him one last time, coming with a roar of his own flung out to the sea, which roared back in return. It was fast and indelicate... and glorious.

Oliver collapsed on top of him, breathing hard. Collin absorbed his body heat, vaguely registering the grit of sand on their skin and beneath his knees.

"I love you," Oliver sighed.

Collin froze, not sure he'd heard correctly. Surely not. It was just the aftermath of the sex talking. He lowered the two of them to the sand, lying flat on his belly with Oliver sprawled on top of him like a heavy blanket. Slowly, the sand beneath him warmed, conforming to his body and cupping it softly. He could lie here like this all night.

"I'm crushing you, aren't I?" Oliver muttered, rolling away.

Collin wanted to wail for Oliver to come back, but instead, he rolled onto his side to face him. In the wake of their chaotic sex, a deep stillness had settled between them. He hated to disturb it. He studied what he could see of Oliver's face in the deep shadows. No trace of stress tightened his features, and no hint of a frown marred his brow.

This quiet, introspective side of Oliver was new to him. He didn't know how to react or what to say. And so, he let the silence lie there and prayed to whatever deity looked over lost fools like him that Oliver didn't regret what he'd said. That this was not an ending but a new beginning.

"You're cold," Oliver finally murmured.

"No colder than you."

"Yes, but I surf all the time. I'm used to it. Not to mention I'm wearing part of a wet suit. You're shivering." Oliver started, swearing.

"I forgot about your wound. Is it still bleeding? We didn't get sand in it, did we?"

"It's good. Bandage is still safely taped over it. And I'm lying on my other side."

Oliver sighed. "As much as I'd like to stay here with you for a week or two and not move, we need to get you back to the hotel."

Collin sat up reluctantly and turned to hunt for his clothes. "Umm, Oliver? We've got a problem."

"What's that?"

"The waves have covered the strip of sand I walked on to get here."

Oliver laughed. "Well, then. I guess I get to rescue you this time."

"Does that mean I'm going to end up saving you?"

Oliver's smile faded. "You already have, Collin."

He didn't know what to say to that, and a wave of shyness—of all things—swept over him. He eyed the water, now a good two feet deep, sloshing against the rocks.

"We need to keep your side dry and not get saltwater in that cut. You could leave your pants off and wade for it," Oliver suggested, "or, I could carry you piggyback around the point."

Collin laughed. "Or I could leave my pants off *and* you could carry me piggyback around the point."

That ended up being what they opted for, in the name of keeping Collin dry and no more hypothermic than he already was from lying naked on the sand for the past half hour. It irritated the hell out of him that Oliver didn't seem to be as affected by the cold as he was. Not that the two of them were ever competitive or anything. The guy must have the metabolism of a blast furnace not to be cold out here.

They paused on the far side of the rocks for Collin to put on his pants and shoes, and they trudged back toward the resort. A few hundred yards shy of El Rocca, Collin stopped. "We'd better say goodbye here."

Oliver snorted. "Wouldn't want my old man to think we're sneaking around making out on the beach."

"Heaven forbid."

They traded wry glances, and Oliver headed up the beach toward the road. "I'll approach from the front. You take the rear."

"There's got to be a joke in there somewhere," Collin retorted.

"Joke's on us," Oliver threw over his shoulder.

It was gratifying to know Oliver wasn't any more thrilled with the situation than Collin was.

"See you at the gaming tables," Oliver added.

"Right, then. Break a leg or whatever gamblers say to one another."

"Around here, they'd actually break your damned leg," Oliver grumbled.

Laughing under his breath, Collin veered toward the water and the hotel's beachside entrance.

Tomorrow, he and Oliver would face each other across a poker table for the first time. It was a prospect he roundly dreaded. He, of all people, knew just how brilliant a poker player Oliver was. Worse, Oliver knew all of his tells. None of his self-effacing amateur shtick would work on the guy. But then, Oliver's half-stoned surfer act wouldn't work on him, either.

Oliver had the right of it. He would lie back when the other top players went on the attack and would do his best not to go head-to-head against Oliver. Not yet.

He fully expected Oliver to win the whole tournament. Thing was, with only six players left, a certain amount of luck would come into play. They would likely play for only a matter of hours before a winner emerged. In so few hands, luck could be a factor. Hell, even he had a shot at winning.

Although he worried how Oliver would react if Collin beat him. They both knew Oliver was the better player. But was he a better loser? Or even a decent one? Collin rather doubted it. Not that he was all that great a loser himself. Oh, he was gracious and polite in defeat, but he didn't like it. Not one bit.

He hated to think what George Elliott would do to him if, by some backward miracle, he came out the winner. Would he even get a chance to find out what they were all job interviewing for and get to tell his superiors and the British government? Would winning cost him Oliver? The mere idea sent him into a mild panic over losing the love of his—

He stopped, staring at the ocean sliding back and forth before him, and finished the thought. *The love of his life.*

Cripes. Had he really fallen that hard for Oliver?

He'd just spent an hour in the cold, wet sand getting hypothermic and ignoring stabbing pain in his side so he could have hot monkey sex with the man. And he hadn't cared at all. He'd been so deliriously overjoyed to steal a moment with Oliver that he hadn't even noticed the cold. Wow. He really was a goner.

OLIVER SAT down at the poker table, studiously avoiding looking across the table at Collin until he caught himself doing it. Crap. His old man had to be watching tonight's play live. No way would he miss it if Oliver and Collin pretended the other one didn't exist. With a sigh he glanced up from stacking his chips and caught Collin peeking at him.

"Good luck, English."

"You, too, Gun."

Play was cautious at first, but all six players were looking for opportunities to strike hard and draw blood. The bets went up steadily, the pots growing bigger and bigger, the risk of making a wrong decision higher and higher. One mistake could spell the end for any player at the table.

Silently, Oliver begged Collin to stay focused, be smart, and keep his wits about him, which was weird. Normally he wished just the opposite for his opponents. Collin had played so well this far; he didn't want the guy to humiliate himself on the big stage like this, where everyone would see every tiny misstep or error he made. Not to mention he needed Collin to stick around and protect his back. Literally.

The tournament directors did not have to force the players to bet big tonight. Everyone seemed to want this long, exhausting tournament to be over. First one player, then another busted out. The chip stacks ebbed and flowed between the players. Oliver went head-to-head against one of the other players, and Oliver's flush beat the inside straight the other guy hit on the final turn card.

And now they were three. Tony Carlotti, a veteran American player with purported mafia connections, was the other remaining player. Regardless of his shady associates, he was a hell of a poker player and a genuine threat to win.

Collin opened the betting on the next hand, coming out strong. Oliver figured Collin for an ace and something else high, maybe a jack or a queen. His own cards were a pair of tens. He followed up Collin's bet, raising it fifty thousand, and Carlotti raised his bet another fifty thousand. Based on the video they'd studied of this guy, Oliver smelled a bluff.

He glanced over at Collin, who was studying Carlotti intently. Oliver knew that look in Collin's eyes. He smelled a bluff too. *Go easy*, he silently exhorted Collin. They would need to slow roll this guy, neither of them overplaying their hands if they were going to sucker Carlotti into sticking with his bluff to the bitter—and expensive—end.

The first turn card was revealed. A king. No help to Oliver, but perhaps it set up a straight for Collin. Carlotti came out betting hard, as if he'd paired up a pocket king in his own hand and was now playing a strong king pair. *As if.*

Collin hesitated to call the aggressive bet just the right amount of time to convey that he was worried about Carlotti's hand. Oliver pulled an aggravated face as he pushed in his own chips, matching the bet.

The next card was a ten. Oliver was now sitting on triple tens, normally a winning hand. He considered the odds if Carlotti wasn't, in fact, bluffing, and still liked his own odds. Carlotti bet aggressively again, presumably on the fake pair of kings, and Oliver matched him more confidently this time. It was Collin's turn to look annoyed at the cards as he pushed his chips in. Oliver couldn't tell yet which one of their hands was the strongest, so he had to stick around to see another turn card. Once he knew whether his hand or Collin's was stronger, he'd know which one of them should bow out and let the other knock out bluffing boy.

The turn card was a queen. He looked up at Collin and spotted the tiniest tightening around Collin's eyes for a fraction of a second. A person would have to know Collin as well as Oliver did, be as fully familiar with every nuance of Collin's face as he was, to have noticed it. Collin had hit his straight.

Carlotti made an outrageously high bet, which Oliver recalled from the video of his play was a standard bluffing tactic of his. Collin had this guy dead to rights, so Oliver folded. No need to bankrupt himself when Collin had this handled.

Except Collin hesitated when the bet came to him. *What the hell was he doing?* Alarmed, Oliver stared at him, willing him to call the bet. He had this hand! Surely, Collin knew Carlotti was bluffing. They'd studied the tape together, for crying out loud.

Collin played with his chips, shuffling two short stacks of clay disks into a single taller stack with a musical clatter. He was obviously thinking hard, running numbers and staring speculatively at Carlotti, who gave him a stone face back. *C'mon, c'mon. Make the bet already.* Jeez. He'd served up Carlotti to Collin on a silver fucking platter!

Finally, Collin reached for his chips. He called the bet and raised it a million chips.

Oliver mentally gave him a standing ovation. If Carlotti stuck out his bluff and lost, Collin's giant bet would cripple the guy. Of course, if Collin lost the hand, he'd be crippled instead. It was a courageous move, and Oliver couldn't be prouder of Collin. It was a play worthy of a world-class poker player.

The heat was now on Carlotti to sacrifice half his chip stack, which was already sitting in the middle of the table, and walk away from his bluff, or to see this thing through and potentially go down in flames. Oliver watched Carlotti watching Collin.

Collin leaned back in his chair to wait out Carlotti, his thumbs hooked casually in the pockets of his pants. Even Oliver had to admit that Collin was a cool customer under pressure. All three of them knew what was at stake with this hand.

Carlotti defiantly called the bet.

Oliver allowed himself a faint congratulatory nod that Collin caught and flashed a momentary smirk back at. Oliver sat up straight in his seat, startled. It had all been an act! Collin had known all along he had Carlotti dead to rights and had been faking all that uncertainty! Son of a bitch. He'd even faked out Oliver, who knew him better than anyone here. Nice.

The final card—the river card—flopped. It was a five, of no use to anybody. Collin was in the clear. Collin made a bet that would gut the remainder of Carlotti's chip stack, and the guy had no choice but to call. He was into this pot too deep to back out now.

Collin flipped over his ace-jack. He had, indeed, made his straight. Carlotti stared at the cards in dismay and shoved his hold cards in, facedown, without bothering to show them. The guy swore angrily in Italian as the next hand was dealt.

Oliver eyed Carlotti's now pitiful stack as Collin raked in his huge pile of chips and counted and stacked them. If Oliver wasn't mistaken, Collin had just moved into the chip lead by a nose. *Jerk*, he thought fondly.

It took four more hands, but Oliver maneuvered Carlotti into going all in—pushing in all his remaining chips—on a mediocre hand. Oliver matched up his queen-nine hold cards with a nine on the flop for a pair. Carlotti matched on the flop to make a pair of sixes, but it wasn't enough. The guy was out of the tournament. He stood up, shook hands with Oliver and Collin, and left the room.

Now it was just the two of them.

CHAPTER THIRTEEN

COLLIN STARED across the green felt expanse at Oliver. A sense of inevitability washed over him. Of course, it had come down to the two of them pitted against each other. Panic hovered just behind his sternum. They both knew Oliver to be the better player. But the cards and Lady Luck were in charge now.

Did he dare try to bluff Oliver? God knew, the man could read every nuance of his body language in bed. There was no reason to believe it would be any different at a poker table.

Would Oliver try to bluff him? Possibly.

A new shoe was brought out. The wooden rack held two new decks of cards randomly shuffled together to minimize the effect of card counting. Which benefited Collin, no doubt. Oliver was hell on wheels when it came to counting cards.

He eyed Oliver's chip stack. They were pretty even in that department, which didn't mean much. This was now all about skill and nerve.

He was shocked to realize he wanted to win. It wasn't so much about finding out what the prize was as it was proving himself worthy to his lover. Or more accurately, proving to himself that he was worthy of a man like Oliver, he corrected. He realized he was scowling in Oliver's general direction.

Oliver looked hurt for a millisecond, but then Collin shrugged and smiled at him, and his bright blue gaze lightened. The fact that he had the power to hurt Oliver warmed him like nothing else could have in this moment. They were in this together, to the end.

As he stared at Oliver, a mischievous glint entered those baby blues.

So. It was going to be like that, was it? One-upmanship had always been part of their relationship, from the very first moment they met. Out in the Mediterranean Sea, he'd tried to save Oliver, and Oliver had insisted on trying to save him. As if either one of them had needed help. Ha! Collin allowed himself a brief smirk, released a slow breath, and girded himself for battle.

The first cards were dealt. He had an uninspired nine of clubs and eight of hearts. Oliver peeked at his cards and didn't look any more thrilled. Collin didn't bother trying to bluff, and it didn't appear Oliver was going to try either. They bet out the hand anemically, and the next several hands in similar fashion, neither one risking many chips. Sort of like their relationship. Neither one willing to commit too much, circling around each other, sizing each other up.

He picked up his next cards. Another ace-jack combo, both spades. Now this he could work with. Although the calculations were worlds easier with only two players in the game, a greater element of uncertainty entered into all his math. He matched up the jack on the flop, bet it strongly, and went down in flames as Oliver turned over a pair of pocket kings.

"Nice cards," he murmured.

"Lucky."

Right. Luck. That ineffable, unpredictable lady who made gambling more than simple math. And tonight, she was a stone-cold bitch who hated his ever-loving guts. As the night progressed, it seemed as if every time he got a half-decent hand, Oliver's cards were just a little bit better. It got so bad he actually started calculating the odds of it happening again and started coming up with some truly astronomical numbers.

After yet another edge out that ate into Collin's dwindling stack of chips, Oliver had the cojones to murmur, "You never give up, do you?"

His competitive instincts flared. He'd show Oliver he could play cards with the big dogs, dammit—

He checked himself sharply. The bastard was playing him! Oliver knew how competitive he was and had poked at him, trying to get an emotional rise out of him. And it had worked!

"Nice try," he murmured back, smiling in genuine amusement.

A flash of frustration passed through Oliver's sapphire gaze. Why was *he* frustrated? The guy had nearly three-quarters of the chips and couldn't buy himself bad cards if he tried. If Collin didn't do something drastic, and fast, to win a big hand, he was going to be finished. Oliver would be able to nickel-and-dime him to death without ever risking a significant portion of his chip pile.

As if he'd willed the cards into his hands, his next hold cards were a pair of queens. A lot of hands could beat those ladies, but they were a decent start. More than a decent start. Oliver opened the betting strongly.

So. He had decent cards too, did he? Well, then, this could get interesting. The first three turn cards were all over the place. Low cards. Two spades, which was mildly worrying if Oliver had two spades in his hand and a possible spade flush. He made the allowance in his calculations and still came out way ahead in the odds. The bets climbed, with raises and reraises back and forth. Oliver seemed to realize that Collin had picked this hand to make his stand.

Silently, Collin asked Oliver to give him a break. To let this hand fall his way. The longer the two of them could draw out this competition, the more time they'd have to figure out what was actually going on with this tournament's endgame.

He noticed Oliver glancing up at the black glass bubble of the surveillance camera directly overhead, and his jaw muscles tightened. It was an unwelcome reminder that George Elliott could see their hold cards. If either one of them failed to bet their cards appropriately, the bastard would know... and no doubt kill one or both of them.

When Oliver looked down from the camera, his expression was resigned. Dammit. He'd made a decision of some kind. And if Collin read him right, Oliver had just resigned himself to giving in to his father.

Oliver announced, "I raise a million."

The huge bet would all but force Collin to fold. Staying in the hand and losing now would cripple him.

So much for them drawing this out.

Collin pushed his entire remaining stack of chips in to the middle of the table. "All in."

He looked up and made grim eye contact with Oliver, whose eyes were hard as chips of blue bottle glass. No sympathy there. Decision made, Oliver was steeling himself to go through with whatever he'd decided, which appeared to be driving Collin out and ending the tournament as fast as humanly possible.

Unfortunately, Collin's gut was screaming at him that it was the wrong move. That something terrible would happen if he and Oliver went down this path. He needed to get away from this table and the cameras. Talk with Oliver. Come up with a plan—

Except none of that was going to happen. He was out of time. They were out of time.

Pain blossomed in his chest. They'd never really had a chance, had they? The deck had always been stacked against them. His job. Oliver's father. The strange circumstances under which they'd met. At the end of the day, they just hadn't been able to overcome all the obstacles between of them.

He had a feeling it was going to be a long time before he recovered from Oliver Elliott. The guy had wrecked his heart. God only knew if and when he would ever take a chance on someone else. It had been hard enough to open up to this man, and Oliver was damn near perfect in every way that mattered. Where would he ever find someone else to compare?

Collin blinked, startled momentarily by the poker table, the cards, the chips, the man seated across the table. Oh. Right. He'd bet everything on the turn of a card. His pair of queens should hold up to anything except paired kings or aces—which he didn't think Oliver had or he'd have bet differently—or a flush. He was good if anything but a spade turned up.

The dealer reached for the final card and flipped it over.

A queen of spades.

Good. And bad.

He'd matched up his queens for three of a kind. But his gut quailed at the possibility that Oliver had hit his flush. Surely the guy hadn't done all that hellish betting with nothing else in his hand but the possibility of hitting a flush.

"Call," Oliver murmured.

Collin tossed out his queens face up.

Oliver sighed. "Nice." He tossed out his own cards. "But not nice enough."

He had them. The spades. Oliver had started this hand bluffing like a big dog on junk—a two and six of spades. And Collin had completely fallen for it. So much for knowing his lover.

He stood, chagrined, and frankly, pissed off. He held out his hand to shake Oliver's. "Congratulations. You completely faked me out. You're a much better liar than I ever could be."

Oliver's eyebrows slammed together as he also rose. He opened his mouth on some undoubtedly snarky retort, but then a voice boomed from across the cavernous darkness of the ballroom. "Not so fast, gentlemen."

They turned as one to face a trio of men striding toward their lone table under its stark spotlight. George Elliott was in the middle, flanked by two gray-haired men Collin didn't recognize. Oliver stiffened across the table as if perhaps he did recognize the other men.

One of the other men spoke in a gravelly voice. "Congratulations on making it this far, gentlemen. You should take pride in your accomplishment. As it stands, Mr. Elliott, you will win the tournament. However, Mr. Callahan, you have one more chance to stay in the running. Although you are out of chips, we are prepared to let you play one more hand and make one more bet."

Collin frowned. He glanced over at Oliver, who shrugged. He didn't know what was going on either.

When the man didn't continue, Collin finally asked, "And that bet would be what?"

George Elliott answered somberly, "You may bet your life."

Collin blinked. His *life*? What the hell did that mean?

Oliver made a choked sound and then demanded, "Are you fucking kidding me? No way! That's insane! I'll concede the tournament to him if he accepts that offer."

Collin glared over at Oliver. "It's not your call to make." To George, he said more calmly, "Could you elaborate on what that bet would entail?"

"Exactly what it sounds like. You win the hand, you win whatever chips your opponent has bet on the hand. You lose, your opponent kills you."

Oliver flared up angrily, "Whoa, whoa, whoa. Stop right there. I'm not killing anybody!"

George glared at his son. "Then you fail the job interview, forfeit your winnings, will be disowned permanently, and my colleagues and I will see to it you never work an honest job again. Furthermore, we'll irrevocably ruin you and your reputation, and we will still kill your opponent. In front of you."

Oliver stared in horror nearly as great as Collin's.

Enough of this crap. Collin spoke up. "And if I turn down the bet? Do I walk out of here ruined instead?"

The quiet man answered with a tiny smile, "You catch on quickly, Mr. Callahan."

"What about my opponent? If I win, does he walk out of here alive?"

"Of course."

"I have your word on that?" Collin pressed.

George Elliott scowled and ground out, "Yes."

"Let's say for argument's sake that I do accept this bet, and that I go on to win the tournament. What will I win? I have a right to know what I'm risking my life over."

"Do you accept the bet?" the man responded.

And there it was. He would complete his mission and finally find out what the hell was going on around here…if he risked his life on a hand of poker.

He also had a sneaking suspicion that if he accepted the bet, he would not be allowed to leave El Rocca tonight. Even if he did flee Gibraltar to avoid this outrageous bet, these powerful psychopaths would find him and kill him, no matter how good Wild Cards, Inc.'s resources might be at hiding him.

"I accept."

"No!" Oliver cried.

"It's not your call," Collin bit out. "My life. My choice."

"Damned idiot—" Oliver started.

George cut off his son, voice raised to talk over him. "Play will resume tomorrow evening at ten o'clock sharp. I'll see both of you then." The bastard strode away into the shadows from whence he'd come. Collin thought he caught a hint of a smirk on Elliott's face as he turned away.

The other two men remained, and the quiet one spoke once more. "The winner of this tournament will be offered a position in the Erebus Consortium. We are arguably the most powerful group of human beings on the planet. And one of you will join us. That is what you are risking your life for, Mr. Callahan."

Collin nodded in terse acknowledgment, his mental wheels spinning. Holy hell. Who on earth was this Erebus Consortium, and why could that guy make such an outrageous claim with a straight face? Why had this bunch never popped up on the Wild Cards' radar? His employer was plugged into every major intelligence agency on the planet, and he'd never heard even the name Erebus Consortium.

"What the fuck are you doing, Collin?" Oliver demanded aggressively.

A pair of goons stepped forward, restraining Oliver when he tried to come around the table, rage hot in his eyes.

Collin looked up at him bleakly. "I'll see you tomorrow night." And with that he turned smartly on his heel and, escorted by another pair of goons, retreated to his hotel room to ponder the nature of self-destruction.

At least he'd completed his mission. After he reported in to Wild Cards ops about this Erebus Consortium, his work here was done. When he lost—for surely, he would—and he was executed, he would die knowing Oliver was safe.

And, big bonus, he wouldn't have to live for long with the knowledge that he'd loved and lost Oliver Elliott. It wasn't much as silver linings went. But it was all he had.

Chapter Fourteen

OLIVER WAS so furious, he destroyed most of the furniture in his room with his bare hands before he calmed down enough to think rationally. Damn his father to the deepest, darkest circle of hell for doing this to him. Doing this to *them*—to him and Collin. Jesus. He would never forget that stricken look in Collin's eyes when he'd realized that Oliver had stone-cold bluffed him, and worse, that sheer dumb luck had cost Collin the tournament. Hell. Cost him his *life*.

Oliver bolted for the toilet. Disgusted at himself for hurting the man he loved, disgusted at his father, he knelt over the porcelain bowl in self-loathing and heaved until his gut was completely emptied.

At length, he sat back on his heels, flushed the toilet, and watched the water swirl in the bowl. His life in a nutshell. And now he'd flushed Collin down the toilet too. And cost the guy his life while he was at it.

It wasn't as if he could throw the poker hand tomorrow. His father would surely be watching the hold cards. If he bet in any other way than what was exactly sensible for his cards, George would likely kill both him and Collin. He was well and truly trapped in a devil's bind. He was damned either way.

There had to be something he could do. But he, of all people, knew the folly of opposing his father. This moment being a case in point. His old man had managed to reel him back in, and oh, by the way, break his heart and destroy his life—and Collin's—in the process.

When would he learn the futility of trying to escape George Elliott's clutches? Hell, maybe Collin was the lucky one. He got a neat escape from the bastard. In death, George couldn't touch him—

His bitter thought train derailed sharply. If Collin were dead, George couldn't touch him.

Collin. Dead.

He had an idea.

Collin's death could be arranged, by God. He dashed for his laptop, but he didn't have much time to work out the details, and he would definitely need help. Thankfully, his hack into the resort's server had never been discovered or shut down, which meant he could go through it to access both the internet and email. Out of curiosity, he tried his phone, but it was as dead as Collin would be if he didn't do something drastic.

No surprise the phone was down, as was his own Wi-Fi access to the internet. Of course, no way were his father's thugs letting him or Collin out of the hotel between now and tomorrow night's showdown, either, to call anyone for help.

No way would he get any access to Collin between now and tomorrow night. He knew his father's tactics far too well. Divide and conquer was a favorite adage of ol' George's. The bastard. He would have to arrange this completely on his own.

What he had in mind would be a dicey gambit. Particularly without Collin's cooperation. But it had to look real. It had to *be* real. George, and everyone else, for that matter, had to be convinced. As much as it pained Oliver to leave Collin in the dark, it was the only way this crazy plan of his would work.

He feverishly worked his way through all the possible outcomes and permutations, looking for holes in the plan, frantically coming up with ways to plug them as he found them. And then he prayed he hadn't missed anything and sent an email to set it all up. Everything depended on this working. *Everything.*

COLLIN DRESSED in the freshly pressed tuxedo a bellboy delivered for him just after he finished the elaborate prime rib dinner that had also been delivered to his room, a condemned man's last supper. Ominously, all the labels had been removed from the clothing. Sheesh. Talk about making him feel like a walking corpse. Oh, wait. He was one.

Grimly, Collin tied the bow tie, brushed invisible lint off his sleeves, and idly admired the fit of the tuxedo. They'd even gotten his shoe size correct. He had wide toes but narrow heels, and the highly shined Italian leather oxfords fit his feet as if they'd been made for him. Impressive on such short notice. He would have complimented the tailor and shoemaker on their fine work, but he would be dead in a few hours, and this would likely be the monkey suit he was buried in. Or, more likely, dumped at sea and eaten in by the fish.

With other cheery thoughts in that vein banging around in his skull, he followed Elliott Senior's goons downstairs after one of them knocked on his door a few minutes before 10:00 p.m. What did a man say to his jailors as they led him to the gallows, anyway? He opted for polite nods and smiles as required and otherwise said nothing.

At least he'd been able to send a quick text to Wild Cards, Inc. last night to alert them to the existence of the Erebus Consortium and that the winner got a job with them. He'd typed it with one hand by touch in the pocket of his suit coat in the elevator on the way to his room.

Funny, but his Wi-Fi had magically stopped working seconds after he'd gotten out that single, short text. His laptop and cell phone had both quit sending or receiving signals by the time he'd gotten back to the room last night. The Erebus boys weren't about to let him send out a call for help.

The elevator opened, and he stepped out into the lobby. With all the other players gone from the hotel, it was eerily quiet in the sprawling resort. Library-like. Or maybe funeral home-like was a more apt analogy. Most of the hotel staff seemed to have disappeared as well, leaving the hallways and lobby strangely empty. Only one man stood behind the front desk, and he recognized the guy as one of Elliott's men from the yacht.

Oliver was already in the ballroom when the goons showed him into the huge, dark cave of a room. Collin spotted his tall frame immediately, shifting restlessly behind his chair. The dealer sat quietly on his stool, shuffling a deck of cards idly under the lone spotlight shining down from the ceiling. The riffling sound of them was all that disturbed the deep silence.

It was a long walk across the room to the table. Now he knew how gunslingers had felt in the Old West when they stepped out into a dusty street at high noon for a quick-draw showdown. His gut felt like water, and a little voice in the back of his brain was screaming obscenities at him for going through with this madness. But something stubborn and maybe fatalistic in his gut kept him placing one foot in front of the next.

"Collin."

"Oliver."

They traded stiff nods with each other.

The doors opened once more, this time admitting a dozen middle-aged men.

"Christ," Oliver breathed.

He had a definite idea of who these men were. Of course, Collin surmised they constituted the board of directors of Erebus Consortium or some equivalent body.

George Elliott was among them. Collin took mental pictures of every face on the off chance that he would somehow find a way out of this death sentence and manage to report back to Wild Cards HQ. Funny how his mind refused to acknowledge that he was about to die and that knowing the faces of his killers didn't count for a damned thing.

"Shall we, gentlemen?" George said.

Huh. The bastard actually seemed to be showing a modicum of respect for the stakes he and Oliver were playing for tonight. Who'd have guessed?

But then the analytic side of Collin's brain kicked in. The man was a psychopath without an empathetic bone in his body. The respect in his voice was more likely aimed at the most powerful person in the cluster of men taking seats on a raised platform beyond the poker table.

Who in their right mind voluntarily watched a man meet his death? They were likely all killers or sociopaths like George. He sincerely hoped his employers found and dismantled the Erebus Consortium sooner rather than later. Too bad he wouldn't be around to help. He only hoped no more Wild Cards operatives had to give their lives before these bastards were identified and taken down.

The dealer shuffled the deck of cards one more time, fanned it facedown on the table, and asked, "Would either of you like to check the deck to make sure it's not marked?"

Collin snorted. He wouldn't know how to spot a marked deck, and besides, it didn't matter. If the suits on the dais wanted him dead, exposing a marked deck wouldn't stop them.

Oliver shrugged.

Collin was offered an opportunity to cut the single deck of cards, which he did.

"Would you like to cut the cards as well, sir?" the dealer asked Oliver.

"Just deal," Oliver snapped.

Oliver sounded ravaged. He knew the feeling. He sincerely hoped they didn't make Oliver witness his murder. The guy didn't deserve that. This had been his choice, not Oliver's.

He deeply doubted that Oliver would do it himself as the men last night had indicated this would play out if he lost this hand of cards. Oliver would rebel one last time against his father and make George do the deed himself.

At least he hoped that was how his death went down. He really would hate to die at the hands of the man he loved, no matter how reluctant Oliver was to pull the proverbial trigger. He only hoped it would be something fast like a gunshot that put him down.

A shudder of horror passed through him. *Eyes on the prize, my friend.* Oliver would walk out of this alive. And maybe one day, he would grow powerful enough to take down George Elliott and his ilk once and for all.

He looked up at Oliver and caught the strangest expression in those blue orbs. Just for an instant, Oliver looked... determined. Focused. Intent on something. But what? Surely, he wasn't any happier about this travesty than Collin was.

The dealer picked up the cards and hesitated for a moment, as if even he were reluctant to get this ball rolling. But then he dealt out two cards to each of them and quickly laid out five cards facedown in front of himself on the felt table.

Oliver didn't pick up his hold cards to look at them, and neither did Collin. What was Oliver up to?

The surfer genius, beach dude, lover, and friend smiled crookedly across the table at him and said, "Let's just cut to the chase, shall we?" Oliver pushed his entire prodigious stack of chips into the center of the table. "I'm all in."

It went without saying that Collin was all in. *With his life.*

Oliver flipped over his cards and winced. An ace-ten of hearts. A strong hand.

Collin flipped over his. A pair of deuces, diamonds and hearts, the color of blood. The suicide hand. "How appropriate," he murmured.

"Turn the cards," Oliver snapped at the dealer.

The guy took a deep breath and turned the first card.

A nine. No help to either of them.

Another card turned. A king of clubs. Again, no help.

The third card was a six of diamonds.

The fourth card, the turn card, was a jack of spades.

The dealer reached for the river card, the final of the five shared cards. His hand paused over the card. Collin's breath stopped. His life depended on a single turn of the card. His face felt hot and cold all at once, and his entire body was drenched with adrenaline and sweat.

"Just turn it," he growled.

The dealer flipped the card over.

An ace of hearts.

Oliver had matched up his ace and beat Collin's deuces. On the last card. Collin stared down at the single heart in the middle of the card, and it swam in his vision as horror slammed into him. He'd lost. He was a dead man.

Shock descended heavily over him, a blanket muffling all sound and sensation as Elliott the Senior surged off the podium to slap his son's back and congratulate him in a hearty voice.

Oliver responded tiredly, "Fuck off, George." But the words sounded as if they came from a great distance away.

Collin stood up woodenly, and Oliver did the same. "Can we get this over with and not draw it out, please?" he asked no one in particular.

Oliver reached into his tuxedo jacket and pulled out a revolver, which stunned Collin out of his shock. Where on earth had he gotten a hold of a weapon? Had George given it to him?

"You? You're going to kill me?" he asked in disbelief. He stared into Oliver's eyes, unable to imagine a greater betrayal had ever been perpetrated in the history of love than this.

Oliver shrugged. "You know my old man. Did you think he would have it any other way? That any of them would? This is my last test to pass before I become one of them. I have to have blood on my hands. Just like all of them."

A note of deep bitterness crept into Oliver's voice at those last words.

Collin stared at him and said candidly, "If I misjudged you this badly, if I loved a man who is able to look me in the eye and gun me down in cold blood, I'm actually glad I don't have to live with that."

"You loved—" Oliver started. He broke off sharply. The revolver trembled so badly in his fist that Collin wasn't sure Oliver would hit him even if he tried to shoot.

Oliver raised the weapon and held it at arm's length with his right hand. Collin stared into the tiny black bore, unable to believe this was actually happening.

In that moment, a dozen images of him and Oliver together flashed through his head. The two of them laughing in bed together. Gasping in passion. Playing cards on Oliver's bed. Naked in the shower. Making love on the beach. Oliver. Always Oliver. At least he'd shared real love before the end. It was something, at least.

"Goodbye, Oliver," he whispered. His voice failed then, and he only mouthed his last words. "I love you."

A huge explosion of sound and a bright flash of light exploded in the dark ballroom. Something massively heavy slammed into his chest just over his heart. Within the powerful blow, something needle-sharp stabbed him, like a jagged bone fragment tearing into his heart wall. He staggered backward, half spinning around from the force of the gunshot.

He felt wetness. Looked down. Spied a blossom of red on his pristine white shirt, just starting to peek out from under his tuxedo lapel.

He tried to draw a breath, but no air entered his lungs. He looked up at Oliver in entreaty, and his legs buckled out from under him as his lover's face—his killer's face—faded to black.

CHAPTER FIFTEEN

HORRIFIED TO the core of his being to see his lover fall, to see that burst of red over his heart, Oliver jumped forward as Collin crumpled to the floor. He had to work fast now. He knelt and pressed his fingers against Collin's neck, checking for a pulse.

He looked up at the cluster of men that included his father and announced grimly, "It's done."

The group seemed to exhale as one in satisfaction. *Cock-swinging, motherfucking sons of bitches.*

Oliver shrugged out of his own tuxedo jacket and tossed it over Collin's head and chest. Then he commenced rifling through Collin's pockets, pulling out his lover's wallet and taking off his watch. He threw over his shoulder, "I assume you removed all identifying labels from the tuxedos you provided us?"

"Of course," someone answered.

"I need a rug or a tarp or something to wrap him up in. I used a hollow-point round to minimize the blood, but I need to get him out of here soon so he doesn't bleed all over the floor and leave behind evidence."

While they waited for a tarp to be fetched, Oliver looked over at his father. "Tell me something. Was this entire tournament a ruse to draw me out and suck me into your world?"

George shrugged. "Would anything less than a chance to prove you're the greatest poker player on the planet have gotten you off that damned beach?"

"Absolutely not."

"There's your answer, then."

He supposed he should be complimented that his father and his cronies had gone to so much expense and trouble to lure him here and then manipulate him into committing murder so they could control him forever.

But still, it galled him to his core to have been maneuvered into this moment, standing over the body of his lover, neatly caged, forced to serve the consortium as his lord and master.

He asked, "What about the attempts on my life? Are you saying your people had nothing to do with those?"

George answered for the group, "The murders were not us. Gathering the best poker players on earth necessitated dipping into some rather bloodthirsty barrels of monkeys."

"Was it Stacy Kiern behind the attacks? She was using the escorts brought in for the tournament, wasn't she?"

"Very good," George said approvingly. To his colleagues, the older Elliott said, "I told you he's sharp. He figured out who the attacker was without our help at all."

Oliver rolled his eyes.

George commented, "Ms. Kiern is interesting. She showed impressive initiative. We may choose to recruit her at a later date."

Initiative? Apparently in George's lexicon, that was a nice way of saying the woman was a homicidal psychopath.

He glanced down in distaste at Collin's awkwardly sprawled body. And apparently, he'd earned his own bona fides as his father's son and as a sociopathic psychopath in his own right.

A big man in a cheap suit stepped out of a door on the far side of the room and walked forward with a big blue plastic tarp folded sloppily in his arms. A second man followed close behind. Oliver had only seconds left to do the last thing he needed to. He palmed two small objects and unobtrusively slipped them into Collin's front pants pocket as he bent over his body. Collin would need them where he was going.

One of the thugs laid out the tarp beside Collin, and Oliver grabbed his limp body under the armpits while the second thug took Collin's feet. They heaved him onto the edge of the tarp and then rolled him in it. The thugs helped him wrap ropes around the whole package to hold it together, and then the first guy hoisted Collin's body over a beefy shoulder.

"Give him to me," Oliver demanded.

"But—" the guy started.

"It's not a request. That's an order," he snapped.

The guy complied, and in the matter of a moment, Collin's heavy body, still warm through the cheap plastic, hung over his shoulder.

"To the marina, I assume?" Oliver asked the thugs.

"Yup," the second one answered gruffly.

"Let's get rolling, then. I've got places to go and things to do."

"You don't have to go with them," his father called.

Oliver spun slowly under Collin's weight and glared at his father, for a moment letting the full measure of his rage flash in his eyes. "I see my work through to the end. Always have. Always will. If you don't like that about me, you can shove it, father of mine."

Actual satisfaction gleamed in George's eyes. Glad to know he hadn't broken his fractious son's spirit, was he? Bastard was in for a hell of a shock when he found just how little he'd harnessed his son to the Erebus yoke.

The two burly men led him outside and across the beach to the marina. Collin was heavy, but he was glad he was the one to carry the man he loved on this journey to the sea.

Thankfully, the thugs veered away from his father's massive yacht and opted instead for a smaller cabin cruiser. He laid Collin's body down gently, but it still ended up lying tangled in an unceremonious heap. There truly was no dignity in death.

Oliver moved into the wheelhouse. The first man stepped up to the vessel's controls and started the engines while the other one cast off the lines. The thug driving guided the cruiser out of its berth.

As they reached the sea, he pointed the prow to the west and opened up the throttles, announcing, "Best place to dump a body is in the Atlantic. Currents will carry it down the coast of Africa a ways before there's any chance of it coming ashore. Locals won't give a damn that some dead guy washed up and won't report it."

"Perfect," Oliver replied coldly. How these goons weren't hearing his heart pounding its way out of his chest, he couldn't fathom. He was so light-headed with adrenaline and icy terror he could hardly see straight. Time was the enemy now. He squinted down at his watch. It had been a scant fifteen minutes since he'd shot Collin. He needed to make sure this little jaunt took at least thirty more minutes. He'd had to hurry Collin's body out of the casino so his father and George's cronies wouldn't examine it too closely. But now he needed to delay.

He commented, "Make sure we're far enough away from land that there's no chance of him being found. I didn't jump through all these hoops just to get sloppy now."

"You got it, sir."

Sir. Right. He was one of the bad guys now. The newest member of the Erebus Consortium. May they all rot in hell, his father in particular.

As the chilly night breeze sprayed a fine mist of saltwater against his face, shock began to set in. God almighty, pulling that trigger had been hard. Harder than he'd imagined it would be—and he had a damned fine imagination. The look of shock and hurt in Collin's eyes—he would never forget that as long as he lived. He suspected it would haunt him to his grave and beyond.

The longer they motored into the night, the farther from shore they went, the more tense he grew. And the combination of terror, shock, and tension proved toxic. Acid rose in his gut and burned the back of his throat.

The more he thought about it, the more violently his gut twisted in horror at what his father had made him do. What kind of monster did that to his own child? The revulsion threatened to spill over, and he mumbled to the other men, "Shit. I think I'm gonna be seasick."

Staggering out of the cabin with his hand over his mouth, he ran to the back of the boat and emptied his stomach over the back end of the vessel. He leaned heavily on the rail, gasping in the aftermath.

Taking the opportunity while he was there, he nudged Collin's body with a toe and murmured low, under the roar of the engines, "You awake?"

A faint groan rose from the tarp.

"Hush," Oliver said quickly, keeping his back turned to the wheelhouse and also not moving his lips in an excess of caution. "If you're conscious enough to understand me, say my name."

"Ol-liver" came the sigh.

"Listen up. Your life depends on it. I faked your shooting. I fired a blank and, using a remote control, simultaneously exploded a fake blood pack one of your Wild Cards colleagues hid in your tuxedo. There was also a hypodermic in your jacket, triggered by the remote as well, that injected a fast-acting sedative into you to knock you out. With me so far?"

"Uh-huh." Collin sounded groggy as hell. Hopefully, he was conscious enough to grasp the next bit of the plan.

"The tranquilizer is wearing off now. I've put a knife and an emergency locator transponder in your right front pants pocket. When the goons dump you in the water, you'll need to cut your way out of the tarp. The ELT will activate when it's submerged. Friends of yours will come pick you up as soon as this boat has cleared out of the area. The water's cold, so try to keep the tarp wrapped around you and don't flail around too much. For God's sake, don't make any noise when you hit the water to let my father's men know you're alive. The cold will be a shock, but don't scream. Got all that?"

"Uh-huh."

"I'll try to keep them from dumping you for another fifteen minutes or so. The sedative should be totally out of your system by then. Don't drown on me, Collin. I love you."

COLLIN LISTENED in disbelief as Oliver's steps receded across the deck from him.

I'm not dead?

Well, that certainly was good news. How in the world had Oliver pulled all of this off? He lay there, waiting for his brain to clear before he tried to puzzle that out.

Did they have a chance, after all? If he managed to make it off this boat and out of the ocean alive, was it possible he and Oliver could be together, after all? Had Oliver found a way for both of them to extricate themselves from that damned poker tournament trap? Hope ignited in his gut, and his heart beat a little more strongly.

He still felt groggy, and it was tempting to drift back into unconsciousness. Must fight it. For Oliver. For the love between them.

Bit by bit his brain cleared, and he began to think more rationally.

He needed to get ahold of the knife in his pocket before he got thrown overboard and risked losing it. His life would depend on being able to cut himself free of the cocoon encasing him. It was probably a good thing he was still somewhat sedated, because he was mildly claustrophobic. At full mental speed, he would be freaking out at being a human burrito like this.

Moving cautiously, he wriggled his right hand up his thigh and into his pocket. His fingers closed around the hard steel of a folded pocketknife. How in the hell was he supposed to get it open with one hand—

Ah. His fingertip encountered a small button on the side of the knife. It was a switchblade. He debated opening it now or waiting until he hit the water. But the claustrophobia made the decision for him. He popped the knife open and winced at the tearing sound of his pocket and pant leg giving way. Sharp little sucker, this knife of Oliver's. Thank God.

He tested his wrappings and felt loops of rope around his shoulders, waist, and thighs. None of them were that tight. Just enough to hold the tarp around a corpse. But the rope felt thick.

Maybe he should get a head start on sawing at it now. He would hate to die because he couldn't get the rope cut before he sank or got too cold to cut it.

Easing the knife slowly up his torso, he poked the tip of the knife through the tarp and started sawing at the ropes around his waist.

It was laborious work, but not because the rope was hard to cut through. Quite the contrary. He didn't want to cut all the way through the ropes just yet. He needed them to hold long enough for his killers to pick him up and throw him off the boat.

When he was done nearly sawing through the waist ropes, he shifted by slow degrees, jackknifing his body a little until he could reach the ropes around his legs. He went to work on those, carefully sawing them mostly through.

He was just pondering how to reach the ropes around his shoulders when the vibrations of heavy footsteps underneath him announced the arrival of his killers. He froze, holding the knife tightly, resting the blade along his pant leg.

Had he been dead long enough for rigor mortis to be setting in, or should he play limp corpse? No telling how long he'd been unconscious. It must still be night, though, or they wouldn't be out here to dump him in the middle of the busy sea lanes near the Strait of Gibraltar. If it was still night, then he'd been dead only a short time. No rigor mortis, then. Limp it was.

As rough hands grabbed him through the tarp, he forced every muscle in his body to relax—which was actually damned hard to do under the tense circumstances. He focused, too, on steeling his mind for the abrupt agony of submerging in ice water. He remembered all too well the shock of jumping into the Mediterranean after Oliver several weeks ago.

He was lifted and swung up and out. There was a sickening moment of free fall, and then a tremendous impact as he slammed into the water. The cold and dark closed around him like a grave, and panic smashed into him. He kicked violently, and the ropes around his legs broke free. Another violent jerk with his arms, and the waist ropes gave way. Rather than try to cut the ropes around his shoulders, he just shoved and tore at the tarp and rope, ripping his head free of the confining materials.

He heard the roar of an engine under the water, and reminded himself not to surface. Instead, he held his breath for as long as he could. Finally, when his lungs were screaming and the sound of the retreating boat had faded, he kicked hard with both legs against the weight of his sodden tuxedo and the resistance of the water.

He opened his eyes underwater, and nothing but painful blackness stung at them. Screwing them shut again, he realized the weight of his clothing was pulling at him. Crap. Which way was up?

He gave an experimental pull with both arms. It felt like the pressure on his ears diminished slightly. He pulled again, more strongly this time. Did he dare surface yet? Was the vessel Oliver and the thugs had dumped him off far enough away that they wouldn't see him surface?

His lungs didn't give him much choice in the matter, however. He must have exhaled partially when he hit that intensely cold water, because his oxygen supply felt almost depleted. He opened his eyes and thought he spied the faintest light overhead. He stroked strongly toward it.

Collin's face popped out of the water. He dragged in a blessed lungful of air. Just to be safe, he submerged again, pushing upward with his arms to hold himself below the surface. He counted to thirty and surfaced again.

This time he turned in a full circle, searching for the boat carrying Oliver and his helpers. Nothing. He was alone. Distant lights on the horizon told him where the nearest land was. Whether it was Spain, Morocco, or someplace else altogether, he had no idea. He was only seeing what looked like the tips of mountains, so he estimated he was a good three miles from shore. Not that it mattered. No way could he swim that far before he succumbed to hypothermia.

Speaking of which, he was starting to shiver. Violently. As in, his teeth were chattering like castanets and his large muscles were starting to cramp up. Belatedly remembering what Oliver had said about the tarp, he grabbed the tattered plastic sheet where it floated beside him and awkwardly wrapped it around himself like a clumsy blanket.

If it helped, he couldn't tell. He still felt as if he was quickly turning into an ice cube.

To keep his mind off his suffering, he shifted the switchblade to his left hand and managed to reach into his right pocket while staying afloat. A small square of plastic rested there. Grabbing it, he pulled it out and brought it to his nose. A tiny green light blinked underneath a piece of tape that mostly obscured the light-emitting diode. Okay. Locator beacon working. Now he just had to pray someone found him before he froze to death.

He grabbed the edge of the tarp and pulled it more tightly around himself. Would he ever be warm again? If he got out of this mess alive, he was finding the hottest, sunniest beach he could and cooking himself on it until he was the color of boiled lobster. Well, maybe he would use sunblock. But he was still going to get as hot as he could stand.

Maybe he would build a sauna in his garage. Then he could cook himself every single day until he forgot what this bone-deep chill felt like. His brain was getting sluggish, and he couldn't feel his face anymore. His fingers and toes were so numb he lost all feeling in them.

He was going to haunt Oliver from beyond the grave if the jerk saved him from death by shooting only to freeze him to death out here because no one came to rescue him.

As if his threat conjured it, the sound of a motor became audible. It was quiet, and he felt the vibration as much as heard it. He looked all around and saw nothing approaching. Granted, he was only inches above the water, and the swells were a couple of feet high out here.

All of a sudden, a shape loomed in front of him. It was low and black and sleek. And two men dressed in black wet suits with something black smeared all over their faces were leaning out of the boat.

"Mr. Callahan, I presume?" one of them said in a British accent.

"Uh-huh," he managed to gasp.

"Need a lift?" the second one said in the broad vowels of upcountry England.

"Can't move my arms," he managed.

The men reached down, snagged him by his armpits, and bodily hauled him over the edge of the boat. He landed in a heap on the cold metal floor of some kind of low-profile motorboat.

Several pairs of hands jerked at him, and he realized with a start that they were efficiently cutting his clothes off his body with knives.

"Don't move, sir. We'll have these wet things off you in a sec, and then we'll wrap you up in nice warm blankets. You'll be toasty in a few minutes."

He would believe that when it actually happened.

They rolled him in a scratchy wool blanket and then in another blanket that sounded like plastic. Someone said something about heat-reflective plastic. A motor revved quietly behind him somewhere, and the vessel felt as if it leapt forward beneath him.

One of the black-clad men explained to him, "Normally we'd take you to the Royal Navy base in Gibraltar, but your employer is concerned that someone might see you there and report your survival to the wrong people."

"Where are we going, then?"

"Rendezvous with a private craft that will take you aboard. We'll reach it in twenty minutes or so. Just sit back and relax, Mr. Callahan."

He spent most of the ride to the yacht shivering more violently than he believed possible, but ever so slowly, he began to regain feeling in his face and fingers. His quads, biceps, and back muscles started to unclench, and somewhere in there, he stopped being an actual icicle.

He didn't pay much attention as the rescue boat pulled alongside a nice but not obnoxiously ostentatious yacht. Conversation floated over his head about how he was still dangerously chilled and to leave the heating blanket on him for another hour at least. And then he was lifted by the men in the small vessel and passed into waiting hands above.

"May I please stand up on my own two feet?" he complained.

Chuckles sounded around him. Someone said over his head, "Irritability is a good sign. His mental functions are returning to normal."

He turned to thank the men in black for saving his life, but the vessel was already nothing more than a small hump among the waves.

"Who were those guys?" he asked the crewmen standing around him.

"British SAS," someone answered.

Whoa. Who'd managed to pull strings and get those guys to come fish him out of the ocean?

"This way, sir."

He was able to walk, but it wasn't pretty. His muscles were still cramping randomly, and he hobbled like an old man, clutching the blankets around himself. He followed a crew member down a hall, up a steep stairway, and into a salon decorated like a posh gentleman's library with dark wood paneling, burgundy carpet, plush wingback chairs, and shelves of leather-bound books. Two men sat in side-by-side armchairs, smoking cigars.

Collin started. "Pere? Martin? What are you two doing here?"

Both owners of Wild Cards, Inc. were present? Had he screwed up that badly?

"How are you feeling, Collin?" Pere asked.

"Cold. And I could use some clothes." He was currently as naked as the day he'd been born underneath the blankets he held around himself.

Martin Wylde picked up a telephone from the coffee table beside his chair. "Emmitt, could you roust up some clothing for our guest and bring it up here?"

It was under a minute before a tall, handsome man with cold black eyes entered the room and handed him a small pile of clothes and shoes. The guy pointed at a closed door. "Restroom's in there."

Collin retired to dress in gray slacks, a white polo shirt, and navy blue wool jumper. He was clumsy as hell and it took twice as long as it normally would. But eventually, he slipped on the deck shoes and availed himself of a comb he found in the medicine cabinet. At long last, he felt vaguely human again. Time to find what in the ever-loving hell had just happened, and more importantly, what came next.

He stepped out into the salon and took the neat whiskey that Pere held out to him before sinking into the club chair that had been pulled up beside the first two. At Pere's urging, he spread the plastic heating blanket over his legs to continue bringing his core temperature back toward normal.

"Quite an evening you've had," Martin commented. "I hate to interrogate you so soon after the shock of being shot, but what can you tell us about the Erebus Consortium? We looked into it, or tried to, and the security we ran into blew up our entire computer network. Our mainframe had to initiate an emergency shutdown to keep from being fatally corrupted."

"That sounds about right," Collin replied. He filled in his bosses quickly on the few morsels of information he'd collected before his death. Erebus was some sort of shadow organization of incredibly powerful men who styled themselves the puppet masters of pretty much everything they touched.

Pere and Martin exchanged loaded looks. Pere was the one who spoke, however. "What can you tell us about Oliver Elliott?"

Collin had no idea where to start answering that one. Instead he asked, "What do you want to know specifically?"

"Will he join the consortium now that he's won the tournament and killed you?"

"I have no idea how to answer that. But I do know Oliver despises his father and everything his father stands for."

"Did the son say anything to you once he found what prize you were playing for to indicate his intention to go to work for Erebus or not?"

Oliver had said he loved Collin. The members of the consortium had forced him to kill the man he loved. Surely, Oliver wouldn't turn around and go to work for people like that. "I have to believe he'll ultimately refuse to work for his father. My guess is he'll go along with George Elliott and company just long enough to affect an escape of his own."

His bosses nodded as if his assessment concurred with theirs.

Collin blurted, "How is it that I'm not dead? Not that I'm complaining, mind you."

"Oliver Elliott contacted us yesterday. Explained what was going on. We arranged for operatives to infiltrate the hotel last night, bring in tuxedos for both of you, and plant the blood squib and sedative injector in your suit coat. We then provided Oliver with a revolver loaded with blanks, a knife, and a locator beacon to slip into your clothing."

"What if I'd won the hand of poker instead of him?" Collin demanded.

"Oliver was going to pass you the revolver and tell you to shoot him."

"But I wouldn't have known about the pickup at sea by the British SAS."

"No. You would have had to labor under the impression that you'd killed Oliver until we could discreetly get in touch with you after you left the resort. But we weren't worried about that."

Collin frowned. "Was everybody so certain I would lose the hand of cards? I'm not *that* horrible a poker player."

His employers laughed. "By no means. You made it to the last two players, after all. Well done, by the way."

"So, you had it all planned. Why in bloody hell didn't anyone bother to share all of this information with me? I thought Oliver actually shot me." He couldn't stop a note of anger from creeping into his voice.

Martin answered, "Oliver thought it best that your reactions be genuine and unscripted. He's well-practiced at deceiving his father, but he worried that you would not be able to bluff George Elliott."

Reluctantly, he had to allow that Oliver might be correct. But it still pissed him off a little.

Pere added, "Oliver was very worried about you. He was unwilling to take even the slightest chance with your life."

"And yet he drugged me and threw me into the frigid ocean in the dead of night."

"You're here, aren't you? The SAS was monitoring you the whole time you were on the boat with Oliver and those men. They had a stopwatch on you from the moment you entered the water and knew how long they had to pull you out before hypothermia became life-threatening. You were never in any danger."

No. Just gut-clenching terror.

"Where's Oliver now?"

"Our surveillance showed him returning to the El Rocca and disembarking just before you arrived aboard this vessel."

"You have surveillance on him? May I see it?"

"We were hoping you would be up to taking a look. You know his body language better than any of our other analysts do."

They had no idea.

"Come with us." His bosses rose to their feet and led him downstairs to a shockingly well-equipped electronics room crowded with computer monitors and manned by a pair of analysts he worked with in England. After a quick round of greetings and congratulations for not being a Popsicle or dead, one of the men stood up and held out a headset to him.

The guy murmured, "Mr. Elliott the Younger gave us direct access to his hack of the resort's security system last night. The yacht, *Erebus*, is currently using the resort's Wi-Fi network, and we've worked our way into the ship's video feeds and established a permanent link. We're streaming them in real time."

"Nice," Collin replied, impressed.

He sat down at the station and donned the headset. Oliver Elliott's voice filled his ears immediately. Something uncurled in his gut at the sound of his lover's voice. Oliver was angry but hanging on to his temper tightly. The video feed wasn't great, but he was amazed there was any video at all on the *Erebus*.

"—satisfied now, Father?" Oliver was pacing a gaudy salon decorated much like the Italianate office Collin had visited aboard the ship.

"I have to say you performed better than I expected, son. I didn't think you'd do it. You clearly had a crush on that British chap."

"That British chap had a name."

"A name you would be wise never to utter again in the presence of my—our—colleagues."

"Tell me something. Did you feel a need to eliminate the best players so I would end up standing here? You let Stacy Kiern kill players because you *knew* it would encourage a bunch of the top players to sandbag to stay out of danger. And you knew the bottom seventy or so players in the top one hundred were going to be summarily dismissed."

"In point of fact, I was confident you could win on your own. You were correct, though, that Stacy Kiern hired some of the escorts to thin the ranks. She personally tried to take out that British-player friend of yours, in fact."

"Was she responsible for the Jet Ski that almost ran me over before the tournament began?"

"We believe so, yes."

"Bitch," Oliver murmured mildly.

Collin had to smile a little. Oliver didn't sound angry about that incident at all. But then, it was how they'd met. He couldn't find it in his heart to be angry about their first encounter in the middle of the Mediterranean, either.

"Tell me something. Why did the British chap come to you to get patched up?" George asked casually.

Oliver answered equally casually, but Collin heard the note of caution in his voice. Thank God. He saw the trap George was laying for him. "He came to me to get patched up because by then he didn't trust anybody. He told me he figured that, since I was the chip leader, I was the one person not trying to kill anybody else to make my way to the top of the leaderboard."

"Smart fellow. Too bad we couldn't hire him too."

Collin made a face. As if he would ever work for a criminal bastard like George Elliott. Hah!

"So what's next, Father? I'm now a murderer with blood on my hands. I assume a quick departure from Gibraltar is in order?"

"The *Erebus* sails within the hour for a private island in Greece. It's one of our bases of operations. You'll receive your full introduction to my colleagues in the consortium, there."

"And then what?"

"Then your special talents will be shaped and honed to serve the organization. We like to keep our enterprise all in the family, of course. Mark my words, boy. You'll be the most successful of all of us. In a few years... the power you'll have... you'll thank me for forcing you to accept the Elliott legacy, son."

"You mean the legacy I've spent most of my adult life avoiding?"

Easy does it, Oliver. Don't be too bitter, or George will get suspicious.

George replied, "It was high time for you to quit fooling around and join the family business. I'm not getting any younger, and I'd like to retire in a few years. If you're going to be trained to take my place, it's time for you to start."

"By murdering someone?"

"The life of one insignificant poker player in return for the world at your feet... it was worth spilling a little blood."

Oliver was silent, but Collin spied a telltale tic in his jaw muscles.

Collin murmured to his bosses, "Oliver's silently furious. He's not swayed by his old man's promises of wealth and power beyond measure."

Oliver left the salon without saying any more. His gait was stilted, his shoulders stiff. Oh yeah. He was beyond pissed. He was livid.

"That ship is a fortress. We'll never get him off of it," Collin declared.

"We don't want him off the *Erebus*. To the contrary, that's exactly where we want him to be," Pere replied.

Collin swiveled in his chair to stare up at his bosses. "What's going on that you're not telling me?"

"Come with us." Pere and Martin led him back upstairs to the salon and made him endure the pouring and sipping of another round of whiskey before Pere finally spoke. "We'd like to develop Oliver Elliott as an asset."

"A spy? Inside the Erebus Consortium?" Collin asked, shocked.

"Exactly."

His eyebrows slammed together. "He has no training whatsoever to pull off something like that. You'll get him killed!"

"That's why he'll need a handler," Pere answered patiently.

Collin snorted. "One does not *handle* Oliver Elliott. Not unless one wishes to make an enemy of him. He's fiercely independent and hates being manipulated in any way." An image of the two of them tangled in bedsheets flashed into his mind. There was *one* way Oliver liked to be handled, at any rate.

Pere and Martin exchanged another pair of loaded looks. What in the hell were they slow-walking him toward?

"Just spit it out, you two. I've had a crappy day, and I'm too tired for these games."

Pere said quietly, seriously, "We'd like you to be his handler, Collin. You know him better than anyone else in the firm."

"Small problem with that. My face is known to the Erebus Consortium."

Martin answered patiently, "That is, indeed, a problem. But there is a solution, if you're willing...."

Chapter Sixteen

OLIVER STRETCHED his arms over his head and cracked his neck as he pushed back from the computer monitor. The sums of money that Erebus controlled around the world were still staggering to him, even after months of managing various investments and banking transactions for the evil mothership.

At the moment, they had him building a complex investment algorithm for shifting the consortium's holdings in and out of various currencies rapidly to take advantage of currency fluctuations. Arbitrage traders did the same thing, but with the inside information Erebus obtained from various governments around the world, they could move in advance of the open markets. It was as illegal as hell, but still an interesting project to the mathematician within him.

He glanced out the glass wall to his right, down the mountain to the brilliant turquoise Aegean Sea below. The surf was up. A few surfers rode the waves, shooting along in front of the whitecaps like seagulls skimming the water. God. It had been forever since he'd surfed.

Giving in to impulse, he strode out of his office. "I'm going surfing, Callista. I'll be back in a few hours."

His secretary and personal watcher replied, "There's a surf shack about five hundred meters south of where the stairs emerge onto the beach, sir. You can rent a board there."

Ever the soul of efficiency, she was. He'd planned on bumming a board off one of the locals, but renting one would work too. He changed quickly into surf shorts and jogged down to the beach. The sun was brutal on his bare shoulders. Fuck. He'd lost most of his tan in the past few months, slaving at a computer day and night.

But his algorithm was almost finished. Then maybe his taskmasters would cut him loose for a small vacation. God knew, money was no object for him now. The numbers of zeroes on the end of the bank account his father had presented him with upon his arrival in Greece still appalled him. He thought he might try Australia. He'd like to surf the big waves there.

Assuming the bastards let him risk his ever-so-valuable neck.

Which wasn't bloody likely. They'd failed to inform him that he was basically their slave until he proved himself loyal and valuable to the consortium. Even this small break to surf for an hour was likely to land him in hot water with the senior members of the consortium.

Tough shit. He was losing his mind.

One of these days, they would start to trust him, and the round-the-clock surveillance would ease up enough for him to make his escape. To where, he had no idea. But he would find some tiny corner of the planet where Erebus and his father couldn't find him.

He'd been stockpiling information on Erebus for months now. He had lists of shell company names and bank account numbers that went on for pages. If he turned those over to the U.S. government, surely they would be willing to put him in witness protection or something. He hadn't found a conduit yet to pass the information through, but one day he would. One day, his watchers would get sloppy or finally trust him enough to look away. And then he was out of here.

He rented a scuffed-up surfboard and carried it down to the water. The warm Aegean Sea lapped around his legs, and he flopped onto his board and paddled out toward the breakers. It was the first time since he'd thrown Collin overboard and known that his lover was free of Erebus that he could remember feeling even a little happy. *Please God, let Collin be alive and safe.*

He'd waited for weeks for Collin to contact him, but there'd been nothing. Total silence. Not that he blamed Collin for not forgiving him after Oliver had shot him. In the absence of contact, he could only assume nothing had gone wrong and nothing bad had happened to Collin. To believe anything else was to court suicidal depression. He had to hold out hope that Collin was okay, and that someday he'd get away from Erebus and find him again.

Oliver had frequent nightmares that involved Collin drowning, alone and terrified. But he dared not look for any evidence that Collin was alive. In the first place, Oliver expected that Erebus's security team monitored his computer usage. And in the second place, the last thing he needed to do was to lead his employers right to his supposedly dead lover.

A blond, tanned surfer caught a wave a little farther out to sea, and Oliver paddled hard to get out of the guy's way. He shot past Oliver, executing a nifty reversal only a few yards ahead of him. Something about the guy's physique, his way of moving, reminded him of Collin. Of course, Collin didn't know the first thing about surfing, and this guy wasn't half-bad. He wasn't an expert like Oliver, but he was a decent amateur.

His path crossed the blond's several more times in the next hour of surfing, and each time, something about the guy vaguely reminded him of Collin. And every single time, a pang of loss and longing twisted in his gut.

Eventually, the blond guy went ashore and flopped in the sand. Whether he was taking a nap or just working on his prodigious tan, Oliver couldn't tell.

Oliver caught a few more waves, but the breeze was abating and the waves were subsiding as well. Tired, but less stressed than he'd been in weeks, Oliver waded ashore. As he reached the beach, he noticed the blond guy peering sidelong at him from behind his sunglasses.

Frowning a little, he slogged through the sand to the guy and sat down beside him. The blond guy stayed stretched out on his back.

"My name is Oliver," he tried in his rudimentary Greek.

"Keep staring at the water," a familiar voice said from beside him in a British accent.

Oliver jolted violently. Collin!

"Don't look at me," Collin bit out more sharply.

Oliver froze, staring at nothing but pointing his face toward the water. "How did you find me? Where have you been? Are you all right? What the hell happened to your face?"

"I've been watching you ever since the night you dumped me."

"What took you so long? I'm so fucking sorry about that—"

"No apologies necessary. And we don't have long to talk. I've been sent to help you infiltrate Erebus, if you're willing. I would act as your handler and give you whatever support you need. The idea is for you and the new me to develop a relationship over the next few months. In case you haven't noticed, I've had facial reconstruction, and your employer should not be able to identify me. And that's what took me so long. I had to heal from my surgery and establish a cover that will hold up to Erebus-level scrutiny."

Collin's voice had shifted to a distinctly American accent in the past few sentences. New Jersey, maybe. And even he hadn't recognized the face of the man he loved.

Collin continued tersely. "If you turn me in to your employer, they will kill me for real this time. If you choose to work with me, your life will be in serious danger. But you will be able to help me and the British government take down a powerful criminal organization that's doing harm all over the world. It's your decision. If you want to accept my offer, meet me here the next time a fresh breeze blows up some decent breakers."

"Since when do you know how to surf?"

"Since I went under deep cover to rescue the man I love."

And with those stunning words, Collin jumped to his feet and jogged off down the beach. Oliver watched him go, so elated he could hardly breathe.

Collin was alive. And he was here. Collin had come for him! Hot damn.

THE NEXT few days passed in an agony of suspense for Oliver. He fiddled around with his algorithm, delaying finishing it with a series of test runs that were entirely unnecessary, but which fooled his supervisors by producing long and incomprehensible lists of numbers.

The winds had shifted to the west, and the sea was glassy calm out his window day after day. He was losing his mind bit by irrevocable bit. And then, on the ninth day since he'd briefly seen Collin, he woke up to a hot breeze through his window. From the southeast. The wind had finally shifted.

He worked through the morning, keeping one eye peeled out the window for a tanned blond working the waves. A little after noon, he spied a familiar physique and a flash of golden hair wading out into the surf.

"Callista!" he shouted through the open door. "I'm going surfing for a few hours. If anyone complains, tell them the program will go live tomorrow. If I don't go crazy staring at these four walls, that is."

"Yes, sir."

He had to stop himself from sprinting down to the beach, and from throttling the surfboard guy, who took forever to rent him a damned board. But then he was paddling out to sea. To Collin.

The Brit—correct that: the American—was straddling his board, watching waves roll in from the open sea as Oliver paddled up beside him and said, "It seems that we're destined to keep running into each other in the middle of bodies of water."

"You came," Collin said with obvious relief, smiling without looking at him.

"Of course I came. So how's this going to work?"

"If you're prepared to work inside Erebus to help me take it down, you and I will meet for coffee tomorrow, maybe have a lunch or two, and then, when it makes sense, progress on to a more serious relationship."

"My father won't stand for it."

"He will when that algorithm you're working on makes him and his buddies an astronomical fortune."

"How do you know about that?"

"Sorry. Classified."

Oliver turned that over in his head for a minute. The authorities—of what countries was anybody's guess—were on to the Erebus Consortium. Outstanding. He'd been banging his head against a wall, trying to figure out how to take it down from the inside, but the bastards at the top had the organization so compartmentalized that he'd found no way to destroy the whole thing at once.

As for his father standing for him taking a gay lover, Collin had a point. George was not in charge of Erebus and was far from the only voice in votes or decisions. If Oliver made them enough money, they wouldn't care who he took to bed.

"I have lists of companies they secretly own and bank account numbers—"

"Hang on to those for now. We don't want to move too fast. First, we want you to make the consortium so much money it stops looking too closely at you."

He snorted. "My program is ready to go live any time. I've been delaying running it until I could see you again."

"Run it," Collin said tersely.

"Okay." He hesitated, then said slowly, "I'd like a do-over with you. I'd like to do the whole develop-a-relationship thing like normal people."

Collin grinned, and Oliver was startled. He'd gotten caps on his teeth, and the faint imperfections from before were gone. His smile was now movie-star perfect. In fact, just about everything about him was now movie-star perfect.

"You clean up pretty good, Yankee."

Collin's smile widened. "The plastic surgeon said the only way to make me fully unrecognizable was to make me really ugly or so handsome no one could see past the razzle-dazzle."

"Thank you for choosing hot," Oliver replied, grinning. "Although, I'd still love you if you looked like Quasimodo. After all, you came to rescue me, yet again."

Collin's gaze, through the same rich, complex, fascinating gray eyes as always, softened. "I'll always come for you, Oliver. I love you." He shrugged and added simply, "You're the one."

"I'd lean over and kiss you if I could."

"Patience, Oliver. We're in this for the long game. There will be plenty of time for kisses later. And I'm not going anywhere."

"Thank God. I'll never leave you again, I swear. And believe me. I've got the resources now to make that happen."

"I'll look forward to hearing all about them." Collin held out his hand for a shake. "My name's Rick. It's nice to meet you, Oliver."

"Likewise. So tell me about yourself, Rick...."

New York Times and *USA Today* bestselling author, CINDY DEES started flying airplanes while sitting in her dad's lap at the age of three and got a pilot's license before she got a driver's license. At age fifteen, she dropped out of high school and left the horse farm in Michigan where she grew up to attend the University of Michigan.

After earning a degree in Russian and East European Studies, she joined the U.S. Air Force and became the youngest female pilot in its history. She flew supersonic jets, VIP airlift, and the C-5 Galaxy, one of the world's largest cargo airplanes.

She also worked part-time gathering intelligence. During her military career, she traveled to forty-two countries on five continents, was detained by the KGB and East German secret police, got shot at, flew in the first Gulf War, met her husband, and amassed a lifetime's worth of war stories. Cindy has turned many of her experiences into novels of military romance and suspense.

Cindy's hobbies include professional Middle Eastern dancing, Japanese gardening, and medieval reenacting. She can also be found often on various social media, hanging out with her friends and fellow readers.

Winner of a Golden Heart and Holt Medallion for writing, Cindy is a five-time finalist and two-time winner of the prestigious RITA Award for Romance Fiction, two-time winner of RT Book Review's Best Harlequin Romantic Suspense Novel of the Year, and is a Romantic Times Lifetime Career Achievement nominee.

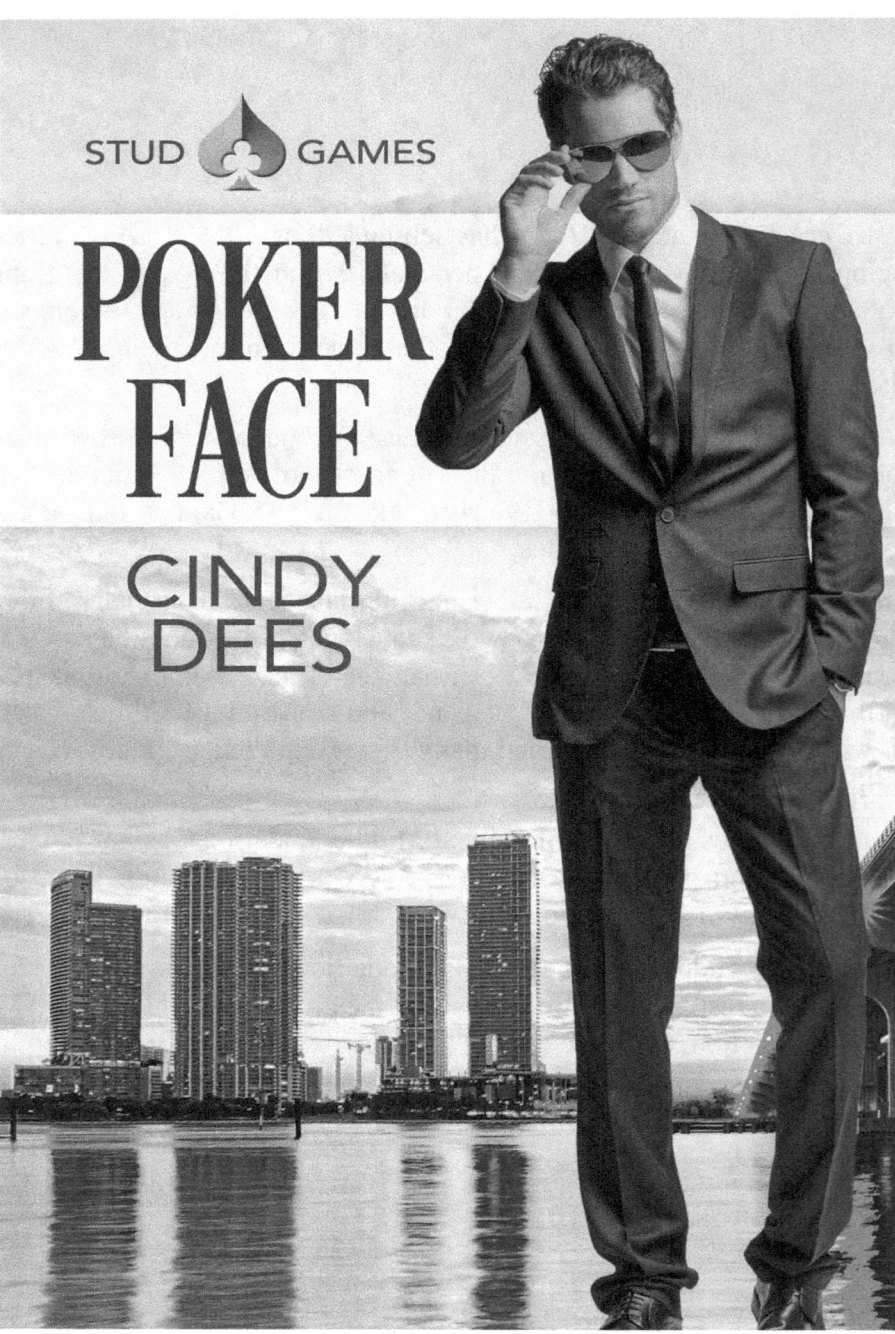

STUD ♠ GAMES

POKER
FACE

CINDY
DEES

A Stud Games Novel

Surveillance, seduction, and extra-dirty politics.

Christian Chatsworth-Brandeis has a problem. A huge one. The US senator he works for has run away with his latest mistress on the eve of a make-or-break fundraising event, and it's up to him to cover his irresponsible boss's tracks.

Stone Jackson, Senator Lacey's new bodyguard, looks enough like him that, with some extensive grooming, he might pass for the senator. Christian and Stone hatch a plan to substitute Stone for the senator, but Miami madness and the incendiary heat between them are throwing obstacles in their way. It's a race to find the senator and pull off the con of the century before the attraction between them spins completely out of control.

www.dreamspinnerpress.com

Also from Dreamspinner Press

BESTSELLING AUTHOR & TWO-TIME LAMBDA FINALIST
RHYS FORD
BACK IN BLACK

McGINNIS INVESTIGATIONS
BOOK ONE

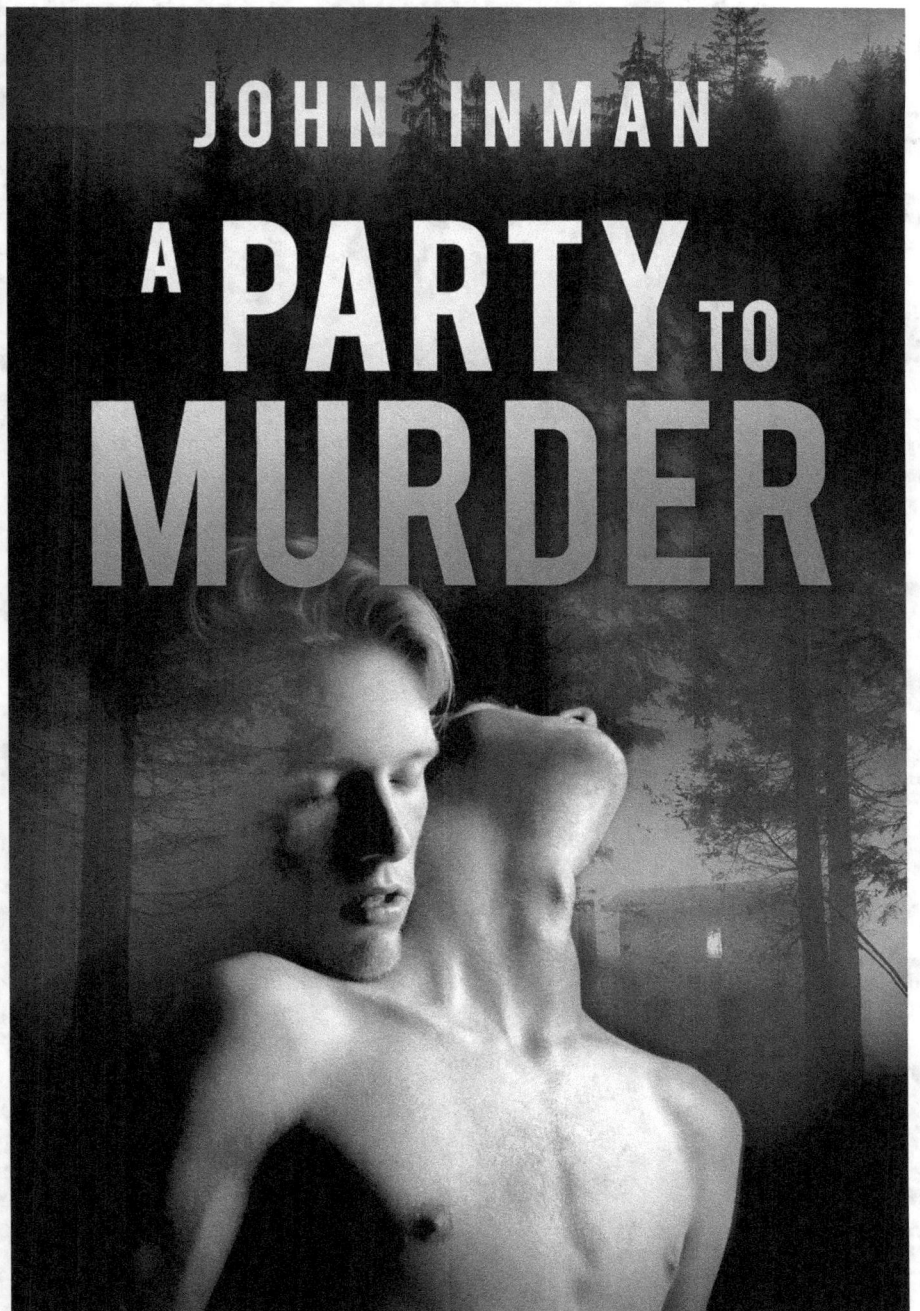